Penny,

THE LOVE LAB

Thank you for your support!
Hope you enjoy reading it!
Love Jill x

The Love Lab
Published 2024 by Jillian Stout

ISBN: 978-1-916544-31-4

Publishing Information
Design & publishing services
provided by JM Agency

www.jm.agency
Kerry, Ireland

Lust, Love, Therapy

THE LOVE LAB

JILLIAN STOUT

To Jean……Mamma Mia

PRELUDE

'Good evening all, and welcome to *Friday Night Live* on RTÉ. I'm your host Rachel Winters and our first guest of the evening is certainly going to pique some interest. Her name is Doctor Anna Floesing, and Anna is a sex therapist. Please give her a warm Irish welcome.'

Rachel started clapping, and the audience facilitator got the audience to join in. Unsurprisingly a few audience members refused to clap and the cameramen zoomed in on those that had their faces set in stone.

Anna walked out from behind the set into the bright television studio. Waving at the audience she smiled and shook Rachel's hand and followed her lead to take a seat on the couch opposite her.

Rachel smiled warmly at her guest. 'Dr Floesing. Thank you so much for joining us here tonight.'

'Please. Call me Anna. I'm delighted to have the opportunity to have this conversation. I appreciate you asking me.'

'First things first. Your accent and name would suggest that you are not from Ireland. Can I ask a little about your background?' asked Rachel.

'Of course. You are correct. I'm from Sweden. From a mining town in the very north called Kiruna. I studied in London, however, and that's where I met my Irish husband, Fergal and we moved here just after we got married.'

'So, you've made your home in Ireland because of the love of an Irish man. They're very charming, aren't they?' Rachel laughed.

'Oh, they definitely are charming. Compared to Swedish men, the Irish sense of humour is very different. It's true what they say about having the gift of the gab' Anna and Rachel laughed companionably.

'How long ago did you get married?'

'We're married three years now. Fergal is an amazing man and I'm grateful we get to do this part of life together.'

The audience broke into a round of applause.

'Look at that,' said Rachel. 'I guess we're all just suckers for romance here on *Friday Night Live*. But I believe your husband and yourself don't have what we would call a traditional marriage?'

'Traditional? No. I'm not big on traditions. I feel they restrict people's ability to develop into the human beings they are meant to become.'

'You do? In what way?'

'I believe we are all here to experience our best lives, and if we adhere to traditions, then that means that we are just walking through life following in the footprints left by someone else. I don't believe that's the way to become who you are meant to be.' Anna shrugged her shoulders and smiled a little at the audience.

'Very interesting Anna. So how does your marriage differ from the more 'traditional' ones then?' Rachel probed more.

'It's fairly simple, really. I'm not a believer in monogamy, so Fergal and I have a non-monogamous relationship, an open relationship.'

'When you say non-monogamy can you explain that a little more for those of us that may not understand?'

'Of course. It's where two people are married but they have agreed they can have sex with other people.'

'Oh. Wow. I'm not sure how I feel about that. Don't you get jealous?'

Anna smiled. 'I love my husband dearly, and he loves me. Jealousy on my part hasn't come into the equation yet, but it may do. We are doing exactly what we agreed upon though. Plus, there's so much more to each other than our sex lives, that being jealous over who we have these fleeting moments with would probably be counter-productive to us. We have full, well-rounded lives that we share with each other.'

'That's a really interesting way of looking at it. I would take a lot more convincing though. I would feel that if my husband slept with someone else, he would be disrespecting me.'

'I get that, I do. But the difference with us is that we 'chose' the lifestyle. Being intimate with someone else behind your spouse's back, well that's different. That's cheating.'

'Yes, definitely, I agree. I think I'd take more time to tease this out than we have right now because I want to get onto why you are here tonight.'

'Yes, yes, please. That would be great.' Anna rubbed her skirt material on her thigh and sat even more upright if that was possible. 'Shall I dive in?'

'Please do; tell us all about The Love Lab.'

'Rachel, The Love Lab is a dream come true for me. For many years I've wanted to try to reach as many people as I could with what I've learnt, and the Foundation is the best way we can do that in real tangible terms.'

'What exactly is it?'

'Ultimately, it will be a platform both on and offline that teaches people about the importance of a healthy approach to their sex lives, their relationships and the sexual energy we all have. Right now, the biggest part of that is 'The Love Lab' we are opening on Monday in our purpose-built facility, in north Dublin. This is where people will be able to come and chat with us, have a one-to-one session and discuss any issues they are having around their sexual wellness.'

'What makes you think that we need a separate clinic to deal with just our sex lives? Why can't traditional counsellors deal with that?'

'That's a really good question. There are many types of therapy, and they all have their place but I believe sex therapy is so important that I decided to study that field and focus my attention on it solely for my entire career. Let me ask you this. Have you ever noticed how you feel when your libido is high, and you have an extended period of intimacy and connection with another human being?'

Rachel blushed a little. 'Well, eh, obviously I feel great.'

'Exactly. Now think of a time when you may go long periods without that intimacy, that connection. What happens to you?' Anna held up her hand. 'You don't need to answer that, Rachel. This isn't about you. But for people in general, when they do go long periods, the disconnection is felt in their bodies but also in their minds. Their productivity suffers, mood suffers, interactions with others even suffer because of that.'

'I suppose I've never really thought of it like that.'

'That is exactly why I wanted to start The Love Lab. You and millions of others never thought of that because we are not taught to think that way. In Sweden, we have a very open relationship with our sexuality, and we are not restricted by years of guilt towards our bodies and our desires. It leads to much healthier relationships in general. Not just healthy sex lives. Here in Ireland sex and our bodies have been a source of embarrassment. Even me sitting here talking about it is probably embarrassing at least half the audience and more watching at home.' Anna lifted her head and looked at the audience. 'But our sexual energy connects us directly to the source, whatever you believe that to be and to spend a lot of our lives afraid of it, embarrassed by it, and many times ashamed about it, means that there are literally millions of us not reaching our potential in life because we are suppressing the very thing that gives us life.'

'But Anna, isn't sex meant to be private, kept between two consenting adults? Why do we need to talk about it and, in particular, talk to therapists about it? It's embarrassing.'

The audience clapped a little and a few coughs could be heard.

Anna smiled before she spoke again. 'And for as long as there are people who feel embarrassed discussing their sexual appetites, there will be a need for people like me. The clinic and the therapists aren't there to embarrass people. We are there to empower people. Men and women are sexual beings. Just because that idea makes people feel awkward and embarrassed doesn't mean it's not true. And something that's been completely missed here is that a healthy sex life means pleasure. Lots and lots of pleasure. Who doesn't want that in their lives?'

A few people chuckled in the audience, and Rachel laughed companionably with Anna. 'Well, we all need pleasure in our lives for sure.'

'Exactly. So, the philosophy behind the clinic is very simple. It is transformation through sex therapy. And I don't take that ideology lightly. I know that we have a mountain to climb, but I'm more than willing to give it everything I have to achieve that.'

'I really hope it goes very well for you, Anna. Thank you for taking the time to join us here tonight, and we wish you every success with The Love Lab. Thank you.'

Rachel shook hands with Anna and waited for the applause to die down before addressing the camera to announce a commercial break.

CHAPTER 1

Anna sat back in her leather chair, the wall of library books behind the velvet sofa caught her gaze. Pleased with the tone she had set she stole a glance around the remainder of her plush office. The artwork was perfect. A bright star, an up-and-coming abstract artist she had found. Wonderfully vibrant abstracts that could hold so much meaning for one or so little for another. She loved how subjective art was.

Smoothing her hands over her black pencil skirt, she absentmindedly paused at the slit that stopped mid-thigh. Her stocking top was visible momentarily before she pulled the skirt closed. Her crisp, white shirt tucked neatly into the band of her skirt. Lost in her thoughts, her intercom rang.

'Mr Harry Eames is here for his one o'clock interview, Anna.'

'Great, thank you, Hilary. Can you show him in and, then you may finish for the day.'

'I will. Thank you, enjoy the rest of your weekend, Anna.'

'You too, Hilary.'

Anna stood when she heard the knock on her door and slowly walked towards it, watching as a tall, dark-haired, extremely attractive man entered her room. She reached out a hand, and he clasped it with a strong, yet tender grasp.

'Anna, it's an honour to meet you. Thank you so much for the opportunity.' Harry smiled his enigmatic smile, and she watched the small lines appear at the side of his eyes. She noted how intense the blue of his eyes was, and how his presence made the energy in the room simmer.

She smiled back at him. 'My pleasure Harry. I'm delighted you've shown such an interest in working with us here at the Foundation.

Why don't you take a seat, and we will get started?' She gestured to the chair opposite her desk and took a seat. She knew she wasn't imagining feeling his eyes on her and she admitted to herself it made her tingle a little, knowing he was looking at her.

Harry opened the button on his blazer before sitting into the chair. Anna couldn't help noticing how the slim-fitting open-neck shirt clung perfectly to his taut body.

'So,' Anna sat back comfortably, the plush red velvet of the Queen Anne chair framing her slim figure perfectly. 'Harry, tell me what you know about what we are planning to do here at The Love Lab?'

Harry removed an invisible piece of dust from his jacket arm and looked at Anna.

His breath caught a little before he composed himself. 'Well, I know it's the first of its kind in Ireland. I believe it is a groundbreaking clinic that will test the boundaries of human sexuality and help many people overcome their deep-rooted sexual repression.' He paused and looked at Anna for guidance.

Anna laughed softly, 'I believe you have just written our mission statement, Harry. But yes, you are absolutely correct in your synopsis. As you are no doubt familiar with my work you will know that I truly believe in the innate power of our sexuality. I believe that it is the gateway to all that happens in our lives, good and bad. My life's work is to help as many people as possible to understand that, to help them break through the barriers they and society have put up and bring them a freedom they never dreamt possible.'

Harry shifted in his seat and leaned forward to address Anna. 'I want to be with you on that journey Anna. I can think of nothing in my life that has come close to exciting me and igniting a passion in me as when I heard what your plans are. I would count myself truly privileged to get to work with you and learn from you.'

Anna held Harry's gaze. Standing she moved slowly to the front of her desk and leant against it. 'You flatter me too much, Harry, but I'm very happy to hear you feel the way you do.'

He noticed the slit of her skirt opening to reveal her lace stocking top. Harry took a deep breath and tried to look away but found his gaze shifting to her sheer blouse instead and felt himself harden.

'Harry, I think you would be an asset to our team here. Your reputation precedes you, and I really just wanted to meet you today to see if the man matched that reputation. I believe it does so I'd like to offer you a position as a sex therapist here at The Love Lab.'

'Wow, that's amazing. Thank you so much.' Harry stood and reached out to shake her hand. 'I'm thrilled and would love to accept.'

She kept hold of him and leaned in, whispering in his ear. 'I know of one very special way we could seal the deal.'

Harry felt her breath on his neck and quickly put two and two together. But his mind wouldn't quite go there, and he reclined back to look at her. He needed to know for sure that he wasn't taking her up wrong. Anna saw the confusion on his face, so she whispered. 'I want you to fuck me, Harry.'

'Anna, are you sure?'

'Very.'

He took her hand from his and placed it at the side of the desk, leaning into her, he devoured her welcoming mouth with his. His hands reached for her face and neck caressing her. Suddenly stopping he pulled back, panting.

'Are you really sure? You're married, right?'

'Yes, I'm married. We're in an open relationship, and yes, I'm very sure.'

'Just one more thing Anna...'

'Yes, Harry?' Anna looked at him curiously.

'If this doesn't go well, do I still get to keep my job?' he smirked.

Anna smiled, 'I think this is going to go very well and either way the job is yours. As to whether we fuck again, well that will wholly depend on how the next few minutes go.'

'Few minutes?' He smiled down at her grabbed her hair with one hand and caressed her face with the other. 'We will be fucking again.'

Harry's lips covered hers and Anna moaned loudly.

CHAPTER 2

Anna absentmindedly wiped the dashboard with her hand. Closing the car door and hitting the lock button, she sat in the dark, empty car park, staring at the clinic building. Her building. A dream only a year before. The bright white letters of the clinic's sign shone in the night sky, The Love Lab. There was certainly going to be some raised eyebrows and some head shaking when the word got out. The traffic that drove by on the M50 in north Dublin couldn't miss it.

A soft smile crossed her lips while she sat looking at the white-washed walls. Anna's upbringing in Sweden had ensured her attitude to sex was very different to her soon-to-be clients and even her Irish husband's. He knew she needed to be in an open relationship. She'd never hidden that side of herself from Fergal. She had been clear to him from the beginning that monogamy was not something she would sign up to. Despite his reservations, Fergal had loved her enough to allow her what she needed, and if it was possible, she fell more in love with him for that.

Even so, she knew if word got out about how the interview ended today, it would be considered that she'd crossed a line. The interview earlier had been as much of a surprise to her as it was to Harry, she was sure of that. He was going to make an excellent sex therapist, and if she also happened to find herself attracted to him, well, that was a little bonus, wasn't it?

The taste she'd had of his skills had left an impression and she was definitely planning on exploring that more.

Anna loosened her hair grip and let her brunette curls cascade down her back. Rubbing her neck, she closed her eyes for a moment and held onto the sensation he'd stirred in her a little longer. Savouring the memories of his kisses on her neck, her lips. Remembering his strong, knowledgeable hands made her come alive again. Her thighs started to tingle.

She always felt liberated after having great sex, and today was no exception. She couldn't help the satisfied smile that escaped.

Opening her eyes, she pressed the ignition button and the engine came to life. She turned the volume up as the raspy tones of Lewis Capaldi emanated from the speakers. She hummed along, turned the car in the direction of the exit and started for home. Putting all thoughts of Harry from her mind Anna switched gears and as always, felt the desire for her husband increase.

She drove the short distance home and pulled into their circular driveway. Reapplying her lipstick in the rear-view mirror, she pursed her lips together and blew herself a kiss, laughing. She was excited to see Fergal and hear about his day.

He appeared in the hallway as she pushed through the front door allowing the light to spill onto the hardwood floors.

'You need a hand with those?' He reached for her leather bag and kissed her hello.

'Thank you.' She handed it to him. 'How was your day?'

'Exhausting but fruitful,' he replied.

Anna removed her trench coat and powder blue silk scarf.

He wanted more and leant in to kiss Anna again, this time full on the mouth, skimming his hand over her hip and letting it rest a moment.

She smiled suggestively at her husband. 'Hold that thought älskling. I'm famished and need sustenance before we go where that kiss is leading.'

He lightly patted her behind and smiled turning towards the kitchen.

'Your wish is my command,' he spoke over his shoulder.

'How was your day? Did you get out at all, or were you tied to your desk for the duration?' Anna asked sauntering in behind him to the kitchen.

'I had one client this morning then I got out for a brisk refreshing walk on the beach. The bitterness is gone from the air, and you can feel spring coming. The rest of the day was quite productive. I got chapters three to seven edited,' he answered.

'Oh, that's wonderful darling. There's nothing quite like a productive day to put a spring in your step,' Anna responded.

She reached for two wine glasses while Fergal handed her an already-opened bottle of red wine. Their evening ritual, more practised now, meant their days had a rhythm to them which was comforting. It was hard to believe they were only in their home for six months.

Anna sat at their breakfast nook with the view over the hillside to the sea below. She could never imagine tiring of the scene in front of her. People had told them how lucky they were to acquire their dream home. She believed people made their own luck with hard work and ingenuity. But maybe, just maybe, she could believe there was a little luck thrown in as she surveyed her surroundings and looked at her husband.

She took a generous mouthful of the full-bodied red. 'I hired one of the final sex therapists today for the clinic, Harry Eames. Do you know him?'

'Eames, I know the name alright. Not familiar with his work though. Is he a Dalkey man? Spent a lot of time in England?'

'Yes, I think that's him. He'd be about your age. Was with the Bracken Clinic in London and spent time in their US one in New York. Very astute, fascinating insights. I think he'll fit in very well.'

'That's truly wonderful, Anna. I'm impressed with how quickly you've managed to assemble your team.' Fergal placed their meals on the polished concrete dining table.

Anna smiled when she stood to join him. 'I'm surprised myself. But it's wonderful that we have a full staff ready to start straight away. The final interview is with a colleague of Harry's tomorrow. A US-based guy who studied with Harry and has an excellent reputation. It's just a formality, as I have spoken to him at length. It's all very exciting. All we need now is the paying public to make appointments.'

Fergal lifted his glass, and she joined him. Leaning towards her, he kissed her lightly. 'Here's to The Love Lab and all that it represents and will achieve in the years to come. Here's to Ireland's sexual revolution.'

Laughing, Anna tipped her glass to his. 'I think sexual revolution may be stretching it, darling. But let's hope it starts the conversation that's so badly needed. I hope you're ready?'

'Don't worry about me. I can deal with scaremongers and the frigid. I've dealt with them my whole life,' responded Fergal.

Anna reached over and kissed him. 'And isn't it a miracle you turned out so sexually liberated?'

'Yes darling, it is. Now eat this wonderful meal your husband has cooked for you so he can show you just how sexually liberated he really is.'

Anna grinned and batted her eyelids at Fergal. 'Why sir, you tease me so.'

He gently lifted her hand and placed it in front of his lips. 'I'm certainly not teasing, Madam,' he kissed her hand and held her gaze.

'I think dinner can wait.' Anna rose from the table and led Fergal upstairs.

CHAPTER 3

Harry unlocked his apartment door and felt the deafening silence. If he wasn't going to let the past haunt him anymore, he knew he needed to change his perspective. He had to learn to accept the silence and live in it. Easier said than done. He knew this was the new beginning he needed. He wanted to take the good from it and savour the feeling.

His view of Dublin City from his tenth-floor apartment always managed to make him think of the past. A past growing up in a city that never quite managed to embrace its own successes. A city of cliches and stubbornness, but a city that held his heart no matter where in the world he travelled. Abigail had never understood that connection. Not being from Ireland, she found his affinity with it hard to comprehend. It was her free-spirited nature that had drawn Harry to her all those years ago and yet ironically, it was the very same free spirit that had somehow come between them. He would never know now if they could have made it work.

Shaking off his coat he reached for the Sonos and let the soulful sounds of Chet Baker surround him. Grabbing the opened bottle of pinot noir he poured a glass and stepped onto the balcony, standing, watching, as life moved below. He leaned on the rail, the wine glass hanging over the outside, high above the city. Harry thought back to earlier in the day and smiled smugly to himself. His mind filled with Anna.

He played the interview over in his mind. The long, lingering looks. The lightness of her touch when she leaned into him. At the beginning, he wondered if he'd imagined the electricity between them.

He thought of her long, lean legs, coated in those silk stockings. He thought of that black lace peeking through her skirt split and could feel himself tingle a little. He thought of her with those cat-like eyes and the way her mouth moved when she spoke. The accent, her lips, red and full, how it felt when he kissed them. How he'd felt sliding inside her.

Savouring a large swig of wine, he felt the blackberry notes coat his throat as it slid down. Breathing deeply with thoughts of Anna filling his mind he looked out across the Liffey.

His eye was caught by a woman trying to hold her coat closed as the wind whipped her skirt a little too high around her thighs, and he smiled. He thought of Anna again, those stiletto heels and what it was like to have her legs wrapped around his body. He remembered the lace of her bra straining at her blouse and felt himself getting hard. Adjusting his pants, he finished the glass and returned inside leaving the balcony door open. The city noise mixed with the jazz tones reminded him of another city long ago, of hot nights sipping wine and listening to the sounds of Chet Baker coming from the club below.

It felt like a lifetime ago, he thought. He trained his thoughts back to Anna. Wondering what he would do if she was with him right now? He knew exactly what he would like to do, and it started with taking her on his couch like earlier, again and again.

He reached for the remote to change the music. 'I fall in love too easily,' was not helping his mood. Clicking the forward button he laughed as Eddie Vedder's voice sang out, 'I'll be sleeping by myself tonight.'

He tried to put all thoughts of Anna from his mind. He knew he didn't want a complication to mess up this new opportunity and sleeping with his married boss was certainly one way to complicate things.

He started putting together a meal that would at least fill a hole if nothing else.

His phone ringing took his thoughts away from Anna. 'Yes?' his tone was a little sharper than it needed to be.

'Well, that's not very nice now is it?' the demure female voice didn't have the desired effect on Harry.

'Sophia, I'm busy what can I do for you?'

'I was kinda hoping there was something I could do for you Harry, but I'm thinking now maybe I shouldn't of bothered,' he could feel her pouting through the phone.

He took a deep breath and stopped pouring the pasta sauce. With a sigh, he relaxed a little and shifted gears.

'I'm sorry, I'm sorry, I wasn't expecting a call that's all, and I was just in the middle of something. Don't get mad, Sophia baby.'

'So you are happy to hear from me, babe?'

'Baby, you know I am. Plus, I have some good news and I'm in the mood to celebrate so why don't you get that pert little ass of yours over here, make sure you are in very little clothing, and we can do some celebrating together?'

'See, that's what I wanted to hear. Well, babe, you're in luck tonight, open the champers I'm downstairs.'

'Well, well, well, aren't we the presumptuous little minx. What if I'd had another woman up here?' Harry couldn't help laughing at Sophia's audacity. Sometimes it paid to like feisty women.

'Well then you wouldn't have answered your phone, and I would have taken myself and my pert ass off home alone. But as my timing is impeccable as always, I suggest you open your apartment door and give me one minute to reach you.'

Hanging up, Harry smiled and grabbed a bottle of Dom and two glasses depositing them in the bedroom.

He was going to enjoy this evening after all. All thoughts of Anna disappeared as Sophia, blonde and beautifully bosomed with her impeccable ass, appeared in his open doorway and leaned against the jam.

'Well?' she looked at him through those long lashes, 'aren't you going to invite me in?'

Harry reached her in two long strides, wrapped his arms around her waist and pulled her in for a hard, deep kiss.

'I'd do you right here if I thought Mrs Murphy across the hall wouldn't have a heart attack if she saw us.'

He pulled her inside and swept the door closed with his foot. Kissing her again, he lifted her dress and felt for her ass, squeezed her perfect cheeks, and moaned.

'Well aren't I glad I called you,' Sophia purred as Harry devoured her mouth again.

CHAPTER 4

Everyone strode into the boardroom and took their seats. Anna and Hilary stood near the top of the table. 'Before Hilary brings you to the business of the day, I'd like to kick this off with a few words,' began Anna, nodding to Hilary, 'if you have no objections, Hilary?'

Hilary coughed, sat down, and looked at her boss. 'Of course, Anna. Please go ahead.'

'Thank you, I won't take long. Firstly, I'd like to say welcome to each of you. We are a small team, but I really do feel we are the right team. I believe The Love Lab is a unique opportunity for the people of Ireland to really shift their perception of sex and relationships. I'm delighted each of you has decided to join us on this journey. I know we will face a lot of opposition and I know our methods are going to be seen as unorthodox at best, but I truly believe, as time moves on and we prove how helpful what we do can be, the voices of, how do you say it in English?' she moved her head side to side in thought. 'Adversity, yes, they will disappear. It would be naïve of us to think we will not get some negative publicity. Right?'

Everyone nodded in agreement.

Hilary interrupted. 'We are already getting phone calls from religious groups Anna, more this morning again.'

'I see, I see. Only to be expected. We will deal with them all and if anyone reaches out to you, please make sure you send them to Hilary or myself?'

'No problem, Anna,' Harry smiled at her. The rest of the group nodded.

'Great, thank you. I also expect to have protesters at some point at the door. But as long as we stay true to our ethos, and keep our clients' needs at the forefront of everything we do, I feel we will be fine. Now, has anyone any questions?'

Karla was the first to speak. Her accented voice was crisp and clear. 'I would like to say how excited I am to finally be able to do something that will have such a huge impact. I am delighted that your dream has finally happened Anna. You are truly inspirational, and I am very excited.'

Anna noted with amusement the nods of approval around the room, in particular from the young American therapist, Matt. She was certain he wasn't just approving of what Karla said. More than likely, it was the approval of Karla herself.

She caught Harry's sideways glance at Matt and realised she wasn't the only one who noticed his interest in Karla. She could understand the fascination. Karla was a real beauty. Her blonde hair cascaded past her shoulders combined with her green eyes and curvaceous figure she was a sight to behold. During their time in college together Anna had witnessed the power Karla wielded over men, time and time again.

Anna continued. 'Thank you, Karla. I think we are all feeling the same way. Yes? It is certainly a very exciting time to be in this business and be a part of the birth of The Love Lab. I hope this professional milestone will be one we can all treasure when we look back in years to come. But, for now, I will hand you over to Hilary. I need to leave, but I am available in my office for the rest of the day. Welcome, and thank you all.'

Anna smiled warmly when she passed Harry and sauntered from the room.

Not long after she left the meeting the knock on her office door took her away from her work. 'Come in,' she responded warmly.

Swinging the door wide open Harry landed in her office like a man on a mission.

'Come in, why don't you, Harry?' She leaned back and smiled. 'You seem in a big hurry?'

Harry was reaching over her desk before she finished speaking.

'Anna, I,' he paused, 'no, we,' he emphasised, 'need to get whatever this is out of our way,' as he gestured to them both.

'Really? What exactly is this that we need to get out of the way?' Anna stood, the smile hadn't left her face, and she pushed her chair back.

Regaining his composure, Harry inclined his head and smiled questioningly.

'Really Anna? Are you trying to tell me that you, Sex Therapist extraordinaire, doesn't feel this?' he waved his hands back and forth.

'This?' she mimicked his hand gestures and moved around the desk towards him. 'This, Harry, isn't anything other than a working relationship, you must know that surely?'

She wasn't sure who she was trying to convince but Anna knew that despite what she was saying, the man in front of her made her feel extremely wanted. He was an exceptional lover and she wasn't sure he was someone she could stay away from.

'Anna.' He stood a moment and held her gaze, rubbing his hand over his mouth, his eyes moving slowly towards her lips and back to her eyes again. He took a step closer until they were within a breath of each other and gently touched her chin.

'Anna,' he spoke softer still, 'This is BS, but if that's what you really want then I can give you that.' He shrugged his shoulders and released her chin.

She would have loved nothing more than for him to kiss her right now. She couldn't help it. But before she could do anything more, she watched him walk towards the door. She knew she wanted him. 'Harry?'

'Yes?' he turned with his hand on the doorknob.

'I know it's not normal. But I need time.'

'Take all the time you need. But just know we're not done. Not by a long stretch.' He nodded at her and walked out closing the door behind him.

Anna folded into her chair and sighed heavily knowing this man was going to be trouble.

Harry walked towards his car feeling satisfied with his control over the Anna situation, but still very frustrated that his longing had just tripled in intensity. Knowing he wouldn't be able to sleep until he sorted his problem he reached for his phone and dialled.

She answered on the first ring. He knew she would.

'Sophia?' his husky voice wasn't lost on the recipient. 'I think you and I need to have a little chat.'

'Baby,' purred Sophia.

CHAPTER 5

Her last client of the day gone, Karla surveyed her office and found herself rubbing the mahogany desk with an admiration she usually only held for her men. She took in her surroundings nodding in approval at the luxurious décor.

She loved Anna's interior design and marvelled at how Anna could pull a room together.

She remembered how during college Anna always had an air about her that commanded attention. Her elegant, timeless style and her confident, and at times aloof attitude, put a lot of people off, but not Karla.

A more pragmatic and loyal friend she had never found. She was going to thoroughly enjoy being part of The Love Lab. She knew that Anna's dreams of opening it had been a long time in the making and was thrilled when she approached her about joining the team. Not only that but being a founding member gave Karla a deep sense of satisfaction.

That satisfaction was intensified when she thought of Dr Harry Eames. Her co-worker had a swagger that Karla could very much appreciate. His confidence oozed out of every pore. Every time she saw his smile light up his face, she felt something stir inside her. She had never broken her golden rule – never sleep with a colleague – but she definitely felt her resolve wavering where Harry was concerned. The temptation was going to be hard to resist. The relationship she was in with Tom had come to its natural end, she just needed to find the right moment to break that news to him. They hadn't had sex in a few weeks, and she had started to get a little concerned that her sex drive was dwindling. But, with thoughts of Harry filling her head, she began to feel a stirring she hadn't felt in a while and decided it was a welcome feeling. It was one she'd missed and was certainly not going to stop her body from reacting to thoughts of him and what he could do to her.

She reached behind her and undid the pins in her blonde hair, letting it unfold past her shoulders. She ran her hands through it and moved her neck to release the muscles. Strolling to the armoire she took her time to savour the ritual and poured herself a Teremana Tequila over ice. Holding the cut glass tumbler aloft she appreciated the amber liquid for a moment, nodding approval, before settling onto the couch. The plush cushions felt soft against her bare legs below her hemline. Feeling the warmth of that first sip make its way through her body she uncrossed her legs. She moved to allow them to spread a little more resting her head against the back of the velvet couch. Breathing deeply her fingers found the sweet spot between her legs and she touched herself gently.

Moaning, she slid her panties aside, let her fingers slide inside her and felt the warmth envelop her. Karla let her mind roam free and fill with thoughts of Harry. She could hear his deep voice, that sexy accent. His face filled her mind. His dark hair, taut body, those strong arms, his sexy smile, she gasped. What she wouldn't give to have him here, fucking her. She let herself go, moaning louder and louder. Her pace quickened and her breath caught as she came, Harry's face felt close enough to touch as she sighed deeply with the release of her orgasm.

Relaxing and smiling for a few minutes Karla pulled her panties back into place, knocked back the remaining tequila and composed herself. She certainly wasn't surprised at how intense and fast her orgasm had been, as thoughts of Harry made her continue to ride the wave. She poured herself another generous glass of tequila with a splash of soda this time, before taking a large mouthful. She felt the deep satisfaction as it slid smoothly down her throat, only waiting a moment before taking more. Karla fixed her makeup and reapplied her lipstick in the bathroom before deciding it was time to leave for the evening. Tomorrow was another day and she needed to have her game face on.

She fixed the knot in her wrap dress and took one last look in the mirror, tossing a hand through her hair before turning off the lights and locking the office door behind her.

♥♥♥

It was the end of the day and Matt was trying to distract himself from thoughts of Karla by studying his practice notes for his roleplay scenarios. It wasn't working. He had only seen two clients for the day, and both had worked out well. He was now more distracted than ever.

No matter how hard he tried to concentrate his mind brought him back to thoughts of Karla.

Matt knew he felt slightly uncomfortable thinking about having sex with Karla. It killed him that not only had she brains to burn but she was damn hot. In fact, she was one of the sexiest women he had ever laid eyes on, and when she did that whole brainiac thing, glasses, blonde wavy hair held up loosely at her neck, well that just sent him over the edge. He wasn't sure how he was going to sit in meetings with her and not think about taking her on the conference table every single time.

Today had been no exception. When she had walked into the room with her hair pinned up, wearing a dress that clung to every curve, with all that easy access, his mind had gone to mush.

He knew the job was an opportunity of a lifetime and he really didn't want to let himself or Anna down.

Matt figured he needed to get all thoughts of Karla from his mind and gave it one more shot with the practice scenarios before he finished for the day.

He had enjoyed the role-play with Anna, but they had the real deal coming in and he needed to bring his A game. There was no margin for error where the clients of The Love Lab were concerned.

These people would be relying on him to help them navigate what was a difficult time in their lives. Most would be reaching out for help for the first time.

Matt knew what it felt like to be the shy guy, the one afraid to approach a woman, let alone ask them on a date. And, as for sex, he knew all the hang-ups people could have, not just from the books he had studied, but from real-life experiences. If he could help even one person navigate the confusing, often embarrassing world of sexual encounters then he would have done a good job. But he knew he had more in him and could help many people.

Focusing on why he had decided to join the Clinic, he felt his pulse slow down and thoughts of Karla moved further from his mind. The men and women who would become his clients over the coming months and years were the ones he needed to think about right now. They were the ones at home absolutely petrified about what they had signed up for. He was enough of a professional to know that they needed his undivided attention and Karla, and all her luscious loveliness would need to be put back in a box in his head, at least for the time being.

CHAPTER 6

Alice dialled the number she had hastily scrawled on the side of the newspaper. Hesitating a moment before pressing the green dial button she took a deep breath and heard the ringtone on the other end. She tried to calm her breathing.

'Good morning. The Love Lab, how can I help you?'

'I'd like, well at least I think I'd like, you see I was told...'

The lady interrupted, 'Would you like to make an appointment?'

'Well, yes, yes I would.'

'That will be no problem, Madam. I have a cancellation tomorrow at 11 a.m. Would that suit you?'

'Oh, right. That soon? Oh gosh, OK, I'll take it. How long do the sessions last?'

'We ask clients to allow a minimum of one and a half hours and a maximum of two. A session won't run over two hours. Either way, the price is three hundred and fifty euros per session.'

'Alright, that's wonderful I'll see you then.'

'Wait, Madam, I'll need some details so I can book you in, please? Your name, address, that sort of thing?'

Laughing nervously Alice felt her nerves jangle. 'Oh, my goodness, I do apologise. Of course.'

'That's perfectly alright, and it's also fine to be a little nervous, but we promise you complete confidentiality and the best help there is.'

'Thank you so much. My name is Alice Metcalf, and my address is 95 Hawthorn Avenue, Clydesdale, Dublin 18.'

'Alice, can I get a date of birth please?'

'It's the 13th of December 1968.'

'Excellent, and lastly, I will need your mobile number and credit card details. Your card will only be deducted the deposit today of €100 and the rest will be taken on arrival tomorrow. Your card will be used to access the building and the consultation room as there is no communal waiting room here at the Clinic for confidentiality reasons.'

'Oh, I hadn't thought of that. That's wonderful, wonderful.' Alice gave the helpful lady her credit card details and mobile number. When they had said their polite goodbyes, she pressed the end button on her phone and sat quietly staring out at her garden.

Wondering what she had just done, Alice dropped her head into her hands and wept silently. Maybe it was relief? With a good dollop of sadness? She felt stupid if she was being honest, sitting crying because she'd made an appointment with a sex clinic. But then again, she was feeling a little stupid about everything lately. She wondered what difference it would make if she added one more thing to the list.

Alice dabbed her eyes and surveyed the mature garden from her kitchen table. She remembered all the parties Brian and her had thrown for their families and friends through the years and the many memories they had made together. If she concentrated hard enough, she could see the kids on the long-gone swing set and hear their squeals of laughter while Brian chased them on those rare hot summer days. The colourful scene in front of her was like an assault on her as the tears came again. Each memory brought both pain and joy in equal measure. She knew there would be children's laughter again in the garden, at least she hoped there would, one day when her children made her a grandmother. But that was some time off yet. And no matter when that happened, Brian would never get to chase their grandchildren around the garden. He would never again hear kids laugh with glee or see another summer come and go.

She missed him something rotten. It didn't matter that it had been five years. Five years of waking up alone, of making dinner for one, of reaching out during the night and realising with a start he was gone.

She had tried to date. At least she had gone on the obligatory blind dates that her well-meaning friends had set her up on. She had listened while grown men droned on about their mothers and what was wrong with women today. She had paid her way and politely made her excuses when halfway through some of the dates she had concluded that she would be better off in her pj's on the couch watching the soaps. She had even gone so far as to kiss a few.

The next step always seemed that step too far. Every time she thought she would enjoy moving things forward, something stopped her in her tracks. It wasn't loyalty to Brian, she knew that. It was more about the voices in her head telling her they would laugh at her stretchmarks or not enjoy the way she did certain 'things.' Brian had been her true love.

She had no idea how you were meant to go from one man your whole life to starting a relationship with another. A wistful sigh escaped.

Rising from the chair, Alice decided a cup of tea was in order before she started on dinner. She then settled on an egg and toast because cooking for one never managed to bring her the pleasure cooking for two had. With an ache deep in her heart Alice ate in silence and retired early to bed, concerned about what she had signed up to tomorrow.

Harry checked his reflection in the mirror before strolling back into his office and taking his place behind his mahogany desk. The phone rang. After two rings he picked it up, smiling at the name on the display. 'Good morning, Anna.'

'Good morning, Harry, I just wanted to wish you good luck on your first official day.'

'Thank you. I appreciate that. I'm all set and ready to go here. Quite excited really.'

'That's great. I know you'll do a wonderful job. Let's debrief around 4 p.m., my office?'

'Perfect, see you then. And Anna?'

'Yes?'

'Thanks again for the opportunity.'

Alice could hear a voice on the other side of the door and hesitated a moment before knocking. But then she heard the 'Come in,' in response and she patted down her short bob before opening the door and peeking her head into the room.

The smiling face and welcoming gesture made her feel a little more at ease, and she felt the carpet beneath her feet soften to the touch as she silently walked across the room. The high ceilings gave the office a wonderful feeling of space so that the heavy furniture didn't feel oppressive, rather, it felt warm and solid and made Alice feel safe for some reason she couldn't quite understand.

Harry stood and rounded the desk to greet her.

'Hi there. I'm Dr Eames, Harry, you must be Alice. Can I call you Alice?'

Alice let out a breath reaching for his outstretched hand.

'Alice is fine, thank you. Very nice to meet you, Harry.'

'Please take a seat.' Harry gestured to a tub chair opposite his at the desk. 'Did you find us OK?'

'Yes, I was a little surprised at how easy it was if I'm honest. I was here so early I ended up sitting in the car park for the past thirty minutes. I can't abide lateness.'

'Well, now you're here can I get you something to drink? We have still or sparkling water or would you prefer tea or coffee?'

'Oh, some still water would be fine. Thank you. My mouth is a little dry. I'm pretty nervous.'

Alice talked to Harry's back as he went to get their drinks.

'Well, I hope by the time we finish our session here today those nerves will be gone and we will have you feeling a lot less nervous for your next visit.'

Harry turned and smiled his most enigmatic smile at Alice before continuing.

'First things first Alice, we need to go through some background information on you that will give me some idea as to what brought you here today. But, before all that, whilst you settle in, I'm going to give you an overview of what to expect here at The Love Lab.

He handed her some water and placed a glass on his desk. Sitting on the edge of his desk Harry looked at Alice. 'What do you know about us?'

'Well, I really only know what I heard on Friday Night Live a few weeks ago. The woman who started the Clinic was on. Very good-looking lady. With an accent. I think she's from Sweden. When I heard her speak, I'll be honest I began to cry. It felt like something inside me reacted. Like it wasn't me. It's hard to explain. I know that probably doesn't make sense, and it didn't make much sense to me then, either.'

Alice took a deep breath. 'But, afterwards, I sat and thought about it and all that weekend I heard different pieces of her conversation popping up in my head. Then I went and watched it again on the player and that was it. I knew I needed to come. I knew I needed to do something to help take back me.'

Alice sighed heavily and looked down at her crossed legs. She noticed her hands had stopped shaking and she raised her head and smiled at Harry. He was sitting looking at her. She noticed how intense the blue of his eyes was. She felt there was a kindness in them which put her at ease. She knew he had listened to her, and it felt right to be exactly where she was.

Harry stood and returned to his chair. The silence was comfortable in the room as he took a sip of his water before speaking. 'Now that was pretty special Alice. Thank you for your honesty. I think we are off to a great start.'

His smile reached his eyes she noticed. She'd always considered that a good sign in someone.

Harry spoke. 'I can tell you about the Clinic if you wish another time. What I'd like to do is for you to tell me in your own words why you think you had such a strong reaction to hearing Anna being interviewed and what 'taking back me' really means to you?'

Exhaling slowly Alice lifted her head, and for the first time in a very long time spoke with happiness and love about her life. 'Well, you see. I was always the quiet one and never liked the limelight. I had some loud, funny, daredevil friends growing up, but I was content to stay in the background. Then Brian, my late husband, came along and in front of a group of my friends he swept me off my feet, quite literally. He ran into me on his bicycle, and I fell flat on my bum. I was mortified naturally, and Brian was so apologetic. He insisted on walking me home to make sure I was OK. When he got to my door, he asked me out. From that day on we were inseparable. I was seventeen and fell in love pretty much on sight. Although he would tell the story that he fell in love first.' Alice paused and glanced at Harry and his encouraging smile was all she needed to continue.

'We married on my twenty-first birthday and we had the first of our four children the day after my twenty-second birthday. The next three followed soon after. We were blissfully happy. All I ever wanted to do was stay at home with the children, while Brian went off to work every day. He did very well in his career and over the years we had a good life. A very good one. We were so happy.'

Her voice broke a little, but she went on. 'Then, just over six years ago our world fell apart. Brian found a lump on his breast. His breast of all places. He hadn't thought anything of it initially because, well, we didn't know men could get breast cancer, did we? Unfortunately for him, it wasn't the only place they found it. Within weeks, after PET scans and biopsies he was told he had stage 4 cancer, that the breast was the primary site and he had secondaries in his lymphs. But he was a fighter my Brian. He outlasted their diagnosis. They had given him six weeks. He fought like a trooper and made it to eight months after that initial diagnosis. Then he was gone. It felt like one minute he was there and the next he was just, gone.' Alice couldn't stop the tears, nor did she want to.

She gratefully accepted the box of tissues Harry handed her and dabbed at the tears trickling down her cheeks.

'I'm so sorry for your loss Alice. It sounds like you had a wonderful relationship.'

She lifted her head and turned to face him, speaking in hushed tones as if someone else in the room might hear. 'I think losing my Brian, I think it broke me. I don't think I have any love left inside me.'

He had to lean closer to hear her. Reaching for her hand Harry placed his on top and patted it.

'You are not broken, Alice. You speak so lovingly and openly about the life you shared and about the heartbreak you suffered. That tells me that your heart may have cracked a little, a lot even, but you have so much love inside of you that there is no way that you are broken, and you most definitely have love left inside you to give.' Harry patted her hand again before rising. 'And I'm here to help you find it.'

Alice smiled through her tears and dabbed again at her cheeks before laughing a little. 'I must look a state. Do you have a bathroom I can freshen up in?'

'Through that door there,' Harry pointed her in the direction of the bathroom. 'Take your time.'

Alice rose and started towards the bathroom, she paused, turning to Harry. 'Thank you. I can't remember the last time someone just listened to me. In fact, I can't remember a time I spoke about our lives together other than with Brian.'

Harry stood and smiled at her. 'You're welcome. I think it's the start of something very special for you Alice.'

CHAPTER 7

Karla felt ready for the challenge ahead. Watching her first patient arrive on the camera that was pointed at the front door, she stood behind her desk for a moment before deciding to move around and stand in front of it. She didn't want there to be any barriers between her and her clients, whether they be physical or metaphorical.

Her office door opened and in sauntered Mark Devine. His playboy smile was evident the moment he laid eyes on Karla.

'Welcome Mr Devine, may I call you Mark?'

'You certainly can.'

Karla walked briskly towards him and reached out to shake his hand.

Mark certainly had a firm, confident handshake and didn't shy away from holding eye contact. Karla was impressed with his audacity and his flirty smirk while he shook her hand.

Not new to men's reaction to her, Karla took his hand. 'Yes, lovely to meet you.'

'Karla, right?'

'Yes, that's right. Why don't you take a seat, while I get us a drink, then we can get started?'

Karla pointed to the chair opposite hers at her desk.

'Don't mind if I do.'

'What can I get you?' asked Karla.

With a smirk, Mark responded. 'I suppose a scotch is out of the question?'

Karla smiled as she walked by him. 'We better stick to the soft stuff I'm afraid. I'm having sparkling water, but I can organise a coffee if you prefer?'

'Sparkling water sounds good, thanks.'

Karla felt his eyes follow her as she walked to the drink bureau. 'While I fix these let me give you some background on The Love Lab?'

'Yeah, great.'

'As you may be aware it was started by Anna Floesing, the pre-eminent Swedish, sex therapist. The mission sounds simple, to bring sexual awakening to the masses, but the implementation not so much.'

Mark interrupted her. 'I'm aware of the controversy surrounding the Clinic's beginnings here. It's part of the reason I decided to give it a go, to be honest. If the church and the locals are up in arms you can pretty much guess it's a good thing you are trying to do.'

Laughing Karla nodded her head in agreement. 'That's a good way of putting it. I guess ultimately Anna, and all of us who work here, agree that human beings are sexual beings and unless we can be open and honest about our sexual needs and desires our lives will only be half-lived.' Karla paused and looked directly at Mark. 'And who wants a half-lived life, right?'

Mark sat silently nodding his head before answering. 'You've hit the nail on the head for me there, Karla.'

'I'm glad to hear it, and that brings us nicely on to you. Tell me a little about yourself, Mark. Your upbringing, what was it like?' handing him his water she rounded her desk and took a seat facing him.

Exhaling heavily Mark uncrossed his legs and leaned forward, 'Well, it was pretty unremarkable if I'm honest. No dark scary moments that would scar me for life or anything like that. My dad worked as a teacher most of his life. My mum stayed at home and looked after myself and my younger sister. They fed us, clothed us, brought us on nice holidays. My parents even told me they loved me.' He leaned back in the chair and chuckled a little. 'Listening to myself, I'm not sure why I'm here. It all sounds perfectly normal when I tell it like that.'

Karla leaned on her desk clasping her hands in front of her. 'I'm not sure there's a definition for normal Mark, and even if there truly was, everyone is different and therefore their perceptions of the same situation are going to be different. Tell me about you as a teen. What did you like to do and not like to do?'

'Ah, that's easy enough. I figured out very early on that I liked women, and they liked me. I usually liked as little hassle as possible and along with fast cars they became the two loves in my life. After my mam of course.'

Karla smiled at his cheekiness. 'Of course. And was there ever love involved with any of those women?'

Mark didn't miss a beat. 'There was always love, Karla,' he laughed.

Karla rose from her chair and came around the desk to lean against the front of it. She knew his eyes were on her. She had ignored the flirty smile and instead looked seriously into his eyes and held his gaze a moment before she spoke.

'I know you, Mark. I've met you a million times in bars all over the world. I now also know why you are here. There's nobody special in your life is there? The ones you thought you were connecting with; they were just using you for sex and all along you thought you were using them.' Karla stopped a moment and Mark just stared. She continued. 'When you eventually figured out you had real feelings for them, they were gone, off getting married to good old Joe down the road or Billy from accounts, the boring but dependable guys. Am I close?'

Mark stood and started to pace the room. 'They weren't all like that.' Running his hand through his hair he turned to face her. 'That's a lie. You're right they were all like that. How the hell did you get there so damn quick, I'm barely here five minutes?'

Karla walked slowly towards him.

He inhaled.

She touched his arm as she circled him.

'Mark, you have it written all over your face. To the trained eye I can see the pain you are in. I can see the hurt of unrequited love and the longing you have inside you to feel real, intimate love, the likes of which you've never felt before. We are here to help you. I am here to help you. Do you think that's what you want?' she paused and looked up at him.

Mark wasn't in a position to answer. Karla could see the emotion across his face. The pain of holding back tears was evident and the embarrassed shake of his head told her she'd hit a nerve.

She guided him towards one end of the couch before he had time to realise what was happening and she placed herself at the other end. Crossing her legs and angling them towards him she placed her manicured nails in her lap, the material of her skirt gathering around her.

'Mark.' She saw the effect of saying his name had on him. He lifted his head and inadvertently licked his lips. His piercing blue eyes were staring at her and Karla understood the magnetism this man exuded wouldn't be lost on the women who garnered his attention. 'Here's my suggestion for you, I think you are ready. I think you want to change. I also think that you are very good at masking your honest feelings with self-deprecating humour. You see, because you are so good-looking you have grown up used to getting your way. You didn't even realise this, because, well, because that's always been the way. You haven't had to fight for what you want, ever.' Karla paused, 'please stop me if I'm wrong?'

Mark smiled at her and gestured for her to go on.

'What you haven't had to do is check in with yourself and ask what those feelings are that now and again would pop up. Those genuine, deep-rooted feelings that would connect you to your very soul. I bet you are successful in everything you do and just expected love to follow suit. No?'

'Well, when you put it like that.' He shifted uncomfortably in the seat.

'It isn't anything to be ashamed of Mark. Being a success in life isn't wrong, but for you to have that success you have, for some reason felt it necessary to bury the part of you that would allow you to find a real connection with another human being. Because that would require vulnerability that you have never allowed yourself to feel.'

Mark just sat and stared. Karla knew what she was saying was hitting home. But she also knew she needed to push his buttons more, not quite knowing how far she could go.

'You strike me as someone who gives one hundred per cent to everything they do. I just have to look at how you are dressed today, how you entered the room with confidence, head high, shoulders back. I bet your car is spotless and tended to with care and attention, and I would lay my life on the fact that every woman you are interested in is given the full Mark Devine Treatment.'

'The full Mark Devine Treatment? I'm interested to hear what you think that is Karla?'

She smiled at him before continuing. 'It isn't a criticism. I just think that you probably do romance very well. You know the right things to say or at least what you think are the right things to say to get a woman all worked up and falling into your arms. I bet you're a complete gentleman, treating her like a lady until you get her into bed and expect her to be a whore for you there.'

Mark stood and looked at her incredulously. 'Now just wait a second, I don't want a whore and I certainly don't treat women like whores. You're way out of line lady.'

Karla stood too but only so she could reach out and touch Mark's arm and gently guide him back onto the couch before she spoke. 'Mark by the fact, that you are angry it means I've touched a nerve.'

'No, no, don't start giving me at all that mumbo jumbo stuff. I'm annoyed at you for painting a picture of me that's not true.'

'Really?' questioned Karla. 'Let's look at it then and you can tell me what's not true?'

Mark let out a sigh. 'The bit about treating them like a whore or wanting a whore or whatever that was that you said. You were right, I am a gentleman and that doesn't stop. I may like to do certain things in the bedroom department and have them done to me, but you of all people should be advocating that. Isn't that what you are all about here, free love, sexual health and well-being? Maybe I'm actually alright in that department and this was a mistake.' Mark rose off the couch and looked down at Karla. 'Thank you for your time, Karla. But I think this session is over.'

He held out his hand and Karla rose slowly and took it. She placed her other hand on top. 'Mark, stop for a moment, think about this. You've paid for the session at least take a few moments and then decide if you still want to leave. Let me say something and at the end, if you still want to go you can walk out that door and I won't try to stop you.'

Karla was composed, and her voice held compassion and her eyes searched his for something to hold onto.

Mark looked away. He took his hand from hers and placed it in his trouser pocket. He strolled to the desk chair and leaned on the back of it. He spoke without looking at her. 'I'll give you five minutes. If you haven't convinced me why I should continue with this then I'm gone.'

He looked up as she walked by him and took her place behind her desk again.

'Deal. Now can you sit down for those five minutes because I'll get an awful creak in my neck if I have to stare up at you for that long.' Karla gave a half smile which Mark received with his own.

'I spoke earlier about the sort of man I thought you were, about how relationships worked for you and for the most part you agreed. In fact, you were quite taken aback that I could understand the type of person you were in a short space of time. Is that correct so far?'

Mark nodded but didn't speak.

Karla took this as her cue to continue. 'I want to clarify the part that seems to be the issue here. What I said was when you get a woman into bed, I surmised that you wanted them to act like a whore for you after treating them like a lady.'

Karla could hear the objection coming so she raised her hand. 'Please, let me finish. What I meant by that was, that I think your issue lies in the fact that these women would react to your gentlemanly behaviour exactly how you wanted them to, demurely, gratefully, and as expected your behaviour got you past first, second and third base. Then once in the bedroom, you have a heightened sexual appetite that you would have expectations of having fulfilled. However, whilst there is absolutely nothing wrong with enjoying consensual sexual activity, your issue lies in the fact that as soon as these women do what you want them to do you lose respect for them. You cannot equate doing all those wonderfully sexy, exhilarating things to each other with the lady you want to bring home to your mom. Because you don't think of them as wonderful, sexy and exhilarating, you think of them as dirty, disgusting and vile, and hate that part of you that loves it all so much.'

Karla stopped speaking and exhaled. She stared at Mark and watched him absorb what she had said, watching how his face changed as the realisation sunk a little deeper. She could feel the uncomfortableness shift for him, and he eventually lifted his head, so his eyes met hers. She noticed the tear at the corner of his eyes, though he didn't seem to feel it as he continued to stare at her.

Mark cleared his throat. 'Karla, I don't know how you did that but you fucking, excuse the language, you may have hit on something and I don't know why. I love sex. I really do. I'm good at it and I know how to satisfy a woman and treat her exactly how she likes. I always ask and I always deliver. But... damn it, I, em, I,' the tear fell, and he wiped it away from his cheek. 'I think it best that I stay.'

Karla smiled sympathetically.

'That's a great decision, Mark. I don't think you'll regret it.'

CHAPTER 8

'Come in,' Anna responded to the knock on her office door, lifting her finger was enough of a sign. Harry closed the door behind him and said nothing while she worked. Taking his cue from her, he helped himself to a nice-looking bourbon from her bureau. Placing a measured glass of the cool amber liquid over ice in front of her, he relaxed on the couch and took a tasting sip, nodding approval as he did.

Anna looked up and smiled. 'Perfect timing, Harry. I just had to get that done and emailed, and that is me finished with computers for the day. Gosh, I really hate them.'

Harry held his glass up and nodded towards Anna. 'To successful days and horrible computers.'

Anna joined him on the couch and touched her glass with his. 'Yes, for sure.' She took a drink of the bourbon and looked at Harry thoughtfully. 'Tell me now, how did it go today?'

He nodded as he answered. 'It was amazing. My clients were all so different but each one of them will have something to gain from this. I know we are here because Ireland so badly needs a sexual revolution, but from the few I saw today, people are ready. They want this. You were right, they just needed someone to give them a space where they felt they could open up. Kudos to you, Anna.'

Harry held his glass aloft again, smiling at Anna as he took a swig of the smooth caramel-tasting whiskey. 'This is good stuff, what year is it?'

Anna laughed. 'Your senses are on high alert, aren't they? I do believe that's a very special bourbon you opened. My good friend Professor Harvey over at MIT sent that to me as a gift for opening the

Clinic. It really is delicious and smooth. You deserve the good liquor, Harry. I'm very impressed with your clinical notes, and your depth of knowledge. I really think those clients are very lucky to have you.'

'As shucks, you're making me blush.'

Anna looked at him and paused before she spoke. 'Take the compliment Harry, you deserve it—another annoying trait of the Irish. You very rarely take a compliment. The Love Lab is very lucky to have you.'

'Thank you, I'll take it gratefully. You're too kind.'

Silence descended.

Catching Harry's eye Anna held his gaze just a moment. It was all she needed.

Those eyes and that laid-back confidence on his six foot two taut frame did things to her that she had hoped would have disappeared by now.

Standing, Harry knocked back the remaining drink in his glass and placed it on her desk. 'I better go, Anna, it's been a long day and tomorrow looks like it's going to be another busy one.'

'Yes, yes, of course, I'll see you tomorrow. Have a lovely evening.' Anna nodded and stood.

As soon as Harry left, she drained her glass, picked up her mobile and dialled Fergal's number, 'Hello my love, how are you?'

'Hey darling, I'm great, what time do you reckon I can expect you?' Fergal asked.

'Well, that's why I'm ringing. How about you come in and meet me? We could stay in the city, make a night of it? I feel like celebrating our first official week.'

'That sounds great, give me an hour or two. Meet you at 37 Dawson about 7 p.m.? Want me to book somewhere or have you got that covered?'

'You know me, Ferg, I'll get it sorted. Westbury, OK?'

'Great, see you in a bit,' Fergal smiled and hit end on the phone. He loved their life. He knew how lucky he was to have found Anna and would never forget the first time she had agreed to go on a date with him. There were a lot of firsts he wouldn't forget. The sweetness of their first kiss, he nearly hurt with the pleasure as he thought of it. He could feel the heat of the sun from that day when he thought back to it. It was the Clapham Common Summer Fair in 2012. He had asked her to go with him, he'd packed a picnic. He'd even splashed out with his student earnings on a picnic blanket, but it was money well spent, and he would never regret a minute of it. He'd kissed her on that blanket as she sat chatting and telling him about her life in Sweden before her move to the UK. She spoke of her parents and their liberal views on sex and marriage, and how they had brought their daughters up to believe in their own autonomy over their feelings and their bodies. Anna oozed confidence on their first meeting. But not an arrogance. She was so self-assured that Fergal found it both endearing and if he was honest, a little scary. He'd never been with a woman who was so sure of who she was and where she was going in life. When she spoke, he listened intently, but somewhere along the line her words started to fade out and all he could hear was the lilt of her voice, the sexy accent, and those beautiful full lips. He kissed those lips that summer day and took his time savouring every moment of it. He knew at that moment this was the woman he would marry. He knew he would never tire of kissing those lips and he hadn't been wrong. Throwing a bag together and switching off lights, he headed to Dublin City Centre from their coastal home to join her.

CHAPTER 9

Karla was busy doing up her notes from the day and she wasn't particularly in a hurry home. She and Tom needed to have a serious conversation; she knew that. And she also knew she was stalling because she hated having tough conversations. Ironic in her line of work. Nobody wanted to break someone's heart if they could help it. She wished he'd just come to the conclusion himself, but she also knew that was a cop-out and she would have to just face up to it. Karla thought back to a book she had read during college, *Fierce Conversations*. But she couldn't remember what they said she should do to ease the pain for someone when you break up. Tom was a big boy. She hoped he'd dust himself off and find someone who could adore him like he wanted to be adored. She just knew it wasn't her anymore.

She was interrupted by the knock on her office door followed by a 'Karla, are you there? May I come in?'

She recognised the voice and smiled. 'Of course, Matt, come in take a seat. What can I do for you?' She gestured to the seat in front of her.

Matt gave her a big cheeky grin and sat. 'I was checking in to see how today went for you?'

'Oh, thank you, that's very thoughtful. It was a very interesting and productive day. I was delighted with my clients, and I really feel like we made some headway with them all. What about yourself?'

'Yes, much the same. I had two today. I found the second more challenging if I'm honest, I'm not sure we made much progress, but I'm hopeful that over the coming days, she'll start to see things a little differently.' Matt ran his hand through his hair and loosened his tie.

'I think I may lose this tomorrow.' He laughed as he pulled at it. 'I know Anna said no ties necessary, but I felt it gave me a more polished look, take away from the baby face,' he rubbed his cheek, 'but I don't think it had the desired effect.' He shrugged.

'I like it. You're right in thinking it gives you a polished look, but I'm not sure anything is going to take away from that baby face other than time and maybe a little stress to add in some lines?' Karla laughed companionably with Matt.

'I've plenty of stress,' Matt started but threw his hands up and laughed, 'Well actually that's not true, life's pretty good and what's there to be stressed about?'

'You better make that a rhetorical question, or we could be here all night.'

'All night's good with me,' Matt couldn't help smiling, and Karla was sure there was a twinkle in his eye. She hoped there wasn't because despite his cheerful disposition, and thoughtful and adorable American accent, Matt wasn't anything like the type of man she went for. She liked them rough and ready, and her preference would be a tattooed musician who liked to ride motorbikes, not an intellectual, baby-faced psychologist, no matter how sweet or handsome they were.

'Listen, Matt, I don't mean to be rude, but it's been a long day and I'm still not finished here, and my boyfriend promised he'd cook tonight as he has no gigs. Well, when I say cook, I mean order take out,' Karla knew she was divulging too much information, but she wanted Matt to get the hint.

'Oh yes, sorry. Sorry, anyway, I'm glad your first day went well.' Matt stood and pulled at his tie. 'Great, well… so see you tomorrow, or not yeah, so see you soon.'

He walked out the door.

Closing the door behind him he palmed his forehead. Not quite believing how flustered she had made him. It brought him right back to his teenage years and all the beautiful women whom he had fawned over and who hadn't looked sideways at him. At that time, he was scrawny with bucked teeth and absolutely no confidence when it came to women. Speaking with Karla had brought all those insecurities rising to the top again. No woman since Janine Zabowsky in eleventh grade had made him feel so tongue-tied. Janine Zabowsky, he hadn't thought about her in a few years. He remembered the pain of the interaction like it was yesterday. It had taken all the courage he could muster to walk up to her at recess in front of all her friends and ask her to spring dance. But rather than just say a polite no thanks, she had laughed in his face and made fun of him in front of everyone. And that had been the turning point for him. Two years of painful orthodontic work and spending every waking moment in the gym meant that by the time Matt turned eighteen every girl at Highgrove High School wanted to his attention. Nobody since then has had such an effect as Karla. He wasn't about to let those old insecurities win. He was no longer a shy, awkward sixteen-year-old boy. He was a twenty-eight-year-old man, and he knew what he wanted. He reminisced all the way to the car and decided there was only one thing for it. He lifted the phone and hit the speed dial number one. Harry answered on the second ring.

'Harry, we need a drink,' Matt didn't waste any time with pleasantries.

Harry laughed. 'We do, do we? And why do we need a drink? Actually, scrap that, I don't care why we need one because I do too. Where and when my friend?'

Matt knew exactly where they should go, '37 Dawson, in thirty minutes?'

'Great, I'll be there, see you shortly.'

It may have been a Wednesday night, but nobody told the revellers in 37 Dawson that. Matt shuffled through the crowd at the front door searching for his friend. Not that he would miss him. At six foot two Harry was usually a head above many in a crowd.

Matt wasn't seeing him, so he made his way to the bar and ordered two pints, scanning the crowd for familiar faces. As he did, he caught a glimpse of what looked like Anna leaning in and kissing a guy full on the lips. Putting two and two together it didn't take Matt long to realise it must be her husband. Then he caught sight of Harry out of the corner of his eye.

Matt threw a hand in the air to beckon him and handed him his drink before nodding in the direction of Anna and her husband. 'Better go say hello to the boss lady, mate.'

Harry followed Matt's gaze and caught sight of Anna, she was laughing at something a guy was saying to her and looking at him like she would devour him at any minute.

Harry swallowed hard before answering, 'I think we may be interrupting something if we do, Matt.'

'Not at all, mate, sure we have to get to meet the famous Fergal and see what's so special about him that he hooked Anna, right?' Matt playfully thumped Harry on the arm and as he turned he caught sight of Harry's expression. 'Hey, what the hell is that look for? I've seen that look before mate, you're not seriously looking at her that way?'

'I'm just surprised to see her here,' Harry took a long drink of his beer and tried to look anywhere but where his eyes wanted to go.

'I've seen that look, Harry, and it was the first night you met Abigail.'

'Leave it, Matt, you've no idea what you're talking about.'

'Sure, if that's how you want to play it. Do you want to leave?'

'No, of course not, let's go say hello and do the pleasantries.'

'You sure?'

Harry was already making his way through the bar to where Anna and Fergal were standing against a pillar. They were thoroughly engrossed in each other, and Anna only noticed Harry when he was standing in front of them.

She was as surprised to see them as they were to see her and took a second too long in Matt's eyes to make the introduction. He knew there was more to this than Harry was willing to divulge. He also knew his friend well enough not to ask anymore, certainly for now.

'Harry, Matt, what a surprise. Nice to see you both.' Anna looked from one to the other and smiled widely. 'I'd like to introduce you to my husband, Dr Fergal McDermot.' She turned to Fergal and introduced Matt and Harry.

'Lovely to meet you. Anna has spoken highly of you both. Harry, I believe we probably kicked back in our youth. I was trying to place you. I know I've heard your name in recent years. You're from Dalkey also. Is that right?'

'Yeah, but we moved away for a while and back when I was in my late teens.'

'Ah, that's probably what it is. I know when Anna was speaking about you, I was wondering why I couldn't place you. Can I get either of you boys a drink? My wife and I haven't managed to make it to the bar yet,' he smiled. 'We were busy catching up.' Fergal placed a chaste kiss on Anna's lips.

'Eh, sure, we're both on Heineken, very kind of you Fergal. Here, let me help you,' said Matt heading to the bar with Fergal, chatting amicably as they went.

Anna looked up at Harry. He couldn't help the way his body reacted when she did that. It was like an ache he wanted her so much.

'Harry,' she said his name so softly, but even with the music playing he heard it. 'Fergal and I have a very open marriage, but I still don't flaunt anything in front of him out of respect and he's the same with me, so maybe we could have a chat tomorrow and keep certain things between us?'

Harry didn't say anything for a moment. He took a deep breath before he spoke. 'Anna, right now I can't think of anything other than how beautiful you look, and yes, you have my word. I would never betray your confidence.' Harry grazed her hand with his own.

Matt and Fergal returned from the bar and pleasantries were exchanged before Anna and Fergal made their excuses and went to dinner.

Matt waited until they were out of sight before pouncing on Harry, 'So, nothing to tell?'

'Leave it.' Harry didn't move, the beer holding his gaze, 'just leave it, Matt.'

'You want to head home?' Matt shrugged his shoulders and took a swig of beer.

'Definitely not. It's all good.' Harry knocked back the rest of his drink and raised his hand to get the bartender's attention. 'I'll have two more Heineken and two tequila slammers please.' Before Matt could open his mouth to protest, Harry raised his hand to silence him. 'We're going old school my friend, and there's some college-going ladies at our three o'clock that are in for some fun tonight.'

Matt laughed, turned to look and found himself locking eyes with a very petite brunette who raised her glass in silent salute to him. Smiling back, he turned to Harry and dusted the salt onto the side of his hand. 'Harry my man, you haven't lost your touch.'

Licking the salt from their hands they threw back the tequila and sucked hard on the lemon wedges before slamming the glasses upside down on the bar. 'Let the games begin.' Harry raised his beer in the direction of the group of girls he had earmarked for them and treated them to his megawatt smile.

Matt raised his beer and added, 'Dublin watch out we are coming for you tonight.'

CHAPTER 10

Harry woke to the sound of his alarm screeching in his ears. He lifted his head an inch off his pillow, it was all he could manage before the thumping started, the headache was too intense to deal with, so he closed his eyes again and reached his hand out to feel for his phone.

Finding it he managed to quell the noise but not before he had woken the woman who was the owner of the limbs he found himself entangled in.

Reaching out again he felt soft, warm skin under his fingers and couldn't help himself as his hand kept exploring trying to figure out what part of a woman he was touching. The curiosity got the better of him and opening his eyes he recognised the petite brunette staring back at him.

Ah, the girl from the bar. It started to come back to him. *Mm...* She returned the soft touch and found him very much awake in the only area she seemed concerned about now. 'Honey, you can't. I can't,' he started to say but he lifted his head as he felt her mouth take all of him in. 'Oh god, I don't think...' but it was as far as he got before his mouth was covered with full lips and the antics of the night before started to come back, and he remembered there were two of them. He moaned wistfully and gave in to the urges that started to course through his body.

He felt for the breasts of the woman now kissing him and found full, wonderful mounds in his hands. There was something special about college girls, that was for sure, he thought as he exploded into a warm inviting mouth. He heard murmurs of appreciation and ohs and ahs, but they all felt like they were behind a wall, everything was muffled, and the sensations running through his body felt so deep they made him shudder.

His ecstasy was shattered by the shrill of his alarm going off again. Sitting up slowly he hit the snooze button once more. He needed five more minutes. He opened his arms as two giggling, eager girls lay into the crook of each one. He thought life was pretty good.

Harry rapped on the door and didn't wait for an answer. He swung it open and entered Matt's office, smiled broadly, and perched himself on the edge of Matt's desk. Matt was busy on the phone and signalled for Harry to take a seat which Harry ignored and continued to sit on the edge of the desk.

Matt finished his call and leaned back in his chair, crossing his feet out in front of him he stretched and returned Harry's broad grin before speaking.

'Well, well, well, I see your trampled heart got some much-needed TLC last night.'

'Too right it did. How did you fair out in the end?' enquired Harry.

'Well, as a matter of fact, I didn't do too bad either, one of mine got cold feet but her friend more than made up for it. I'm wrecked today, it's been a while since I went all night like that. She was insatiable. Couldn't get enough of Matty Jr here,' Matt tapped his crotch and laughed.

Harry laughed with him and recounted his night before getting up to leave. 'I've only one patient today, so I'm going to get myself out of here as soon I've finished with that. I'm pleasantly tired but I think a power nap might sort me out later. You fancy watching the footie round mine later?'

'Yep, sounds like a plan, if I make it through the day. I've two clients so I'll finish up when I can and head over to yours. Takeaway?'

'Yeah, sounds good, let me see if I'm up for cooking I can throw something together either. I'll figure that out later when I'm awake and thinking better.' Harry headed for the door. 'Catch you later, mate.'

'Great.' Matt gave Harry a small wave as his phone rang again and he pressed the button to answer.

After Harry's patient left, he set about typing up his notes so he could get away for the day. He was just coming to the end of it when the knock on his door surprised him. For a moment he thought he had another patient that wasn't on his booking system.

When he said 'Yes,' followed by, 'Come in,' and looked up from his work, he saw it wasn't a stranger that stood there. It was Anna.

His breath caught and he stood, he wasn't sure why. He ran his hand through his hair and watched her. She stood at the door and slowly closed it behind her. She stared at him, tilted her head slightly, and with a half-smile leaned back and turned the lock. Harry's brain took a moment to catch up with what was going on. She sauntered towards him.

The silk material of her vibrant red skirt floated just below her knees. Her red heels looked exquisitely sexy at the end of her bronzed slim legs. That was all he could take in before he realised she had stopped, she was on the other side of his desk, facing him. She still hadn't said a word, but her eyes said a thousand things all at once to him. He was afraid of his voice, so he didn't speak.

Harry walked around the desk, tentatively placing his hands on either side of her. Anna with her back to him leaned forward slightly on the desk. He took it as compliance and slowly, as steadily as he could with how he was feeling, traced the line of her right hand with his, followed it up her arm and let his hand rest on her hip.

The silence in the room was heavy and still, they didn't speak.

Harry reached under Anna's skirt and slid her panties aside finding a warm, wet space waiting for him. 'Oh Christ,' he murmured, and a moan escaped. He devoured her neck, sucking and kissing like a madman. His hand left her hip and found her beautiful pert breast under her blouse, her hard nipple greeted him as he moaned again. Anna bent over further on the desk as Harry's fingers brought her to the edge of ecstasy. Whipping open his buckle and trousers he grabbed himself and ploughed into Anna.

'So tight,' he murmured into her ear. She pushed back and moaned as he ploughed into her again and again, and the more she bucked against him the deeper he drove.

'Fuck me, Harry,' she said deep and low making him nearly lose his mind.

'Jesus, Anna, you're fucking amazing,' he moaned before biting at her neck and reaching round to find her lips and kiss her. With both hands now on her breasts he squeezed and rolled her nipples as he drove faster and faster feeling the crescendo coming, and not sure how much longer he could hold out. 'I want you to cum in my mouth,' she whispered. Harry didn't need telling twice, pulling out of her he spun her around. She was on her knees with him in her mouth before he had time to think and he was sent over the edge letting go when he saw her look up at him and smirk. *My cock is in Anna's mouth*, was the last thing that went through his mind before he came, and his legs started to lose power. He half fell, half grabbed for the chair behind him and watched as Anna licked her lips and pulled her panties back into place.

She reached over and kissed his flaccid cock before kissing his lips, smiling, and walking out the door.

Harry sat motionless, waiting for his breathing to return to something that was semi-normal.

He looked down at himself and started laughing. 'Anna, Anna, Anna.' He shook his head. 'You are fucking amazing.'

Harry figured he'd better make himself half decent and then remembered the report he was finishing when he was interrupted.

Knowing it wasn't going to finish itself, he forced himself to try to concentrate but couldn't quite contain the satisfied smirk that escaped and sat on his lips, still not quite believing what had just happened.

♥♥♥

Matt could hear the Kings of Leon banging out of Harry's apartment when he stepped out of the lift. As he walked in through the unlocked door, he saw Harry rocking out in his kitchen to 'Sex on Fire,' an apron tied around his waist and a myriad of pots and pans on the go on the stove. Matt placed the six-pack on the dining table and watched his friend for a moment before starting a slow, loud clap.

Turning, Harry grinned from ear to ear and reached for the remote, greeting Matt. 'Welcome my friend, it's a fine evening for footie and a home-cooked meal, isn't it?'

Laughing Matt grabbed a beer and handed one to Harry. 'Well, I don't know where you got your energy from, but I'll have whatever you're having.' Matt closed the fridge door and leaned against the counter.

'Amazing what a bit of afternoon sex does for a man. You remember that don't you mate?' Harry opened his beer and took a swig.

Matt looked impressed. 'Did you hook up with those college girls from last night again?'

'Nope,' was all Harry divulged before turning to stir the sauce. Matt was sure he was only doing that to avoid eye contact with him.

'Is that all I'm getting? No deets at all? Come on man, who was she at least? You owe me that!' Matt laughed when he saw Harry's amused expression.

'Yeah, you would swear you were starved of women's affections. Deets will follow if there's anything worth reporting. All you need to know right now is that because of my surprisingly happy mood and sudden burst of energy, you get to enjoy a home-cooked meal tonight. So, take a pew, turn on the footie and be grateful she hasn't joined me tonight, or you my friend would be out on your ass.'

Matt saluted, 'Yes sir,' he mocked and ducked when Harry threw a bottle top at him.

Karla stood looking at her mobile. Leaning against the countertop she toyed with it being a good idea and a stupid one. She tried the pep talk route and it usually worked, but this time she wasn't feeling it. She knew she was being ridiculous and started to dial his number. She stopped and chuckled, embarrassingly shaking her head. She knew she didn't want to chicken out and had thought this through. Before she had a chance to think any further about it, she had dialled Harry's number.

Just as she was about to hang up, she heard Harry's deep voice at the other end of the line.

'Karla, hi, what can I do for you?'

'Harry, hi, I'm sorry I hope I'm not disturbing you?'

Karla heard the hesitation in Harry's voice, 'Eh, no, no go ahead.'

'Oh gosh, I am. I'm sorry, it can wait. It's just a work-related question.' Karla exhaled.

'If you're sure? It's footie tonight and Matt's here to watch the game. I have time in the morning at about ten we could chat then?'

'Ten would be perfect, Harry, and sorry I don't know what I was thinking calling you after hours. My apologies. Hi to Matt.' Karla hung up before she said anything else.

Dropping her head, Karla felt the heat rise in her cheeks and felt foolish. She poured herself a glass of wine and caught sight of the remainder of Tom's belongings by the window in the sitting room. She didn't remember a time when she had ever felt so nervous about asking a man out. Granted it had been a few years because she had been in a relationship. But now she just felt like a prize idiot, and on top of that, Harry and Matt were no doubt wondering what was wrong with her randomly ringing about work like that. They'd probably see right through her feeble excuse.

Harry stood looking at the phone, slightly puzzled.

'What was that about?' Matt asked over his shoulder from his seat on the couch.

'Karla, looking to ask me something about work she said.'

'That is one hot piece of ass right there.' Matt flicked the channels with the remote to see if he could find other coverage of the soccer game.

'Matt, we work with that hot piece of ass. A little respect please.'

Matt turned and looked and Harry. 'Really?'

'Yes really. Although in fairness she is smokin', just not my type.' Harry came around to take a seat.

'Since when was a smokin' hot woman, with a brain, not your type, Eames? This afternoon sex person has you all caught up, hasn't she?' Matt looked at his friend and shook his head at Harry's protestations. 'Don't even think about it, bro. I'll get it out of you who it is, don't you worry. Now, what the hell is going on with the new commentator on RTE? Let's watch this on Sky.' Matt flicked the channel over.

Harry sat silently listening to his friend, with memories of Anna bent over his desk running through his head and smiled sweetly. He certainly had enough memories in there to keep him warm tonight.

❤❤❤

Karla took a deep breath and answered the knock on her office door with a 'Come in.' She watched Harry stride through the door and marvelled at his swagger. She could feel her pulse quicken and had to remind herself that after the embarrassment of last night's phone call, she had decided that she wasn't going to pursue the Harry thing, whatever that was. If the man wanted her, he could show his hand. In the meantime, Karla, would save face and carry on like her loins were not on fire.

'Harry, thank you so much for this. And again, I'm so sorry about calling you last night, I was going through my notes, and I really don't know what I was thinking.' Karla sat back down and offered a seat to Harry.

'Listen, don't even think about it. It's no problem. What's this dilemma then?'

Karla cleared her throat. 'Well, it's a guy who came in because he claimed to have impotency issues. But it was very clear after a short discussion that there were no physical issues in that department,' Karla looked knowingly at Harry. 'The problem for me is that he has gotten a slight attachment now and I've tried all the usual techniques, but nothing seems to be working to get him to understand that I'm not the answer to his prayers.'

Harry nodded knowingly. 'I think you'll have to bring this one to Anna's attention, you know her rules, and there's an ethical line here that you have to be careful not to cross.' Harry hesitated before he spoke again. 'You're not attracted to this guy, are you?' he held up his hands when he saw the incredulous look on Karla's face. 'I know, I know, I'm sorry to even ask, but it's been known to happen.'

'I know, but that's not me. I know the line and I would never cross it with a client. Harry, I know we haven't known each other that long as colleagues, but you have to know my client's needs come first, and despite the position this guy has put me in I want to help him. I just think his care is compromised now because of how he has convinced himself he feels about me.' Karla exhaled heavily.

'OK, so let's look at this in its entirety,' Harry shifted forward in his seat. 'This guy thought for, how long has he thought he was impotent?'

'A year.'

'OK, so this guy thought he was impotent for a year. He's come to the clinic thinking we can help him deal with it. In fairness to him, he figured out that there's not a medical reason for it, rather, something is going on in this head,' Harry paused and looked at Karla. 'Right so far?'

'Yes. Continue.'

'He comes in, starts talking to you and his little soldier starts to stand to attention all by its lonesome. He can't believe it and looks at you and looks and it and goes, well, blow me down, this woman can work miracles by just being in the same room as me.'

Karla smiled at Harry's description and gestured for him to continue.

'So, then he goes home, but his little soldier doesn't stand to attention as it had in here, and once again he comes back in and it's standing ramrod straight for the lovely Karla.'

'Not quite, Harry, but go on.'

'Now, it's not a far reach for this guy to think that you have cured him, though for him to stay cured he needs to be with you. Then all his problems would be sorted. But he has forgotten about the wife and kids at home that he has made the commitment to, and the reason he came – excuse the pun – in the first place.' Harry paused and sat back in the chair holding out both hands to Karla, inviting her to add her piece to the story.

'You have the story fairly accurate, but you missed the part where I tried to convince him that it wasn't standing 'ramrod' straight as you put it, for me, rather it was just because I was something different. I am outside of the ordinary and possibly a little exciting, as it's forbidden.'

'Ah, I'd neglected the "exciting because it's a forbidden bit," very important.'

'Yes, my professional analysis was that he needed to go back in time to when he and his wife had a healthy, exciting sex life, remember those feelings, and try to recreate them with her. However, his answer to that was to come back in two days later and tell me he no longer loved his wife, she didn't turn him on anymore and no amount of going back in time was going to change that.'

'Wow, OK, that was a quick decision on his part.'

'Yes, and when you know, you know, so that would be fine, except he also said that the reason he didn't love his wife anymore was because he was in love with me.'

Harry exhaled slowly and looked at Karla. 'Oh, that certainly is an awkward one, Karla. I presume you put him straight?'

'Of course, I did, Harry. I told him that what he was feeling wasn't love and perhaps he was confusing it with gratitude because he may have felt that I had helped him. I also explained that I had not helped him overcome his impotency, rather, in talking about his issues he had realised that he no longer loved his wife and that maybe the guilt of that was what had caused his problems, but now that he had admitted it, the issue was no longer there.' Karla took a deep breath. 'He pointed out that wasn't true, because he was still impotent with her and any other woman, it was just when he saw me that the problem disappeared.'

'Oh,' exclaimed Harry. 'A little more awkward, so... This guy has it real bad, Karla. You don't really have a choice, do you? You've got to speak with Anna and let her take it from here.'

'I thought you might say that, but I was hoping there was another way. I feel like I've failed at the first hurdle with this one.' And she didn't just mean with her client.

CHAPTER 11

Fergal ended the call he was on and sat back in his office chair. The view over the cliff and out to sea was one he adored and hoped he would never tire of. He loved the beach and felt at home when he was close to it. It was where he had grown up; kissing his first girl in the dunes on Breezy Point strand. Most of his childhood memories came from gloriously content days spent playing in the cold Irish Sea. Sandwiches filled with sand were a staple of his growing-up years when going home before dark was never in the cards. Lunch was eaten in a rush standing with teeth chattering, sand blowing all around, amid typical Irish summer weather including patches of sunshine interspersed with rain showers and windy spells. He wouldn't have it any other way.

Lost in thought, Fergal wondered about his kids should he be lucky enough to have any. Would they have the same freedom he had growing up? Probably not. Things had changed in Ireland since the 90's and they were changing at lightning speed now. He wasn't sure that was the best thing about the internet age and technology. He loved how many jobs had been made easier with the development of technology, but what about all the advances that weren't so good, mostly to the psyche? He had kids coming to see him now younger and younger with mental health issues. And technology definitely played a very large role in their lives and the issues they were having.

He was finding it very hard to shake the melancholy today and knew he needed a walk and some fresh air before his next client was due. He reached for his windbreaker and headed for the back door and down the steps to the beach. Fergal loved that Anna had taken to his hometown so quickly and had grown to love it nearly as much as him. That she had wanted to set up her clinic in Dublin was a source of great happiness for him. When they had met in college, he never dreamt she would fall for the pasty Irish nerd. He always felt he was punching above his weight with her, and his friends constantly reminded him that they thought so too.

He knew the reason for the mood but was reluctant to go there in his mind. He admonished himself as he strode purposefully down the steps, the coastal wind whipping at his face. He had never doubted that Anna loved him. But he also knew Anna was a free spirit, and a woman who knew her own mind. It was part of what had attracted him to her in the first place. She'd been honest with him from the beginning. Monogamy was never something she had believed in and yet she had agreed to marry him; with one caveat. She needed to have an open relationship. All along he had thought he could deal with it. He convinced himself that if he allowed her what she needed and loved her enough, she wouldn't need to act on her desires. He was sure that her knowing she could be free within their marriage would be enough for her. But lately, it was getting so much harder to ignore the fact that he knew there was someone else she was seeing, and the thought of it was slowly eating him up inside. He had been crazy to think he could handle this. It didn't matter how many nights they had discussed it before they married. It didn't matter what his friends and family had said to warn him off the idea, and it certainly didn't matter that she had said she was happy for them both to be open in the relationship. Fergal knew the only person he wanted to be with was Anna, and knowing he wasn't enough for her was what was tearing him up inside. He heard what he was saying to himself, but it didn't seem to ease the ache that was creeping into his heart. Everything was getting so much harder to handle now.

Fergal decided to put his marriage problems to the back of his mind and increase the speed of his steps. He needed to focus on his patients for now. He shook his head as he thought of the ten-year-old he had seen that morning. His parents had brought him to talk to Fergal because he was talking about killing himself. It turned out the poor kid didn't want to kill himself, he just wanted someone to listen to him, not to try to make it right. Just to listen to him. Even though Fergal had gotten him to admit there was no plan behind the words, he knew the child wasn't out of the woods and needed help figuring out how to navigate this crazy world.

He let out a roar into the biting wind of the empty beach, in a futile attempt at releasing the pent-up frustration that seemed to be consuming him lately. Just to be sure there was no doubting his determination he picked up his speed turning the walk into a jog and eventually a full-on sprint knowing there was little hope he could outrun the problems taking up space in his head.

CHAPTER 12

Anna sat facing her client and felt herself getting slightly aroused. He was a fine specimen of a man. She had a weakness for working-class men who worked with their hands, and the client in front of her most definitely had hands that she knew would do some marvellous work.

'Padraig, I'm really glad you decided to come back,' Anna spoke softly relaxing back into her chair. 'Would you like to tell me what happened after our first session when you went home?'

Padraig looked a little uncomfortable and cleared his throat before leaning forward on his tanned muscular legs. Anna couldn't help noticing the bulging shoulder muscles through his tight t-shirt.

'Well, em, I,' he stopped and coughed again. 'Sorry Anna, this shouldn't be so difficult for me.' Padraig gave her a half smile before continuing.

'I decided on my way home that I wasn't going to mention anything to Sandra about the sessions, at least not yet. I want to get my head around them first. I know she doesn't see anything wrong, and she hasn't done anything wrong. My sex drive is very high, and I thought after we got married that she would just go along with things, and we'd be grand. But, as I said last week, I don't know how much longer I can hold off before I do something stupid like cheat on her. I really don't want to, and I know it wouldn't mean anything, it would just be sex,' Padraig paused and looked at Anna for guidance.

She nodded and said, 'You're doing great, continue.'

'Well, you see, I thought about that afterwards and what you said about maybe looking at it from her side and well I got to thinking that me being more thoughtful about her and what she needs might actually work. At least I wanted to give it a try.' He lifted his head and looked at Anna. 'I love her so much, I really do. I never want to hurt her but it's like another part of me is pushing my buttons and these urges come over me. If I can't satisfy them with Sandra, I'm afraid I'll take up one of the offers from the young one that I get all the time down the pub.'

Anna smiled a little as she looked at him. 'That's great insight after just one session Padraig, so tell me what you did?'

'Well, like you suggested, I tried to talk to her more and I even brought her flowers one evening. Although that near backfired caused she was convinced I'd done something wrong, 'cause I never bring her flowers,' Padraig paused and Anna smiled knowingly.

'But, I bet she was grateful once you had convinced her nothing was wrong?'

'Yeah,' Padraig grinned wildly. 'She was very, very grateful if you get my drift.'

'Explain that more to me?'

'Really? Oh, well. She, eh, gave me a blow job right there in the kitchen. That hasn't happened since we were first going steady.' Padraig looked embarrassed as he caught Anna's eye.

'How did that make you feel?'

Laughing Padraig shook his head, 'Like a million fucking dollars.'

Anna joined him and laughed too, 'I'm delighted for you and all because you brought your wife a bouquet. Imagine what could happen if you were that little bit more attentive all the time?'

'Yeah, you see I was thinking about that after what you were saying in the last session. But then my problem is that the more I get it the more I want it. It's like the switch has been turned on and I can't turn it off. Sandra's been great, but she's busy and tired a lot and I don't always want to do the whole foreplay thing with her. She needs that. I'd love a quickie when I get in from work some days. No talking even, just a fuck against the kitchen counter for the release. Is that awful to say?'

Anna took a moment before responding, 'What you described to me Padraig is exactly what you wanted. Your wife gave you something she hasn't done in years and all because you gave her a little more attention than usual. Have you ever asked her about the quickie?'

'Well, no, not directly. But I know she wouldn't be up for it, just a wham bam type thing, it's never been her style.'

'And have blow jobs been her 'style' as you put it?'

'Eh well, now that you put it like that, no, but, well I, shit, I just presumed.' Padraig paused and looked at Anna shrugging his shoulders. 'I just presumed, didn't I?'

'I think you just answered your own question, Padraig. What do you think your wife would do if you told her how you feel?'

'I think she'd be asking me if I'm sleeping with someone else.'

Anna nodded and asked, 'What If you sat her down and told her how you were feeling? Explained that you love her very much and you just feel that having different types of sex with her is what you need but you want to know how she feels and what she needs?'

'I think she'd keel over with shock if I said any of that to be honest. But you know what Anna, I'm willing to give it a shot. I've everything to gain, haven't I? And everything to lose if I don't do this, right?' This time he looked questioningly at Anna.

'You're absolutely right Padraig. You and your wife have so much to gain from being open with each other. You have no idea where it may lead. She might even surprise you again.'

'I'll take that.'

'Great, well I'd love you to check in with us and let me know how it goes. But unless there's anything else I think we're all done here?' Anna briskly stood reached out and shook Padraig's hand.

Padraig shook hers and smiled. 'Anna, I have to say, it was definitely easier to talk to you than I ever imagined.'

'Thank you.' She released Padraig's hand and walked with him to the door. She couldn't help admiring his rugged handsomeness. 'You know where we are if you ever need another session, but I have a feeling that once you talk to your wife you won't be needing us here at The Love Lab anymore,' Anna smiled and closed the door behind him, leaning against it and blowing out her breath.

Feeling very frustrated and dare she say a little turned on Anna found herself fanning her face before reaching down and unbuttoning the top button on her blouse. She felt inside her silk blouse, cupping her breast gently, feeling aroused and thinking about what she could do about it. It didn't take long. She strode towards her desk leant over and felt her thighs press against her pencil skirt, the pull of the fabric against her bare legs felt enticingly hot and she quickly lifted the receiver.

Harry answered on the third ring, just as Anna was about to hang up.

'You look your time,' she practically panted.

Harry wasn't paying attention when he picked up his phone until he heard Anna's voice.

'Anna, gosh sorry, in the middle of finishing notes here. I was in another world, what can I do for you?' He was still trying to finish his final paragraph.

'Could you come into my office for a moment?' Anna's voice sounded weird.

'Of course, are you OK?'

'Yes, yes, I'm fine.' She tried to control her breathing, but just thinking about having Harry inside her was sending her into a spin.

'You don't sound it. I'll be right there.' Jumping up from his desk he rushed to Anna's office, swung open the door and then realised why Anna had sounded weird. She was leaning against her desk, her skirt riding her thighs and her blouse open revealing her white lace bra. Her erect nipples pushed through the flimsy material as she looked straight at him, with eyes that were devouring him in the time it took him to take in the scene.

'Holy shit Anna,' was all Harry managed before two long strides had him grabbing her into his arms. He couldn't get enough of her, his mouth found hers, and one hand roughly grabbed her breast while the other found that soft, wet, and wonderful place between her legs.

His mind was going crazy, filled with her. She was devouring him. She had his trousers open, and he was in her hands within seconds. They were both lost in their lust, taking what they needed from each other, getting hungrier for more until he ploughed into her. Begging him not to stop, she moaned loudly, his name tumbling from her lips. She begged him to go deeper, again and again until they came simultaneously. Anna screamed his name with pleasure, Harry moaned deeply calling out hers.

He barely had time to catch his breath when he heard her say, 'Again, I want more.'

He pulled back and smirked at her, 'Are you trying to kill me?'

'Don't tell me you can't satisfy me Eames; I may have to look for a younger model.'

She kissed his neck teasingly.

'Oh, I can satisfy you Anna, and you know damn well I can.' Leaning in so he could whisper in her ear he said, 'I think it's time you turned around, this one is going to be much, much slower and then we are going to see who satisfies who.' Harry grabbed her face with both hands and kissed her before pulling back, smiling and placing his hands on her hips he turned her to face away from him.

Leaning over he stripped her blouse and brassiere off, slowly tracing the lines of her back with his fingertip. He leaned down and whispered. 'This is going to take some time.'

CHAPTER 13

Matt was doodling. The knock on his office door took him out of his revere and he caught a glimpse of the scribbles he had been making on his notepad. He had written Karla's name over and over again across the page. He laughed at himself before chuckling an answer to the knock with a quick 'Come in' and rising to meet his patient. He put all thoughts of Karla out of his mind and tried to concentrate on the task at hand.

'Hello,' said a meek voice that belonged to a very petite brunette who poked her head around the door. 'Should I come in?'

'Sorry, of course, come in,' Matt strode towards her and held out his hand.

'I'm Matt, lovely to meet you. Veronica, right?' he checked that he had the right client.

Softly she replied. 'Yes, I'm Veronica, nice to meet you Matt.'

He guided her towards the chair and offered her a drink.

'To be honest, I'd kill for a gin and tonic, but I know that's not what you meant,' giggled Veronica. 'I'd love an iced water please.' She placed her bag at her feet and sat in the bucket chair Matt had pointed out to her.

'Coming right up, Veronica.'

'Vonny, please call me Vonny. Only my mum calls me Veronica, or my boss at work.'

'Vonny it is. It's lovely to meet you.' Matt handed her a glass of Evian and sat down at his desk.

'You seem a little nervous, which is totally understandable, but please try to relax.'

'Oh, I am nervous, does it show? I'm sorry, it's just well, I've never done anything like this before and I, well, I don't know where to start.' Veronica stumbled over the words as they raced from her mouth.

'Well, why don't we start with both of us taking a few deep breaths, having a drink of water and then when you are ready you can tell me what prompted you to make an appointment?'

She smiled weakly, took a sip of her drink placed it on Matt's desk and took a deep breath before beginning. 'Well, you see I'm engaged.'

'I see that, I couldn't help noticing that huge diamond on your finger. Congratulations.'

'Thank you,' Vonny sat back in the chair and took another breath and relaxed a little more.

'Well, you see, my fiancé,' she giggled. 'I'm still getting used to saying that word. My fiancé, Sebastian, is gorgeous. He's handsome, intelligent, popular, interesting, and has loads of friends.' Vonny gasped and continued, 'And well, I'm not really any of those things, and to top it all off well, you see, I'm still a virgin. Oh god, I can't believe I just said that out loud.' She dropped her head into her hands as embarrassment crept up her face.

Matt took a moment before he spoke. 'Well, that's amazing. That's great that you've told me. We can work from there.'

Lifting her head, she peeped at Matt through half-closed eyes. 'Oh god, I think I'm going to die of embarrassment right now. I really can't believe I shared that with you.'

'Vonny, believe me when I say, that over the next few weeks that will most likely be the least embarrassing thing we talk about. I'm going to help you realise that what you are offering your fiancé is a wonderful gift, and he is most likely very grateful for that gift.'

'But, that's the problem.'

'I don't understand. Why is that the problem?'

'Well, because he has all this experience and I have zero. Well, close to zero. I mean we've messed around and stuff and I like to pleasure him and he's very good at pleasuring me. But he's had several very advanced women if you know what I mean, and I don't want to disappoint him.'

'OK, I get it. I do, you've come to the right place. Can I ask how your best friends would describe you?'

'My best friends?'

'Yes.'

'Em, well, I'd say maybe they'd say I'm a nice person, I'm kind, helpful maybe?'

'Great and no doubt we could add beautiful and now thoughtful to that too?'

Vonny blushed. 'Why do you say I'm thoughtful?'

'Because you are here, despite your embarrassment to see if you can do anything that will help your relationship. I think that shows a very thoughtful person indeed.'

'Oh thank you,' Vonny replied.

Matt continued. 'Your fiancé put that ring on your finger because I'm guessing he's a bright man and he figured out that if he didn't some other guy was going to come along, pretty soon, and put a ring on it.'

'Well, when you put it like that,' she giggled.

'I can teach you all you need to know about pleasuring a man and yourself so that when you get married you will feel more comfortable and at ease. Is that what you want?'

Veronica smiled and looked at Matt, 'Yes, yes please, that's exactly what I want. Thank you, Matt.'

'It will be my pleasure, Vonny. Now the first thing we need to figure out is what makes you tick. What turns you on?'

'Well, I know I love kissing Seb and I love when he touches my, my, oh god OK, I love when he touches my breasts. There, I've said it. I have very sensitive nipples.'

'That's great. What else?'

'Em, I like it when he massages me. He's very good at massages and he can make me cum just by giving me a massage.'

'He is obviously skilled at them so. What about pleasuring yourself, can you do that and bring yourself to orgasm?'

Coughing first, Veronica dropped her head a little before answering. 'I've never used anything on myself if that's what you mean. I've rubbed myself a little down there and it feels nice but I'd rather it when Seb does it. He does know how to turn me on, I just want to know how to do it to him.'

Matt leaned in and spoke softly. 'I bet you already do, but I know what you mean, and I can show you what to do, Vonny.'

'Yes, please. I'd like that.'

'The first thing you need to know about your fiancé is that, like most men, it doesn't take a lot to turn him on.'

'Oh.'

'Well, when I say that, I say it with the utmost respect to my gender, but really it's all about the trifecta.'

'The trifecta?'

'Yes, it's simple really. One, he must find you attractive, some part of you, you don't need to be perfect, there just needs to be some part of you that draws him in. Two, he either must know, from previous experience, or believe, that you are going to be able to satisfy his carnal desires, and three, you have to be willing. After that, it's pretty much a forgone conclusion.'

Matt saw Veronica's surprised expression and followed up.

'Don't get me wrong. For it to become something more he has to develop feelings for you but that's the basics to get you off the ground. Now I know you and your fiancé are past the 'does he find me attractive' stage, but parts two and three of that trifecta are wide open for you, and you have to close them down. Once you do, he's putty in your hands.'

'Really?'

'Yes, really.'

'So how do I make sure two and three happen?'

'Well, does he know from previous experience that you can satisfy his carnal desires?'

Veronica dropped her head a little and blushed. 'Well, if you mean have we engaged in oral sex, well I, oh gosh, this is so embarrassing,

Matt. I've tried, a little, but I didn't quite manage to do anything other than kiss his penis if I'm honest. I'm so mortified right now,' she hung her head again.

'Veronica there's nothing to be embarrassed about, there are plenty of women and men for that matter that don't feel comfortable engaging in oral sex. There are lots of reasons for this, from not feeling confident enough that they will know what to do, to not being sure if they actually even like it, giving or receiving. Everyone's experience is different in this respect.'

'Well, I know for a fact that Seb loves pleasuring me and is particularly amazing at it. I just don't feel comfortable doing it to him if you understand.'

'OK, so let's look at that. What is it that you enjoy about Sebastian giving you oral sex?'

'Oh my. This is so awkward, isn't it Matt?'

'Vonny, there are two ways to look at this. You can look at oral sex as something embarrassing to talk about, or you can look at it as something amazingly pleasurable done between consenting adults. As it happens, it's amazing when done right, and it would be a shame if you walked out of here still uncomfortable about it because your embarrassment got in the way.'

'OK, you're right. When you put it like that, that's why I'm here. I deserve to have a healthy sex life and I want to learn this. So yes, Matt, I want to know how to pleasure my fiancé. Please teach me.'

Chuckling, Matt shook his head and smiled at Vonny's reactions. 'So let's go back to my question, what is it you enjoy about Seb giving you oral sex?'

'Em, honestly, with Seb I can do something I was never able to do with anyone else, it's why I remained a virgin, I feel so safe and loved by him I can be fully present when I'm with him and enjoy everything in the moment.'

'Awesome, now let's teach you how to be fully present when not just receiving but giving oral. So first of all, I think you need to take a couple of deep breaths and relax.'

Veronica looked shocked, 'You're not going to make me do it to you are you?'

'No, no, honestly,' Matt responded, ' I understand that's not something you'd feel comfortable with, but it is something we would offer here at the clinic if we felt it was warranted.'

'Seriously? Oral sex? You'd make me do it to you?'

'Gosh no, I'd never make you do anything you didn't want to. But, if it was something that I felt would help the client, then yes, we would. But in your instance, I have a different method that I think would suit you better.'

'Oh gosh, Matt, I can't tell you how relieved I am,' she chuckled.

He laughed. 'I hope you're good at taking direction Vonny and also at a little role play. Would you be comfortable with that?'

'I'll certainly give it a go,' responded Vonny nervously.

'Great, let's get straight into it so, first things first. Let's talk about a man's penis.'

'If we have to,' she smiled.

'Well it's central to the theme, isn't it?'

'Yes, yes, sorry. Go ahead,' she giggled.

Matt smiled and tried to help Vonny feel relaxed. 'There are many erogenous zones in the human body and a person finding pleasure from these depends on lots of factors. But let's concentrate on the male genitalia for this purpose. Is that all right?'

Matt reached behind him for the plastic 4D model of a man's genitalia.

'Sure, sure, go ahead.'

Pointing to the model he stated, 'There are so many areas of pleasure for a man in the genital area that it's very hard to get it wrong, to be honest.'

'Oh, that's good to hear.' Her nervous laugh hung in the air.

Matt smiled warmly and continued. 'There's nothing proven definitely, but some reports state that the foreskin has huge erogenous sensitivity, but when you take into account the scrotum, anus, and perineum,' he made sure to point out each area to ensure Vonny knew what he was talking about. 'You've got yourself so many areas to work with you certainly won't be lost for pleasure zones for your man.'

'Wow, wow. I had no idea if I'm honest.'

'Most people don't Vonny, it's not just you. If Seb is circumcised the frenulum may be removed so there are fewer nerve endings but don't worry either way there's plenty to work with. Most people stumble on the various erogenous zones by accident but don't give them the attention they require, because they just don't know to. But I think it might help to look at oral sex this way. You adore Seb, you're crazy in love with him, you're planning on marrying him, and you want to spend the rest of your life with him. All right so far?'

'Yes, yes, that's all correct. But I have to ask, what's that got to do with oral sex?'

'Ha, OK, well, a lot of people, through no fault of their own, tend to compartmentalize sex. They put lovemaking, on a pedestal like that's the ultimate goal,' Matt used air quotes for emphasis. 'They tend to put oral somewhere way down the list, past kissing, petting, heavy petting etcetera. But sexual encounters aren't meant to be compartmentalized. You should be having sexual encounters every day with your fiancé, and then your husband. Every single day is an opportunity to tap into those human sexual desires, to touch the erogenous zones, and remember the brain is one of the biggest erogenous zones, in men as well as women.'

'Really?'

'Yes, really.'

'All you have to do is let go of any negative connotations you have around pleasuring Seb. You love him, he's your best friend, you're going to marry him, and for the rest of your life, your mission should be his pleasure, his happiness, just like your pleasure and happiness should be his. Respecting and loving him run hand in hand but loving all of him means loving his desire for you and wanting to give him pleasure. When you take him in your hand you need to have this at the forefront of your mind. You can't be thinking, 'Oh gosh, I've Seb's penis in my hand and I'm meant to suck it or something.' You're meant to look at that penis as an extension of him and think, if I wrap my mouth around this, I'm touching so many erogenous zones and he will go wild. If I gently move my hand up and down it will add to his pleasure. Add in cupping his scrotum with your other hand and if you feel like moving your fingers and running them, or indeed your tongue, along his anus perineum the man will curse himself for not marrying you sooner. But do any of this with a begrudging heart and I promise, your new husband will know, and while in the moment it will still be pleasurable, it will be something that you and he will grow to hate not to love.'

'Oh, my Lord, Matt, you make it sound so normal. But that's the point, isn't it? What if I get it wrong?'

"Vonny, honestly, if you work all of that into a night of pleasure for Seb you won't do anything wrong. Remember the penis isn't a balloon pump, you don't need to pump so hard that you hurt anything, or worst-case scenario, rip anything, but when you go to grip it put enough pressure on it that you have control. Take it all in your mouth, no biting, and no blowing, despite the name.' They both laughed. 'Instead, suck, lick, explore, kiss, even treat it like it's your very own magic wand and it will do things for you you've never imagined. I promise.'

'Wow.' She retreated a little in her chair. 'Wow, I hope I can do everything you've described.'

'Have faith Vonny, I bet you can. Just remember the golden rules. Don't compartmentalise sex. It's an all-encompassing desire and need in a human being. Fulfilling that need is one of the most natural things in the world. And the second rule is, despite the name, don't blow,' they laughed companionably.

'OK, OK. I think I have it. I want to try it out as soon as I see Seb. Thank you, Matt, I've never, and I really mean never, had such an honest conversation about sex before, not even with my girlfriends.'

'That's what we are here for. You'd be surprised at how many people can't open up about sex. That's why The Love Lab was opened in the first place. You're not alone. I just hope that after today's session, you can walk into your new life with Seb and feel empowered and ready to take it all on.'

'Oh gosh, I feel ready, nervous, but definitely more ready. Eek.'

'If you want another session before or even after the big day give us a call, but I think you're ready.'

Vonny stood and took Matt's hand, shaking vigorously, 'Thank you, thank you so much.'

'My pleasure,' Matt walked her to the door. 'The very best of luck to you and Seb.'

❤❤❤

The text came through on Harry's phone as he was getting into his car. 'I need a drink. Are you up for it? Pop over to mine?'

Harry didn't need convincing. He knew that a drink and a chat with Matt was exactly what he needed after the day he had. He texted him back before getting into the car. 'Yeah, sound. I need whiskey & and a very wide perimeter around me to protect me from women throwing themselves at me ☺ C u shortly.'

Driving home Harry's thoughts drifted back to that afternoon and his time with Anna.

He still couldn't quite believe his luck. He kept thinking it was a dream that he'd wake from very soon and have to return to a very different reality. But the fact remained that he was fucking Anna Floesing, and she had him at her beck and call. Shaking his head in disbelief he wondered how he had gotten here so quickly. She snapped her fingers and he jumped. All he was short of asking was how high. He had never been like this with another woman. Not even Abigail had the hold that Anna had over him. Thinking of Abigail made him feel a little nostalgic. The pain wasn't as intense anymore, and he had spent the best part of the five years ensuring that when it reared its ugly head, he had a woman on speed dial and a whiskey in hand. Grief did funny things to the human psyche. He never allowed himself to go back to the day of her death. It was easier that way. But the months and years since had perhaps managed to confuse his mind enough that his memories were contorted. After all, they had just broken up. One week and two days before she was mowed down by a drunk driver with no license in the middle of New York City. Abigail had wanted to be free again. She had told him that she needed to 'find' herself and had felt stifled by the life they had built. Even though New York had been her choice and he had followed her there, she left him, with little more than a chaste kiss goodbye and a promise that she would come find him again. One week and three days later he was identifying her body in the city morgue and cursing every human being that walked the earth.

He hated that when he started to get feelings for another woman, thoughts of Abigail would creep into his mind. He knew why, but that didn't help. He thumped the steering wheel wishing with everything he had that he could leave the past where it belonged, and yet here he was, his head filled with Abbie and what could have been. Punching the infotainment system on, the voice of Eddie Vedder and the music of Pearl Jam surrounded him, and the songs of his youth flooded the car. Turning the volume up he screamed the words to 'In Hiding' as loud as he could and wiped at the tears as they fell freely. *Damn it.* He cursed and kept singing.

Matt answered his door with a whiskey in his hand. He handed it to Harry as he greeted him. 'What took you so long, mate? I'm starving, I ordered Chinese.'

'Yeah sorry. Thanks. Needed to get a few minutes with the bag when I got in.'

Matt turned when he reached the open-plan lounge area and noticed Harry didn't seem his normal effervescent self.

'What happened, mate? I thought you were exhausted from more afternoon sex with your mystery woman?' Matt picked up his whiskey to take a slug.

'Yeah, well. It turns out my sleeping with Anna has got me thinking about Abigail as well. You know, I just needed a bit of time.'

Harry stopped talking but Matt was too shocked to say anything. He took another gulp of whiskey before topping up his glass.

'Eh, I'm not sure which part of that to address first. I'm sorry mate that the Abigail thing is still affecting you like that, really I am, but I can't concentrate on anything else after that bomb you just dropped. You're sleeping with Anna? Not just, I slept with Anna, it was amazing, but she's married, oh, and my boss, so we decided not to go there again. Not that?' Matt took another gulp.

'Yeah,' was all Harry managed before he finished his whiskey and handed Matt the empty glass to refill. 'I think you better take a seat, mate.'

'I better take this too,' Matt grabbed the bottle of whiskey. 'Start at the beginning. Actually, start with what the actual fuck, I bet she's amazing in the sack?' Matt stared at Harry questioningly, begging for an answer from him. 'Come on, Harry, give me something.'

Harry wasn't saying anything, he sat looking into his whiskey glass, swirling the amber liquid looking lost in his thoughts.

Matt shook his head, sat back, and waited. He knew Harry. He knew that if he let him, Harry would speak when he was ready.

A few minutes of silence followed and then Harry let out a sigh. 'It was my interview, I fucked her in her office. She offered me the job and then the next thing I know she's begging me to fuck her. So, I obliged.'

Matt let out a long low whistle and shook his head, 'Un-fucking-believable. I mean she's smoking hot. I would need to be dead inside not to notice that, but she's married and your boss Harry, what's the deal there?'

'She wanted it again, and again, and each time it was in her office or mine. One time, we didn't even speak, she just walked in, grabbed me, we fucked, and she thanked me and left. I swear I keep thinking when did every day become my birthday?'

'This is like every teenage fantasy coming true.'

Laughing Harry nodded. 'I guess you're right. Where's that food you promised me, I'm starving. It's been a tough day at the office dear.'

Matt still couldn't believe what he had heard. He shook his head in disbelief on his way to the kitchen to dish up their food. 'You lucky bastard, Harry, you always did come up smelling of roses.'

'Ah, it's not all sweetness and light, Matt, come on. You're right she is my boss at the end of the day, and she also happens to be married. We're just fucking right now. No strings. We haven't talked about it all, other than for her to say, 'Get in here,' and then I go in and she's half naked and ready for me. She's insatiable, to be honest, I thought she was going to break me today.'

Matt was standing staring at Harry, so Harry took over dishing up the food and heating it in the microwave.

'Mate, you'd swear you'd never had sex in an office before yourself, eh? You even did it in a theme park, so don't look so shocked at me screwing the boss. It will finish soon enough, I'm sure. But, in the meantime,' Harry paused for effect and lifted his glass, 'I am going to enjoy every goddamn minute of it.' He touched his glass to Matt's.

'Cheers to that mate, fair play to you.'

CHAPTER 14

Karla was glad it was Friday. She'd had some difficult clients that had stretched her during the week, and she was ready to decompress and enjoy the weekend. Before the Clinic opened Karla had never worked more than three days a week, and she had only promised Anna to work more to help get the Clinic up and running. She was sure that was adding to her feeling completely out of balance today.

Her desk phone rang as she was about to close her computer, and she was surprised to see Harry's extension flash up. Her initial thought was excitement which quickly changed to wonder. 'Harry, hi, what's up?'

'Glad I caught you, Karla, couple things. First off, I was wondering how you got on with that patient. Did you speak with Anna?'

Karla tried to hide her disappointment, for a moment she had thought Harry was calling to ask her out. Maybe hoped was a better word.

'Oh yes, I talked to her, and she took over the case. The best outcome all around I think, thank you for your help on that one. You said there were a couple of things?'

'Yes, I was just wondering if you fancied joining Matt and me for a drink and a bite to eat after work. We're both finishing up soon.'

'That's very sweet. I'd love to, thanks. Where did you have in mind?'

'We usually go around the Dawson Street area. Thought we'd head over that way and find somewhere to eat when we get there?'

'Great, I'm finished now I'll drop my car home and meet you guys in Dawson Street in an hour. I'll buzz you when I arrive to see where you are?'

'Super, look forward to seeing you then, Karla.'

She hung up the phone and stared at the receiver. Karla normally didn't sweat over men. They tended to just be there when she needed them, but she felt different when she thought about Harry. She felt feelings she wasn't accustomed to. She didn't feel calm and in control, rather the opposite was true, and this made her uncomfortable.

Realizing that she was overanalysing, which was ironic in her line of work, she decided that she was right where she should be. She would put a pin in the Harry situation, whatever it was, and just let it be, and go out and have fun with her colleagues.

She finished shutting down her computer, switched off her office light, and couldn't contain the big smile on her face. Having some Friday night fun was just what she needed.

Matt stomped up Dawson Street much to Harry's amusement. 'I can talk to women and sort out my own damn dates Harry. You know this. I only told you what I thought about Karla to shut you up about Anna. You're sounding obsessed and I wanted to talk about something other than your sex life.'

Harry didn't rise to the bait. His mood was too good. He and Anna had made plans for the weekend, so nothing was going to spoil how great he felt.

'Matt, I didn't ask her to go on a date with you, I asked her to dinner and drinks with us. You and I are work colleagues, nothing more. She has no inkling that you would walk over hot coals for her, although if you stay mad at me, she'll figure something out tonight.' Harry tried to keep up with Matt's furious walking.

'Slow down, Matt, for Christ's sake, I want to take in the scenery.'

'So much for you being all loved up,' teased Matt.

'Hey, I never mentioned the L word. We are having a great time together that's all it is. Anyway, we aren't getting side-tracked here.

You're mad at me because you think I tried to set you and Karla up. I didn't mate and you better snap out of it because here she comes.' Harry inhaled loudly, 'Oh, holy smoke.' Karla was striding towards them, long, bronzed legs in a barely-there mini dress. She smiled brightly when she saw them and waved.

Harry didn't need to look at Matt to know the man would be struggling to even breathe when he caught sight of Karla.

'Hi, Karla.' Matt held out his hand just as she leaned in to plant a kiss on his cheek, and instead of her hand, he sideswiped her breast before turning red from embarrassment and shaking his head. 'Oh gosh. I'm sorry, I thought, actually, I don't know why I was going for a handshake that seems completely stupid now, sorry.' Matt placed his arm on Karla's shoulder as she leaned in again for an air-cheek kiss.

'Don't worry it's fine,' she smiled widely and turned to Harry to kiss his cheek.

Harry returned the kiss and turned to Matt, 'See, simple, mate.' Smirking, Harry shrugged his shoulders at Matt and turned to go into the bar walking purposefully beside Karla.

Matt made up an excuse when they arrived at the bar and headed for the bathroom.

'Thanks for inviting me, Harry. It's nice to get out and have a few drinks after work. I don't do it too often. My boyfriend always had gigs on a Friday, so I got used to either being his groupie or staying in on my own. There was never an in-between for me.'

'No problem, glad you could join us. So, who is this boyfriend you speak of?'

'Ha. I should say, ex-boyfriend. I'm just not used to saying it yet. We've only been broken up a short time.' Harry nodded at Matt when he returned holding up his drink for him.

'Karla, I just want to say sorry about that whole misunderstanding out there, never meant to do the boob graze.'

Harry shook his head at Matt, 'Mate, I think Karla's good now, no harm done, right, Karla?'

Laughing, Karla responded, 'Honestly Matt, I had already forgotten about it, but if it makes you feel better how's this?' Karla leaned over and gently cupped Matt's manhood. She looked into his eyes saying, 'Now we're even,' before removing her hand and kissing him on the cheek. But just as he thought she was pulling away, she leaned a little closer and whispered, 'Nice package by the way,' and then smiled sweetly and raised her strawberry daiquiri to her lips to take a sip.

Harry burst out laughing when he saw Matts's shocked reaction and his quick comeback. He watched the display with interest and noted that his friend was getting his mojo back. He could see it in the way Matt stood and how he eyeballed Karla after she grabbed him.

He wasn't used to seeing Matt all over the place over a woman, and it didn't suit him. He knew Matt had been painfully shy as a teen but by the time they had met in college Matt had grown into the happy, confident man Harry had become friends with. He was normally able to handle any hot woman that came into their vicinity and ultimately have them falling at his feet. They always commented on how 'sweet' he was. His blonde hair and blue-eyed all-American look gave him just enough of a talking point for women to give him plenty of attention.

Harry cleared his throat, 'Well, now that we've got that out of the way, how was your day, Karla?'

Jogging alongside Harry the next morning Matt had a megawatt grin on his face. 'She wants me, I know she does.'

'Yeah? Do you think so? I didn't get that vibe mate, I really didn't. I think you might have found the one girl who's immune to the Matt Fallon charm.'

'You're shitting me, right? That woman, because she's way past the girl stage, couldn't stop looking at me all night. It was a classic flirting technique. Come on you must have noticed the hair flicking, the light touch on my knee when I said something funny, which was a lot in case you didn't notice, and all the, 'Oh Matt, you're so funny.' She wants me, she definitely wants me.'

Harry laughed along with his friend and thought back to the night before. He couldn't help thinking that Karla was being quite flirty with them both, maybe she was keeping her options open. But Matt wasn't going to take kindly to hearing that theory, so he figured he'd keep that one to himself.

'Matt, why don't you play it cool for the next while and see where it leads? I know I can't talk, but a relationship with a work colleague can be tricky.'

'Are you joking me? You're about to spend the weekend with your boss and you're warning me off workplace relationships?'

'Yeah, but Anna and I are just fucking, no strings attached. You and Karla getting together would be a lot more complicated than just being fuck-buddies and you know that. For a start, you're crazy about her.'

'Well, yeah, I think she's pretty awesome, but don't you think Anna is too?'

'Yeah of course I do and if things were different, well, if she wasn't married, then maybe it would have a chance of being something more, but she is married and is very happy.'

Matt couldn't help snorting a response that made his feelings very clear. 'Harry, you are sailing very close to the edge there, mate. No shag is worth the potential fallout from bonking your boss, come on you've got to know this.'

'Look, all I know is that if I don't head for home right now and shower, I am going to miss my hotel rendezvous with the most sensuous, sexy woman I've ever had the pleasure of fucking.'

Laughing, Matt gave Harry a friendly thump on the shoulder. 'Go, go, but don't come crying to me when you're jobless and your dick falls off from overuse.'

'What a mate,' chuckled Harry as he turned and started to run back in the direction they had come. He shouted back to Matt, 'Don't text Karla, stay cool man.'

Matt gave him the finger in return and ran off laughing.

CHAPTER 15

Anna sat poised at the hotel bar and ordered a vodka martini. She had gotten a taste for them in New York and indulged whenever she was in a decent hotel with a bartender who looked like they knew what they were doing.

She thought about Harry and was surprised at how strong her reactions were to him. She had slept with other men since she married Fergal, but they were only an aside when she needed a release or Fergal was out of town. With Harry, it was different. She only had to look at him and she felt herself getting hot. He had a way of walking into a room and making her feel like she was the only thing that mattered. His eyes devoured her, and she could feel the heat between them before he even touched her. She had to admit she would miss Fergal this weekend but what better way to deal with that than spend the night here, with Harry, doing all sorts of wonderful things to her body.

Breathing deeply Anna took a long slow drink of her Martini before calling the bartender to order another. Her back was to the bar entrance, but she felt the change of energy in the room as soon as Harry entered. The bartender placed her drink in front of her and smiled longingly at her. She didn't even notice because Harry was standing behind her barstool, so close she could feel his breath on the nape of her neck.

'Anna.'

She turned and smiled seductively at him, her eyes heavy with a desire she could not hide.

'Harry.' She found herself staring into his blue eyes.

He placed twenty euros on the bar and took Anna's hand, without saying another word he walked with her to the elevators.

She retrieved the keycard from her clutch and handed it to him.

The lift doors opened, they entered, and he swiped the card and punched in the number for the penthouse. He didn't let go of her hand, and he didn't devour her as she expected. Instead, he stared straight ahead and so did Anna, wishing the lift was as fast as those in the US that took ten seconds to go thirty floors.

After what felt like an age, they reached their floor and the lift opened into their suite.

Only when the doors had closed behind them did Harry turn to Anna, speaking each word slowly and steadily. 'You ... are ... by ... far ... the ... sexiest ... woman ... I ... have ... ever ... seen ...' As he spoke, he reached behind her undoing the zipper of her dress and let it drop to the floor. She stood before him in stockings and black lace underwear that left him mesmerized. Slowly he leaned into her, barely touching her lips with his tongue coaxing her to open and allow him to enter. They kissed slowly, his hands exploring her beautiful body, caressing her breasts, still held captive with the lace of her bra. She undid the buttons of his shirt with precision and gasped as she removed it and felt his bare skin against hers.

'Walk ahead of me, I want to watch you,' he whispered.

Anna didn't need to be told twice. She sashayed in her heels towards the bedroom of the suite and Harry eagerly followed, salivating as he watched her long lean legs and pert behind sway in front of him.

Turning to him Anna licked her lips and beckoned him to her with her finger.

Harry strode over and started to open his trousers. Grabbing him, she pushed him onto the bed and began pulling his trousers down, smiling knowingly at him as she disappeared below his waist and took him into her mouth. He gasped loudly at the unexpected quick turn of events and lay back on the bed soaking up every sensation he felt. Anna's mouth and hands were like magic. He had never experienced a blow job like this, and he tried very hard to control himself, but the more she teased and licked and sucked, the more control he lost until he couldn't hold it anymore. The sweet release was wonderful, and Anna made her way slowly up the bed to join him afterwards, smoothing her hands over his body as she did.

Once he caught his breath again, he turned and found her playing with herself beside him, he groaned and looked at her, 'Anna, Anna, what am I going to do with you?'

'Well, I can think of a few things, but we should probably start with you replacing my fingers with yours down here.'

Harry moved closer and moaned deeply as he felt the warm, wet, welcoming space between her legs. He moved down her body until he could taste her with his tongue, using it to bring her to climax as she had done for him.

She writhed on the bed, moaning at him to go deeper and harder, and each time she did Harry could feel himself getting harder and harder until he was rock hard again. Need overtook him. Grabbing her hair with one hand and her breast with the other he slid inside her and felt himself enveloped with the warmth of her. Kissing her he drove, deeper and deeper, biting her lip and sucking her nipples. He was sent to crazy heights and wanted to consume her and be consumed by her. Anna felt the animal instincts of Harry take over. She grabbed his taut behind and pushed him into her, she returned his fervour and matched it with her own. Harder, deeper, grabbing, pulling, licking, kissing, they tormented each other with their lust. She wrapped her legs around him and lifted herself off the bed. He moaned, calling her name.

Anna pulled on his hair and found his mouth, covering it with hers as she too found a deep, sweet release, over and over. 'Don't stop, yet,' she begged. 'Keep going, I have more to give,' she whispered to him.

Harry, tried to catch his breath, 'I don't think I can,' he said as he could feel his legs growing weak.

'Yes you can,' said Anna, and drove him into her again and again. Harry lifted his head and smiled at her, kissed her lips, and fell to the bed, no longer having the strength to hold himself up.

Satiated they rested happily together, chatting and laughing companionably. As night fell, Anna and Harry took what they needed from each other over and over until eventually, they both fell into a deep satisfied sleep.

The next morning, trying not to disturb Anna, Harry gently moved away from under her body. Her nakedness wasn't lost on him nor his manhood which was standing to attention for what he hoped would be a very thorough morning inspection.

Looking down he grabbed hold of himself and chuckled, as he found himself nearly talking to his dick to remind it that if last night was any indication, he would be very well looked after this morning. Finding ice-cold water, he returned with a bottle for them both and climbed back into the bed beside Anna. She stirred beside him and slowly opened her eyes. Harry reached out and pulled her into his arms kissing the top of her head. 'Morning.'

'Morning,' she reached down to touch him. 'Oh, it is morning, I guess someone is wide awake?'

Harry let out a deep sigh as Anna's head disappeared below the covers and he relaxed back against the downy pillow. He had a fleeting thought of her being a goddamn rock star, and then he lost all ability to think straight and gave in to the sensation of Anna's warm mouth devouring him.

Harry was luxuriating in the afterglow of his orgasm when the shrill ringtone sounded from the bedside locker. Lazily Anna reached out and lifted her phone and answered it sleepily.

'Hey,' she mumbled.

Harry tried to lift his arm so he could move away and give her some privacy, but she shook her head and remained in the crux of his arm. He didn't quite know where to look so he turned his head and face away. Anna spoke in hushed tones and hung up after a brief conversation.

'Sorry about that.' She reached up to kiss his cheek. He couldn't help how stiff his body had gotten during the conversation, and Anna felt his coldness towards her when he didn't respond to her kiss.

'Hey, what's going on?' Leaning up she looked at him. 'You're not seriously bothered by the call, are you?'

'Well, yeah. I don't have any right to be, but Jesus Anna, it's weird.'

Sitting up and straddling him, Anna grabbed his arms and held them over his head. Her breasts skimmed his chest and he looked at her beautiful face and ached a little more. 'Harry, you know I'm married, I haven't hidden anything from you. You also know I love Fergal and that our marriage is an open one. He knows and accepts that. Everything is fine and there's no need for petty jealousies.' She started to writhe her body against his and the involuntary rising of his cock made him curse it for being a traitor. Harry didn't look at Anna and he tried in vain to think of something he despised but to no avail. His body was telling a different story and she could feel it between her legs.

'Damn it, Anna, I know you're married, but I like being with you, and I can't help it if your husband calling while we're in bed together gets my goat.'

Anna started laughing 'I've been in Ireland a long time Harry, but I've never heard 'gets up my goat' before. I'm presuming you mean you're pissed off?'

He tried to lift his arms from her grasp, but she held on tighter and lay on top of him. 'Anna, this isn't helping.'

'I beg to differ, if I let your arms go will you put your hand between my legs and feel for yourself what you do to me? I don't want us to have a silly fight over something that we already know and that isn't going to change. I had much better plans for us today.' Anna traced her finger down Harry's arm and let her palm sit on his hip. She lay still against him listening to him breathe and feeling him grow under her.

'You'll be my undoing Anna, you really will.' Harry grabbed her ass and squeezed before flipping her over in the bed. He raised himself into a press-up and coaxed open Anna's legs with his own. Sliding skilfully inside her he held her gaze and pumped hard into her, one, two, and three times, before pulling slowly out, and then in again as she gasped and called out his name. Grabbing her to him, he drove deeper and harder, kissing her lips into a swollen mound. Driving away any thoughts of another man being inside her he fucked her harder. 'Say my name,' he moaned at her, 'say it.'

'Harry, fuck me harder, Harry, I want you. All the fucking time, I want you,' Anna whimpered at him.

It was more than he expected, more than he could bear. He came in a torrent of expletives, cursing her for making him feel so desperately possessive but not wanting to stop.

'Damn you, Anna, I love fucking you.'

'And I love being fucked by you, Harry.' Anna demurely kissed the side of his head as he lay depleted beside her.

CHAPTER 16

The smell of freshly brewed coffee and warm pastries filled the early morning air. Harry watched Hilary get everyone's attention to get the morning meeting started.

He was hoping this wasn't going to take too long. He was having a hard time being in the same room as Anna and not ripping her clothes off. Ever since the previous weekend, he had felt seriously possessive about her and being around her sent electricity flying through him. He'd had a tough week concentrating.

He glanced in Matt's direction who was very obviously smitten with the lovely Karla. Harry could understand the attraction. He knew Matt was in trouble with this one. Karla returned Harry's glance with one of her own and a nod in his direction.

Anna sat at one end of the table reading a report and slowly eating pieces of her Danish pastry between sips of her black coffee. Harry purposefully hadn't looked at her in the few minutes they had been gathered in the boardroom, but stealing a glance he caught her eye in the exact moment she looked up. Neither acknowledged the other and Harry put his head down again. All he wanted was to get out of the meeting to the inner sanctum of his office.

Hilary spoke, 'As you all know it's been three months since the Clinic opened and Anna has called this meeting to go through some information with you. Firstly, I'd like to go through some housekeeping issues.'

Harry tuned out at this point and started doodling on the paper in front of him. The next thing he heard was Anna.

'So, in conclusion, I want to thank you all for your hard work so far. The Love Lab is flourishing. It is building a solid reputation for no-nonsense sexual healing, advice and guidance, and I couldn't ask for more from any of you. All I do ask is that you keep doing what you are doing.'

Harry swiftly removed himself from the boardroom once Anna had finished speaking. He needed air and space to think. His dick was doing most of the thinking for him at the moment, and that wasn't a good place to be.

He had barely closed the door to his office when Anna strode in and locked it. 'You're acting very strange Harry. Are you OK?'

He swung around at the sound of the door closing. 'What do you mean acting strange, Anna?'

'Well, for one thing, you may have physically been in that room, but your head wasn't, and you have been avoiding me all week. Are you sure everything is OK?' Anna started to walk towards him, but he put his hands up.

'Stop, don't come any closer.'

Anna laughed and kept walking. She slowly and seductively unbuttoned her dress as she walked.

'Anna, I mean it, stop. Don't do that.' Seeing the hurt and confusion on her face, Harry spoke softer. 'I'm sorry, it's just you're killing me. I can't get you out of my head and I need to concentrate on something other than you, your amazing body, and what you do to me.'

Anna smirked and took the final step that separated them. Reaching for Harry's face she touched it tenderly. 'Harry, my darling, why would you want to stop thinking about me? I like thinking about you too, and what you do to my body.' She started to unbuckle his belt. 'Let me show you how much I think about you.'

'Don't Anna,' Harry groaned and placed his hand on her, stopping her. 'I have no idea why I am doing this but I'm going to stop you there. If you go any further, you'll get about two minutes out of me. I spent most of the meeting thinking about bending you over the table and I swear I could hear you moaning. You're in my head and I need space for other things.'

Anna gently removed Harry's hand that was blocking hers and despite his moan of protest, unbuckled his belt and reached her hand down his trousers.

'Your body doesn't lie Harry. You want me, and I want you, and as for being in your head? You're in mine too, but you need to put thoughts of me in a box and take them out at moments like this.' She took hold of him and moved her hand gently up and down.

'Oh Anna,' Harry moaned and grabbed her roughly around the neck pulling her mouth to his. He kissed her. The desperation and need poured out of him into the kiss and still it wasn't enough. Anna could do nothing but respond. She could feel the urgency increase and relished in his need for her. She let go and let him lead this dance knowing he needed to.

Harry tried to find some control in the situation. He came up for air and looked into her eyes. He wanted to be inside her, needed to be. Grabbing and lifting her, she wrapped her legs around him. Her pert breasts were within licking distance of his mouth, and he took advantage of the proximity as he made his way to the couch. Frantically unbuttoning the rest of her dress he whispered, 'You wore this dress for me, didn't you?' He was almost gruff in his question.

'Yes,' Anna moaned as he devoured first one and then the other breast.

'I need you now Anna.' His mouth was consuming her, any piece of her he could lick, squeeze or kiss, he did, again and again. And then without notice, Anna felt him enter her, hard. She shouted out his name and he grinned widely. 'You fucking drive me crazy,' he said as he pummelled her harder. 'You fucking know what you do to me.' Harry devoured her mouth again and started to slow his pace. He drove deep and slow now, and his tongue played with hers making Anna moan with intense pleasure. He made his way down her neck, and she could at last catch her breath. 'You're fucking amazing Harry.'

Harry stopped and looked into her eyes. 'You mean that, don't you?'

'Yes, yes, I do. Don't stop please.' It was her turn to devour him, and their kiss deepened as they brought each other to climax.

Laying half undressed on the couch, Harry let his breathing come back to normal and lifted himself to look down at a half-naked Anna. Tracing a line from her breasts down to her thigh he said gently,

'We need to talk Anna.'

'Harry, don't. We don't need to talk. Let's just enjoy this. Let it go.' She started to move.

'Don't. You can't tell me to accept things like this when you know there's a lot more to how we both feel.'

Anna shuffled under him and sat up. Turning to face him she reached out and touched him, gently stroking his cheek and tracing his lips with her finger. 'You knew what this was from the start. Whatever we are feeling is inconsequential. We need to put those feelings away and take it for what it is, what it can only ever be.'

Harry shook his head and sat up. 'You know you don't mean that. You can't. What's happening here isn't just sex and you know it, goddammit.'

Anna finished buttoning her dress and stood holding out her hand to Harry. Reluctantly he took it and stood looking down into her face.

'I mean it Harry, leave it alone. Maybe we should stop this altogether?'

'No. Absolutely not. We can't. I'll take what I can get if that's what you want. But know this, I'm not happy about it. I don't like sharing you and I don't care that you told me from the start that you would stay married no matter what.'

Anna leaned into Harry's chest. He placed his arms around her.

'If you aren't sure that you can handle this as it is, it might be better to finish. I don't want to, so it's your decision.'

'I said no. I'll take it as it is. I mean that.' Harry let her go and walked around his desk. 'I better get to work. I have a client in a while, and I want to prepare for her.'

Anna nodded and walked out without another word.

As soon as the door closed behind her Harry threw his pen onto the desk and pushed his chair away. Looking at his couch he went over and fixed the cushions, absentmindedly rubbing the back of the couch where they had given each other such intense pleasure only moments before. Not for the first time, Harry questioned what the hell they were doing with each other. He already knew letting her go would be torture.

CHAPTER 17

Karla greeted Mark with a wide smile and gestured for him to take a seat before pouring them both a still water over ice and sitting down.

'It's great to see you come back, Mark. I was hoping after the progress we had made at the last session that you would want to continue.'

'I'll be straight with you. I wasn't coming, then I was. Well, anyway, I'm here now. This is much damn harder than I wanted it to be.'

She smiled warmly at him knowing he needed to feel comfortable so that he would stay and not try to walk out again. 'Can you tell me what's been happening with you since our last session four weeks ago?'

'Like everything, or just sex life, or what?'

'Well, start with what happened after you left here.'

'Em, I kinda went a bit nuts if I'm honest. I spent the guts of a week drinking and shagging. I called girls I'd been with in the past and tried to hook up with them. I don't mind admitting it was crazy.'

'And then what happened?'

'Well, that's the weird part. After about five or six days I was wrecked, and something just told me to stop.' Mark leaned forward on his chair and looked at Karla earnestly. 'I could feel something in my belly,' he pointed to his mid-region. 'It felt strange, almost like a dull ache. At first, I thought I was having a heart attack, but then I realised that's not where my heart is,' he laughed, and Karla joined in. 'But you know like I didn't feel right. I went to bed that night and slept for about fourteen hours. I haven't done that in years. Then the next day it felt like I'd had this, OK this is going to sound strange, like this out-of-body experience.' Mark dragged his hand through his hair and looked at Karla. She nodded and encouraged him to continue.

'Anyway, I felt kinda empty. Oh, shit I'm not doing a very good job of describing this. I'll just come out and say it.' Mark paused and took a deep breath continuing. 'I started to cry. I haven't cried since my dad died when I was eight years old. I cried like a fucking baby, sorry for the bad language.' Mark held up his hand. 'It went on for ages, I couldn't stop it and then when I did stop,' Mark's voice had gone up an octave, 'I just felt different. I don't feel like myself, I haven't for the past few weeks. I've no interest in hooking up with anyone. Haven't gone out with the lads. Nothing.' He was incredulous. 'Like, what's that about? You need to help fix me Karla, I'm afraid I've lost my mojo.'

Karla sat back and let what Mark had said filter through. She needed to process what he had said and let him hear it too. After a few moments, she spoke. 'Mark, I'm so damn happy for you,'

'Eh, happy for me? I don't think you heard me, Karla. I cried like a baby and now I'm acting like a little girl, talking about my emotions. Jesus, you've turned me into a sad, pathetic loser.'

Karla smiled a little and leaned on her desk, holding eye contact. 'Mark, you have had a breakthrough that some people spend years in therapy looking for. I haven't turned you into a girl and crying doesn't make you a girl, but you know that. You, Mark, have given yourself a wonderful gift. Now, all we have to do is dig a little deeper, which will be a whole lot easier now that you've already had a breakthrough.' Karla was excited and watched Mark's face for clues as to where he was at. 'Do you get that?'

'Well, I hear what you're saying, but if I'm honest, not really, no. I don't know where we go from here.'

'That's what I'm here for.'

Mark stood and paced the room. 'I'm not sure I can do this. I feel uncomfortable and a bit mortified if I'm honest. I don't feel like myself.'

Karla stood too and walked around the desk so she could rest against it. Mark leaned on the back of the chair.

'Let's look at that a moment, Mark. You came here because you knew something was missing. You want to be able to find real, lasting love in an intimate relationship, and that has eluded you so far in life. Is that correct so far?'

'Well, yes.'

'OK.' Karla continued. 'So, what if I said to you because you feel different, not yourself, it means the process is working. These are all things you need to feel in order to change what has become just a habit. This is what we call getting out of your comfort zone. You are capable of deep love Mark, everyone is, but every time it comes close you do something to sabotage it because deep down you don't believe you are worth it.'

Mark stood in silence shaking his head. It hung low so Karla couldn't read his face.

She walked slowly to her desk, sat down, and waited.

Mark didn't move. The room was silent.

Eventually, Mark sat in his seat and covered his face with his hands. 'I'm so lonely, I don't think I can do this.'

'You can, and I can help you.' Karla spoke softly before coming around to him and kneeling by the chair. Reaching for him, Karla drew him in for a hug as he cried. 'You've got this.'

Neither said another word for a long time, and as Mark wiped his tears away Karla handed him a tissue and returned to her seat.

'Are you ready to talk a little more, Mark?'

'Yeah, I think so.'

'Tell me what you mean when you say you are lonely?'

Mark hung his head again and spoke. 'I could be in a bar filled with my mates, lots of hot, young women and any number of offers and I get this feeling sometimes that I'm just so goddamn alone. I hate it. That's why I'll pick a girl, any girl and go home with her instead of just going home alone. But the same thing happens the next night or the next weekend. The loneliness doesn't go away though.'

Karla nodded, 'What do you think may help?'

'I've never thought about it before all this happened. But maybe meeting someone who I want to spend time with, who I don't push away?'

'How would you feel if I said that even if you met someone who you didn't push away, the loneliness would still be there?'

'I'd say give me a break. Why wouldn't it go away? She'd be in my bed every night so I wouldn't be lonely anymore.'

'Think about what you are saying, Mark. You told me that when you are in a crowded bar you can feel lonely, but you expect that falling in love with one woman, just one, and having her with you would take all that loneliness away? I'm afraid it doesn't work like that.'

'Well, what works then Karla, tell me, because if it's not that then what goddamn works?' pleaded Mark.

'Think of it like this. If I could help you deal with the loneliness, and I don't mean by meeting someone else, but truly dealing with it, then that would help when you went on to meet someone. Would that sound like something you could get behind?'

'If you can promise me that, then hell yes I'll take it.'

'There are no guarantees in this world Mark, but if you are willing to put in the work, then I am going to help you.'

'Great.' Mark rubbed his hands together. 'Let's get started.'

'Let's look at what gets you going. What do you love to do?'

'Baby, I can show you exactly what I like to do.'

'Seriously, Mark?'

'Sorry, sorry, only messing.'

'Let's start with hobbies and take it from there.'

'Well. I love going to the gym, obvs.' He pushed his shoulders back and nodded at this body. 'I go six days a week. I eat healthy. I like watching all sorts of sports and hanging out with the lads. That's it really.'

'No other hobbies? Other than the gym, watching sports and eating healthy aren't really hobbies, more just habits.'

'Eh, well. I like my cars, I work hard, and I don't have much time for anything else. Do you mean golf and shit? Hate that fucking game. It's not a sport anyway. Apologies for the language, Karla.'

'Golf seems to elicit a strong reaction from you, Mark. Why'd you hate it so much?'

'Seriously? Well, it's not really a sport now, is it? Old men driving golf buggies around a manicured green and getting frustrated that they can't get a little ball in a hole? Sounds to me like it's a substitute for a bad sex life. Gives them loads of excuses to be away from the missus who they don't particularly like anyway.'

'Whoa, like I said, a very strong reaction.'

'It's not really, it's just how I feel.'

'Yes, but you've been very vocal about it. Did you play golf in the past?'

'Nah, well, maybe once or twice. But as I said, it's shit.'

Karla stood and walked to the armoire. 'Can I get you another drink, Mark?'

'I'll take another still water if you're having one, thanks.'

Taking her time, she placed the ice and lime in the long glasses, deliberately pouring the water slowly. She spoke, her back still turned to him. 'Who did you play golf with Mark when you played?'

'Eh, I can't remember, it was that long ago,' he replied, staring at her back wondering where she was going with this. 'Why?'

'Oh, I was just curious. Maybe have a think who it could have been?'

'It was probably a couple of lads I grew up with. They all started joining the local golf club a few years back once they got married. Yeah, now I think about it, it was with them. There were a couple of charity events a few of the lads were involved with. Had to pay to sponsor a tee and all that shi... sorry all that stuff.'

'Did you play well?'

'Did I play...? I guess, Yeah, our team came in second in the first competition, and I think we came in third or fourth in the next one.'

'Very good.'

'What difference does it make how I played?'

'Now, I'll preface this by asking you not to respond straight away.'

'Ah Jesus, Karla, what are you going to say now?'

'Just listen for a moment. It's only a theory and we can tease it out.'

'OK, OK, go ahead with your theory.'

'These guys you grew up with, the ones who've gotten married and started having kids. The ones who play golf to try to get away from their wives according to you. Do you think that maybe you are a little jealous of these guys?'

Mark scoffed, 'Are you for real? Me, jealous of them?'

'Yes, Mark. Hear me out please.'

'OK, go on, this should be interesting.'

'Well, these guys seem to have everything you are chasing. They've found someone to love, married them, and have started a family with them. They get to go out with their friends and have a bit of fun and a few pints, all with their wife's consent. Then they get to go back to their warm, welcoming homes at the end of it all. You, on the other hand, may have a successful business, a great car, an incredibly fit body,' she smiled when he lifted his head in surprise. 'I may be your therapist, Mark, but I'm still a woman. Anyway, I'm glad to see you're listening. But even listing what you do have, none of that compares with what you don't have and what you truly want. Which is someone to love you for you, and for you to feel worthy of that love.'

'Ahh shit-balls, Karla. You do this, don't you? You reach in and find my weakest spot and then just keep going.' Mark's shoulders slumped, his face grim with pain.

'Mark, I don't do this to hurt you, I do this to help you.'

'Doesn't feel like it at the moment.'

Karla passed the box of tissues across the desk and watched Mark reach for one.

'Feels like you just sucker punched me again, Karla.'

'Tell me more.'

'Those pricks aren't any better than me. I know for a fact Keith goddamn Whelan has the smallest dick in the whole world, and there he is with four fucking kids. Seriously, how the hell did he manage one, let alone four? We used to take the utter mick outta him in the locker room after soccer each week.'

'You know the old saying, Mark, it's not the size that counts. But that's a little irrelevant at this minute. Why'd you call them pricks? I thought they were your friends?'

'Well, yeah, they are, sorta, but they also think they're better than me. All of them do.'

'Really? What makes you think that?'

'I just know it.'

'Again, what makes you think that?'

'Christ, you're like a dog with a bone. I see it when they look at me, that pity in their eyes. They're all smug bastards going home to their wives. Talking about having sex on tap, not having to go out searching for it anymore, as if it's a good thing to have fuck the same woman for the rest of their long, sad pathetic lives.'

'Wow,' Karla looked at Mark. 'Don't stop, you're on a roll.'

'Well, since you asked. They've even said to me. Told me to my face how they felt sorry for me having to go out every weekend and look for some stranger, like that's a hardship, when I've any number of women in my phone right now I can call for just about any type of sex I want. If I wanted a threesome tonight, I've got twins in here who are always up for it. You know that?'

'I did not know that, Mark. Good for you. So why does it annoy you that they don't understand that you have what you want, and couldn't think of anything worse by the sounds of it than to have a wife and kids at home?'

Mark leaned back in the chair and sighed deeply. 'You know damn well, don't make me say it.'

'I think you'll have to, Mark.'

He hesitated, and Karla let the silence fill the room. 'Because none of that is true, I want what they have, but I've never found it.'

'Can I add that maybe you feel undeserving of it, and that brings up a jealousy in you that takes over and you make your decisions from that space? Decisions like not playing golf. Not because you think it's stupid, but because you feel uncomfortable talking about your life with the lads because deep down all you want is what they seem to have, and you don't feel worthy enough to have it.'

'Ah, bollix. Sorry.' He held up his hand. 'Sorry. I don't hate myself you know. I've done well for myself. Maybe I do feel like I deserve it.'

'Do you honestly think that, Mark? Can we go back to our last session when we talked about your sexual appetite? You have a very healthy sexual desire in you, the more sex you have, the more your desire increases. You want what you consider more explicit sexual encounters, and yet, the more you get, the more you want, and it doesn't seem to stop. You're still scared at the strength of those desires.'

'Yeah, you haven't convinced me it's all normal yet.'

'Well let's look at that a minute. When you sleep with a woman, you guys perform oral sex on each other, you probably go in for anal sex a lot right? You like her rimming you as well?'

Coughing, Mark smirked a little. 'No messin' round with you Karla, yeah, I like all the above.'

'The women you do that with, why do you think they shouldn't enjoy it?'

'I never said that.'

'Not in so many words, no, but you imply it when you treat them differently after the first time you do it. They go down in your estimation. We agreed that at the last session. You start to see them differently.'

'Well, yeah, but… well, yeah,' he shrugged.

'What if I told you I enjoy all those things and more?'

'Ah fuck, Karla, why'd you tell me that?'

'Do you think less of me?'

'Well, actually no, you're different. Look at you.'

'What makes me different?'

'Well, you,' he hesitated, she waited. 'Well, you're beautiful, sexy, intelligent obviously, and then you tell me you enjoy good sex, shit, you're the full package, Karla.'

'And what if I said, I bet there were plenty of those women you slept with in the past that are equally as sexy if not more so than me.

They are intelligent and beautiful and happen to enjoy a healthy sex life. They're not afraid to ask for what they want, but you can't see past your own self-loathing to recognise that.'

'Eh? No, no way. I have never been with a woman that has it all like you.'

'Really? I don't believe you. Think about it for a minute. You're selling yourself short, Mark. I'm sure you have impeccable taste in women, just like you have in your clothes, cars, and business dealings. You're the one selling yourself short here, as well as doing a disservice to those women.'

Mark sat staring at her for a few minutes. Letting the words wash over him. Karla could see the confusion on his face, he got up and paced.

'Shit. Shit. I did this to myself? Is that what you're saying?'

'You haven't necessarily done anything to yourself, Mark. We do better when we know better, and you weren't able to see that your behaviour was causing the problem. But look now, you came here because somewhere inside you understood.'

'But some of those women were shit hot. Christ, what the fuck have I done?'

'Relax, take a seat. They weren't your future. They may have been great, but it would never have worked because you weren't ready to accept that it's OK for a woman to have a sexual appetite that matches yours. You need a woman like that otherwise you'll spend your life looking elsewhere for what she can't give you, and who wants half a relationship?'

'OK, OK, that makes sense. Keep going.' He rolled his hand to hurry her along.

'Ha, Mark, there's not much more to say. We've got the crux of it. It's up to you now to accept the normality of your sexual desire and find a woman who matches it. With whom you can have a full, loving, and respectful relationship.'

Mark smirked, 'I don't suppose?' he flicked his head in her direction.

'Ha, don't even, Mark. Plus, you better work on that pick-up line if you think that would work on any woman with my level of intelligence.' She roared laughing with him.

'OK, I hear you. Thanks, Karla. Phew, that's a shitload of info there to take on board.'

'Well let me make it digestible for you. Go off and be yourself. Do things you enjoy, not because they are good for your ego. Do things that challenge you, and don't be scared of a strong woman who knows her mind, embrace that. She might surprise you and you might surprise yourself.'

'So, just be myself and she'll come along?

'Not quite. Do the things that fill your soul. If you start doing the things you love, and not acting from a place of jealousy or hurt, then yes, she'll come along.'

'But what if I do what I've always done and can't see the good in her?'

'Do you think that Mark 1.0 would have even known to ask that question?'

'Ha, Mark 1.0, I love it. So, I'm Mark 2.0 now, am I? New and improved?'

'Something like that, yes.'

'I'm going to do this, Karla. She won't get away this time.'

'Maybe focus on being the best version of you and then she won't want to leave. Treat her with the respect and love she deserves, and she will return it to you, I promise you that. The woman for you will not look for you to change because you'll already be what she needs.'

Standing, Mark reached out for her hand across the desk

'Karla, seriously, well, wow, just wow. I really appreciate all this, thanks.'

'It's been my pleasure Mark, and you know where we are if you need anything else. I wish you the best and I look forward to hearing about the marriage and kids.'

'Ha, thanks, one step at a time, but yeah, I feel like it could be in my future now.'

Mark strode to the door and threw a, 'Take it easy,' behind him as he walked out.

CHAPTER 18

Harry looked at the text again and smiled. He knew he needed to stop and concentrate on his notes before his next client, but Anna had him all worked up again. In fairness, it didn't take much and a reminder about meeting her later was enough to get Harry all hot and bothered. He had no time to respond as the knock on his office door told him Alice had arrived.

'Come in,' he rose to greet her. 'Alice, how lovely to see you again,' Harry motioned to the seat.

'Harry, lovely to see you too. What a beautiful spring day it is.'

'Yes indeed. I love days like this, the air is crisp, and the possibilities feel endless.'

'My goodness, that's a lovely way of describing the day,' smiled Alice appreciatively.

'Take a seat, please. So, tell me, how have you been since our last session?'

Alice sat in the tub chair, placed her bag at her feet and crossed her hands in her lap. 'I must say I was quite melancholy after our session for a few days. I found myself seeking out places that held some memory of Brian. I have gone through our photo albums which I hadn't been able to even open before now. Five years it's taken me to be able to do this.' Alice paused and looked at Harry. 'It wouldn't have happened without your help and kindness the last time I was here.'

'That's very kind of you to say Alice, but it was all you. I'm here to listen and by sharing what you did, you started yourself on this healing journey. Would you like to tell me what it felt like when you visited the spots and looked at the albums?'

Alice seemed lost in her thoughts for a moment before she spoke.

'It felt,' she paused. 'It felt like I could lay him to rest, and I could let go of the guilt,'

'Lovely. But the guilt? Tell me more?'

'Honestly, I hadn't realised that I had been feeling guilty ever since Brian died. Guilty that I was still here when he was gone. Guilty that I get to live, make more memories with our kids, and see them turn into the wonderful adults we tried to shape them to be. I guess for a long time I believed that it wasn't fair, that he had worked so hard all his life and given the kids and me such a wonderful home. He'd given me the privilege of staying at home with them, and then when it was nearly his time to step back a little, it was too late. He never got the chance. That's what I have felt guilty about,' Alice took a deep breath and exhaled slowly.

'And now?'

'Now, I no longer feel guilty. I'm so grateful that we got to spend the life together that we did. When I looked through the albums, I started to understand that Brian wasn't waiting for retirement to live, we lived a full life, even when he worked so hard. We had wonderful family holidays, weekends together, camping trips, and made so many memories. And to top it all off we created two of the most caring, thoughtful people in the world, together. He did all of that, and yes, I wish we had gotten to do more, but guilty? Me? No more.'

'I'm so happy for you, Alice.'

'Thank you. I wouldn't have been able to do it without your help, Harry. You see I figured out that staying stuck in the guilt meant that not only had Brian died, but I may as well have died with him because I was only existing some of the time. That's no way to appreciate how lucky I am. I started to think if he saw me grieving all the time, he would be so annoyed at me wasting my life when he would give anything to still be here making memories.'

When Alice looked at Harry, she had tears in her eyes. He handed her the box of tissues, which she took gratefully.

Dabbing at her tears she continued. 'These aren't tears of sadness by the way. They are tears of relief. I'm so grateful, Harry, that I get to talk to you, and you listen so well.'

'You're too kind, Alice.'

'I mean it. Do you know how often I wanted to open up to my friends and family over the past few years, but didn't because I knew they didn't want to have the conversation? They didn't want to hear me talk about Brian or try to dissect how I felt. It's been great to have someone impartial and non-judgmental listen to me.'

Leaning back on his chair Harry smiled. 'Alice, I bet they would have been very happy to have you tell them how you felt. A lot of the time friends and family just don't know what to do to help. But that's for another day.' He joined his hands together and looked at her earnestly. 'Now what about that initial statement you made about getting back to yourself? Do you feel closer to you?'

'Well, when I made that statement in the first session it just kind of came out. I wasn't even sure what I meant; it was more a feeling if you understand that?' Alice twisted her hands in her lap.

'But, over the past three weeks, I've started to understand what I actually meant. I think I was lost. I've never known me without Brian. Over the years I picked hobbies that I thought I might like, and some stuck, and others didn't. I never felt a need to figure out anything else about who I was. But suddenly, I was plunged into this unknown world, where I was Alice, not Brian and Alice anymore. It was a strange place to find myself. Does that make sense?'

'Absolutely,' Harry gestured for her to continue.

'I think some of what I was feeling after he was gone was the loneliness, some was guilt for being alive, and some of it was just fear.'

'Fear?'

'Yes, I think it was fear of suddenly being exposed because Brian wasn't there anymore and it was just me. And I had no idea who I was without him.'

'Wow, Alice, you blow me away with your insights. That's pretty amazing. When you had these realisations how did you feel?'

'Scared if I'm honest. But equally relieved and free if that makes sense. Where do I go from here?'

'That's entirely up to you. You spoke about going on dates and meeting someone, do you still want to be able to do that?'

'Yes, I think I do. I want to know who Alice is, but I also don't want to be on my own for the rest of my life. I have a lot to give, and I'd love to find someone to share life's many precious moments with.'

'That's wonderful. Well, let's start from there then.'

'But, how do I start?'

'You've already started, believe it or not, just by allowing yourself to understand what you are truly feeling. By being vulnerable, and opening up, the healing can begin. All you have to do now is keep going.'

'You make it sound so simple, Harry.'

'I believe it is. We tend to overcomplicate things so that we can try to control outcomes. But, in these situations what we need to do is let go and let the feelings take us where they are leading, regardless of the pain. It's only when we do that, we can untangle ourselves from that comfort blanket we've become so used to. When we do that, watch out world because here comes Alice.'

Chuckling, Alice thought about what he had just said. 'Harry, can I ask you something?'

'Of course.'

'What happens when that comfort blanket doesn't want to leave?'

'The comfort blanket never wants to leave, that's why it's clung to you. It's your job to remove it, Alice. And to do that, you take a step each day into the world you want to create for yourself. The new world of Alice, without Brian. However scary that might be at times. Because for as long as you stay put, nothing changes.'

'I feel like I've tried to take it off and even managed to a few times. But then it seems too hard and I crawl back under the blanket.'

'What if you leave it here?'

'Sorry?'

'What if, metaphorically, you leave your comfort blanket here this time? When you step outside this office you choose to do things the old Alice wouldn't do. Each step is a step into the new Alice. So, decisions you make are based on what the new Alice would do, sans comfort blanket.'

'Oh, I can already feel the nerves start to jingle.'

'That's OK. That's understandable. But aren't you safe right now?'

'Well, yes. Yes, I am.'

'So those nerves are just that comfort part. Holding you where it thinks you want to stay because it's safe. But you're safe, Alice. Making new and different decisions doesn't make you unsafe. It might make you uncomfortable but get used to that because that's where you'll find what you're looking for.'

On a deep exhale Alice smiled at Harry. 'I feel like I can trust what you are telling me.'

'You can. I promise you are stronger than you even think is possible right now.'

'What if you have too much faith in me?'

'Well, then borrow my faith in you until you can give it to yourself.'

A solitary tear trickled down Alice's cheek. 'I think I might be able to do that.'

'I know you can Alice. I definitely know you can.'

CHAPTER 19

'Hey Fergal, where are you?' Anna called out from their hallway.

'I'm here, you're home early.' He arrived out to the hall to greet her and kissed her tenderly. 'Not that I'm complaining.'

'Everything is running smoothly. I had no more clients booked in and I feel like I've been neglecting you since we opened.' Anna wrapped her arms around Fergal's neck and leaned in for a deeper kiss.

He kissed her back with pleasure. 'Well, if this is what I get when you feel you are neglecting me, I must tell you I feel neglected, all the time.'

'Very funny,' she smiled. 'I'm also feeling a little neglected by my husband, so what do you have to offer me to make up for that?'

Fergal wrapped his arms tighter around her waist and drew her to him. 'I have this gift for you that gets bigger and bigger the longer we stand here wasting time.'

Anna threw back her head and laughed. 'Look at you acting like you are in college. Should I be asking, oh my, what big present do you have for me?'

'Well, if the cap fits and all that jazz.' Fergal leaned in to devour her exposed neck.

Anna, still laughing, grabbed hold of Fergal's manhood and gently squeezed. 'I think we need to build this up a little longer, don't you? Where would the fun be if you savaged me now?'

'I could savage you now and later if you wish.'

'How thoughtful of you dear. How about we spend the evening working up to the savagery?'

'Oh, you old romantic you. That's why I love my wife. She knows all the right things to say,' he kissed the top of her head before releasing his grip and taking her hand.

'Come on, I was just starting to prepare a feast for this Friday evening. Join me in the kitchen and we can do it together.'

Anna grabbed her bag on the way. 'Let me just get changed into something a little more comfortable and then I'm all yours.'

He leaned over and kissed her full on the lips, Anna felt her insides stirring and dropped the bag so she could hold him tight and deepen the kiss.

When they came up for air Fergal eyed her curiously. 'Are you sure we can't do some of that savagery now? It seems we both want it?'

Anna placed her finger on his lips and softly said, 'Later my love, I'll be yours to do as you wish.'

Fergal shook his head and smiled. 'I'm already looking forward to it darling.'

Anna made her way upstairs and closed the bedroom door.

Fergal had heard the texts come through on her phone when they were saying hello. He decided to let it slide for now. But he knew what was coming, and knew he needed to keep calm and stay focused. He adored his wife and wished he could have these beautiful moments with her without the intrusion of all the other thoughts in his head. The ones where she was kissing other men with the same passion she held for him. Anna returned to the kitchen a few moments later and he marvelled at how much she could still take his breath away. She really was beautiful, and his heart tugged a little when she spoke.

'So, what's on the menu tonight?'

'Apart from me?' he smiled.

'Yes darling, apart from you.'

'Well, I made a trip to Caviston's today and I have commandeered some delicious, fresh-off-the-boat scallops for our enjoyment tonight. I also have a bottle of Sancerre chilling in the fridge, and I have made my world-famous McDermot Salad,' he grabbed Anna to him and kissed her.

'World-famous?'

'Yes, of course. We have friends all over the world who rave about it, you know that.'

'Yes, of course, your salad is truly world-famous,' laughing Anna released herself from Fergal's embrace and opened the fridge. 'It's time to start on that wine, my love. Would you like some help with dinner or should I let the master continue?'

'You relax, I won't be long here.' Fergal lit the gas under the pan for the scallops.

'I have no problem doing as you wish.' Anna kissed his cheek before sitting at their dining table.

Lost in their tasks they worked silently for a few moments. Fergal knew he needed to say something to Anna. But he was also far too aware of the can of worms he would be opening. Despite his reservations, he knew it was something he could no longer ignore. His heart was breaking more with each passing day. Stealing a look at Anna he noticed how happy she looked, and couldn't help himself when he wondered if it was because of them, or someone else in her life, that she was so happy. Fergal finished cooking the scallops, placed the fresh bread and large salad on the table, and served them dinner.

Anna planted a kiss on his cheek in thanks and sat down across from him. She raised her wine glass, 'To my wonderful husband. I love how you look after me. I love our home and I love you.' She clinked her glass with Fergal's, and he smiled with her.

'Cheers.' He couldn't bring himself to make eye contact, instead, he began to eat.

'Is everything alright?'

'Mm, yes, why do you ask?'

'Because you don't seem as happy as you were when you greeted me this evening. Has something happened that I'm unaware of to change the mood? I was having a lovely evening.' Anna reached out and placed her hand on top of Fergal's.

The diamonds of her engagement and wedding rings caught the sun as he looked down.

'Anna, I can't...' He lifted his head and looked her in the eye, 'I can't do this anymore.'

'Do what, Fergal?'

He gestured to the room with his outstretched hands. 'This. Our marriage. I married you because I love you. I am crazy about you. You are the first person I ever want to turn to when something good or bad happens in my life.'

'And you are mine too. I don't understand.'

He reached out and covered both her hands with his. 'I'm saying I don't want to...' he hesitated, 'I can't share you anymore.'

'Oh.' Anna took a drink of her wine. She looked at Fergal and said calmly, 'I hoped this day wouldn't come Fergal. We spoke at length about this before we married. You knew how I felt.'

'Yes, I know, but I was crazy in love, I would have said anything to ensure we became man and wife. Don't you understand that every single person in my life spoke about the fact that I was punching way above my weight, but I was confident in our love, and I knew how I felt about you.' He paused and looked at her earnestly, 'I guess I always hoped I'd be enough.'

'It's nothing to do with whether you are enough. Whatever that means to you. You know that. I love you, but monogamy is not something I believe in. That doesn't diminish the love I feel for you.'

Fergal finished the wine in his glass and topped himself up. 'Anna, I can't bear the thought of someone else being with you. It's eating me up inside. I know you have someone at the moment in your life other than me, and I'm struggling to deal with it.'

'Oh,' Anna took a sip of her wine. 'I don't have 'someone' as you put it. I always told you I'd never flaunt it in front of you and I'm sorry if I haven't been discreet, but there's nobody else that makes me feel the way I do when I'm with you. I've explained this before, Fergal, it's just sex, a connection with another human being, it's nothing else.'

Dropping his head into his hands Fergal rubbed his face. 'Anna, that's just it, it's not just sex, it's so much more than that. You know that. Your life's work is about teaching people the connection between a healthy sexual appetite and fulfilment in life for Chrissake.' Getting angry wasn't part of the plan, but Fergal was struggling to keep himself composed. 'If a client came in and said they were getting married, but they didn't believe in monogamy, what would you say to them?'

Exasperated, Anna replied, 'Fergal this isn't about my clients, this is about us. You knew what my feelings were before we got married.'

'Yes, but Anna, my feelings have changed, that's what I'm saying. That's what I'm trying to explain to you.'

Anna reached for his hand and held it across the table. 'Mine haven't Fergal, I love you as much today as the day I married you.'

He lifted her hand and kissed it. 'I love you, Anna, now even more than the day we married, with all of me, but I'm not sure I can share you anymore.'

Sipping her wine slowly she looked at him. 'So, what are you saying? Is this an ultimatum?'

He shrugged his shoulders. 'I don't know. All I do know is that I am struggling to deal with having an open marriage with you. I guess I was hoping this conversation would go a different way.'

'What you're saying is that you were hoping I'd listen to you and instantly change my belief system to fall in line with how you're currently feeling?'

'No. What I'm saying is that when I vowed to love you, I wanted it to be 'forsaking all others,' but I went along with you because I thought once we settled into our marriage you would grow to love me as much as I do you, and you wouldn't need to be with anyone else.'

'My need to be with someone else is completely separate from my love for you, Fergal. You don't seem to get that. No matter who I have been with during our relationship, my love for you has never diminished. If anything, it was growing stronger because you have allowed me to be who I am.'

'It was growing stronger? What does that mean? Because I am telling you how I feel suddenly you're reassessing how in love with me you really are? Are you serious? I can't even express my honest feelings because you are going to re-evaluate yours now. Is that it?' Fergal stood and started pacing the room.

'Calm down,' Anna said as she also stood up. 'I'm sorry, maybe my choice of words was a little wrong. What I mean is, that my love has grown deeper and more satisfying since we married, and I feel that is a direct result of the fact that you have allowed me to be who I intrinsically am. I am aware that not every man could do that, and I am very appreciative.' She reached out to touch him and Fergal couldn't help himself, he reached for her too and they kissed passionately.

Fergal looked down at Anna and spoke tenderly. 'I adore you, my darling Anna, I don't know what to do.'

'Take me to bed and let's sleep on it, my love. Tomorrow we can take some time and see if we can figure it out.' Anna stroked his cheek before kissing him again. 'I want you to make love to me like you did on our wedding night.'

Fergal smiled softly and said, 'Oh Anna, I need you so much,' before kissing her deeply.

The next morning Fergal lay wide awake as the sun rose and the light streamed in through their unadorned windows. Anna slept soundly beside him, and he found himself listening to her breathing and wondering how they had gotten where they were.

What makes you tick Anna? He thought to himself while he stroked her thigh gently. *I thought I knew, but I'm not so sure anymore.*

'Em,' Anna looked up at Fergal. 'Good morning, darling.'

Fergal reached down and kissed her bare shoulder murmuring, 'Good morning to you. I was just about to put the coffee on. Stay where you are and I'll rustle us up some breakfast.'

'Sounds like heaven to me.' Anna closed her eyes again.

Fergal felt his movements were slower this morning. His good mood was evaporating as he began to remember the conversation from the previous night before his wife did what she does best and distracted him with sex.

Going through the motions he prepared their coffee and returned to their room.

'Coffee is served, Madam.' Fergal placed a steaming mug of black French blend on the nightstand and leaned in to kiss Anna.

'I'm making breakfast and as it's a beautiful morning, I figured we could have it on the terrace?'

'Sounds wonderful, darling, thank you.'

It didn't take long for him to rustle up their breakfast and sitting on their terrace the sunshine felt good on his skin. The warmth, however, couldn't quite penetrate the chill he felt watching her. He knew no matter what, he couldn't keep living like this. He watched her in silence for a moment. Her legs were tucked up to her chest as she ripped a warm croissant apart, taking nibbles of it between long luxurious sips of coffee. Fresh fruit and yoghurt sat untouched on the table. He knew she was thinking about it too and the silence started to become oppressive. 'I think we need to talk, Anna.'

'I thought we had said all there was to stay last night?'

'Really? I don't. I think I told you I am struggling to deal with you sleeping with other men, and you, in turn, did what you always do, which is distract me with sex.'

'Whoa. That's not passive-aggressive at all.' She placed her mug back on the table and her feet firmly on the ground.

'I distracted you? Really, Fergal? I wanted to make love with my husband and show him how very much in love with him I am, despite his belief that that is untrue, and you think it was just me trying to distract you?'

Anna leaned over toward Fergal, 'I am not a sixteen-year-old-school girl darling, I'm a grown woman who is very capable of not only understanding but explaining her feelings. If you don't understand that, then I think I may have married the wrong man.'

'Really? So now we are getting to the truth. You've been wanting to say that to me for some time now, haven't you? But it's only because I brought up my reservation about our marriage that you've managed to voice it.'

'Bullshit. I'm not the one who's been having reservations, Fergal. You are. All I'm saying is that I didn't realise that you thought so little of me and how I deal with my feelings.'

'Now, you're putting words in my mouth, Anna. I didn't say, or imply…' he held his hand up to stop her from interrupting. 'Let me finish. I didn't say, or imply, that you couldn't deal with your feelings. I am very impressed with how you manage to compartmentalize those feelings so damn well.'

'Am I meant to be grateful that you are impressed? This is why I chose Ireland to open my clinic in the first place. This obsession you Irish have with monogamy, and yet everyone is fucking everyone, but nobody has the balls to say it. Nobody has the balls to just say, 'I want to fuck you even though I'm not in love with you.' Instead, they all pretend everything is, how do you say it? Rosy. Yes, rosy behind closed doors, and they go out and pick up girls and get a blow job down an alleyway, and then go home to their wives like good little boys.' Anna sat back down in her chair and ripped at her croissant before throwing it back on the plate.

'Is that what you want? Do you want me to just go out pick someone up and fuck them? Get a twenty euro hand job from some woman on a street corner?'

'No. I would expect you to at least get a hotel room and some champagne for the poor girl.'

'Jesus Christ, you are unbelievable. So, you're telling me that if I leave here right now, you are OK with me meeting up with say, a colleague and fucking their brains out in some hotel room, and then coming back home to you for dinner?'

Anna threw her hands up, exasperated. 'That is what I have been saying all along. I don't care if you do that if that is what you want. I don't want you to fall in love, and I don't want you to be stupid and not use protection and take precautions. But yes, that is what our open marriage has always meant to me. You knew this Fergal. This isn't new.' Anna stared at him and held his gaze.

'Anna, Anna,' Fergal shook his head. 'I love you; I really do love you. And that said, I can't do this anymore.' He rose from the table, grabbed his phone, and headed out the back door without another word.

Anna sat silently in the kitchen, watching Fergal make his way down the steps to the beach, and hesitated before deciding to leave him be at least for now.

CHAPTER 20

Matt decided it was time to bite the bullet. Picking up the receiver he dialled the extension.

Karla answered on the second ring.

'Hi, Karla.'

'Hi Matt, what's up?'

'Well, I was wondering if you fancy a drink later?'

'Oh, great. I'd love that. What time are you guys heading out?

'Actually,' Matt took a breath, 'I was kind of hoping it could be just you and I?'

The silence extended so much that Matt had to check if the phone was still working.

'Hello? Are you there, Karla?'

'Yes, yes, sorry Matt, I would love to go for a drink yes, thanks.'

'Oh great. How does eight o'clock sound? I could pick you up if you like.

'No, there's no need. I'll meet you. Where did you have in mind?'

'How about 9 Below?'

'Oh, I love that place. Great, see you there.'

Matt hung up the receiver and continued to stare at the phone. Hardly believing she said yes, he grabbed his mobile and sent Harry a quick text. 'You're not going to believe who I'm having drinks with tonight…' He smiled as he typed the message and then retrieved his wallet and jacket from the hook on the back of the bathroom door. He couldn't hide the excitement he felt, and laughing, he fist-pumped the room.

'Who?' Harry responded as he leaned against the office door.

'Ahh. Mate don't do that.'

'Who are you having drinks with, and who's making you do fist-pumps as if you were back in college?

'Close that,' Matt said pointing at the door.

'What's with the cloak and dagger stuff, mate?' Harry's interest was piqued.

'I asked Karla out for a drink; I don't want her to walk past and hear us.'

'Ah, nice one.'

'Yeah, so right now I'm heading home, and changing the sheets if you know what I mean.'

Harry laughed at Matt. 'Mate, you've gotten laid a million times, what's with you? You're acting like a schoolgirl.'

'I like her, Harry. She's smoking hot and has brains to burn. I find that sexy and yeah, I want to sleep with her, so I don't want to mess this up.'

'OK, OK, but if you keep at this, you're going to scare her off. She strikes me as the type of woman that wants a confident, cool man.' Harry pointed at Matt. 'What I see in front of me is a high school girl excited about prom. Come on, man. Women love you. You don't need to be this anxious. That's one sure-fire way of turning Karla off, and you know it.'

'OK, fair point. Less of the high school girl comments though, mate. I'm at least a college senior, right?' Matt pushed out his hips and tilted his head to the side, cracking Harry up.

'Yeah, mate, a college senior. Now go get those sheets changed. I hope you get the action you're looking for.'

'I will.' Matt smiled as he picked up his jacket. 'Come on get out, I want to lock the office door.'

'That's my boy,' said Harry, patting him on the back as they walked out of the office.

Karla looked at herself in the mirror appraising her dress with a critical eye. She didn't want it to be too flirty. She drew her hands down her hips and swung her head from side to side.

Noticing how it hugged her curves she decided against it. She peeled the mini dress over her head and threw it on the bed where the rest of her discarded clothes lay.

Her blue baby doll Anrada dress caught her eye, and she smiled slowly. She wanted to feel sexy without going over the top, and she wasn't about to give Matt the wrong impression. It was sweet of him to ask her out, but she didn't want him getting the wrong idea. She checked herself in the full-length mirror. Choosing her nude wedges, she finished with a simple silver necklace and bracelet. Karla deemed herself ready to have a chat with Matt. She knew she would have to be very clever to ward off any advances, but it wasn't like she hadn't had experience with that before. She liked being in Matt's company, and it would also give her time to grill him on Harry.

Matt saw the bartender's eyes being drawn to the staircase and knew she had arrived. He slowly turned and tried to compose himself, as long, golden legs descended the stairs. The blue dress she wore looked like something that should only be worn in a bedroom, its flouncy material just skimming the top of her thighs. Matt struggled to keep from drooling onto the counter by the time she reached the bottom of the stairs. She caught his eye and smiled her megawatt smile.

'Karla, hi,' he waved unnecessarily, and immediately put his hand back down when she reached his side. Leaning in to kiss her cheek she started to laugh.

'I wasn't sure if you were going to go for the handshake-boob-graze-hello or a different one. I'm glad you chose the kiss on the cheek.'

'Ha, ha very funny!' The ice was instantly broken, and his composure returned with it.

'Let's take a seat over here, I think they'll be more comfortable.' Matt gestured to a plush booth and grabbed his jacket and drink, following Karla to the corner seat.

'What would you like to drink?'

'Is that a bourbon or Irish whiskey that you've got?' Karla asked.

'Oh, this is bourbon, but they have an extensive drinks list if you would like to take a look?'

'I'll have what you're having, and then I'll take a look at the menu.'

'Perfect.' A waitress appeared, and he placed the order. 'So, how was your day?'

'It was fine. I had a client cancel, which I wasn't thrilled about. I'm not sure he'll come back. It was meant to be his third session, and he was really starting to have some breakthroughs.'

'Oh, he may surprise you yet. Sometimes us guys need a little more time to process stuff.'

'I suppose you're right, but with that, and the attachment issue with another client, I have a feeling Anna won't be too happy with me.'

'Oh, attachment issue? What was that about?' Matt was curious.

'It was the reason I called Harry that night when you were in his apartment. I was looking for advice because I had a client who felt I was the answer to his problems. Harry was right, I needed to tell Anna. I did, and she removed him from my client list, no big deal really, it happens I know, but, well, you know yourself. Makes you feel like you've failed at the first hurdle.'

Matt felt an unwelcome feeling and recognised the jealousy straight away. Pushing the nagging feeling aside, he smiled at Karla and decided he needed to try to steer the conversation away from work for a while.

'You look stunning tonight by the way.'

'Oh, thank you. That's very nice of you to say. So, Matt, tell me a little about you?'

Matt savoured a taste and replaced the glass before answering.

'It's pretty straight forward really. I grew up in a nice neighbourhood in California. My parents had a strong and happy marriage.

In what is becoming rarer, they're still happily married today, nearly thirty-five years later.'

'Wow, that's certainly some achievement. To be happy and married after that long takes a lot of work I would think, no?'

'I agree, they make it look easy though. It's one of the reasons I believe so strongly in marriage and love, I guess.'

Karla sipped her whiskey and looked up at Matt. He was smiling at her, and she wondered if she had done the wrong thing by coming here tonight.

'So, how did you and Harry meet then?'

'We met in college. I wanted an East Coast college for a change of scene, and Harry was at MIT on a soccer scholarship, believe it or not.'

'No way. Was he that good?'

'He was OK, but he had more of an interest in the ladies than the soccer ball, and when he decided on a psych major, it made sense for him to study human sexuality in more detail. In fairness, he was pretty good at whatever he turned his hand to, it's probably how we became friends.'

'How so?

'Well, I saw him knock it out of the park with the team, women, and his academic studies. Plus, we had already started to get to know each other through some mutual friends. So, I see this guy pretty much ace everything and I thought to myself, that's the sort of guy I want to be friends with. You know what I mean?'

Laughing Karla replied, 'I do, yeah.'

'You know how they say you are the sum of the five people closest to you, well, I wanted one of those people to be Harry. There was just something about him that kind of drew me in. There still is. He's my best mate.'

'That makes sense. I know what you mean, and after hearing you explain it like that, it helps me understand him a little more. It's a little like how Anna and I met.'

'Really? I had no idea. Were you two in college together?'

'Yes, that's where we met. A bit like you two, we were drawn together through some mutual friends. It didn't take me long to recognise that Anna was a very talented and interesting woman. Even though we are the same age, I have always felt that Anna is the sort of woman I would like to be when I grow up.'

Matt laughed with her, trying desperately to hide his lustful thoughts. Her laugh was the sexiest laugh he had ever heard. He didn't think he'd ever met anyone more perfect.

'Hello Matt, are you with me?' Karla was waving her hand in front of Matt's face.

'I'm sorry, I was in another world for a minute.' He hesitated a moment. 'You know, you have a great laugh, has anyone ever told you that?'

'Maybe one or two have. You're embarrassing me now.' She hung her head a little before taking a sip of her bourbon. 'I think I'd like another drink if you would?'

'Yes, great idea. What would you like?' He motioned for the waitress to come over.

'I'll have a Bombay and tonic please, with a slice of cucumber.'

Matt nodded in approval. 'I'll have a JD and coke, please. Hold the cucumber.'

'So, tell me about growing up in California. It must have been fantastic.'

'Yep, it was good, it was great, actually. Myself and my family had a wonderful life. My siblings and I got on really well.' He smiled and added, 'Like any family, we killed each other half the time too.'

'How many siblings do you have?'

'Three sisters and four brothers. Considered a big family nowadays, I guess.' He lifted his glass and tilted it in a silent salute before taking a large swig.

'It certainly is. Beats my one brother. I always wondered what it would be like to have a large family like I saw on American TV Shows. It always looked so chaotic but fun.'

'Chaotic is one way of looking at it, but you're right it was lots of fun, and I wouldn't change it for anything. We're all spread around the world now though, so that makes family reunions a little tough.'

'Oh, that's a shame. But still, wonderful to have so many siblings and still be close.'

'Yes. Can't beat it in fairness. But what about you, Karla? One brother? Are your parents still in Sweden?'

'Yes, they've been divorced for a long time now, but they are close, so we spend time together still as a family. They both have new partners, and they join us too.'

'Really? I couldn't imagine seeing my parents with other partners. How do you find that?'

'Oh, it's fine. We're so used to it and to be honest it's much better seeing them happy apart, than miserable together.'

'That's a fair point. Very progressive. I guess that's what Anna means when she talks about pushing boundaries here in Ireland. We could probably do with The Love Lab in the US as well.' Matt laughed and Karla joined him.

The night flew by and before they knew it the waiter was calling last orders. Declining another drink, Matt suggested he'd walk Karla home. She surprised him by saying yes.

As they strolled through the park, Matt wanted desperately to reach out and take Karla's hand, but somehow, he felt that wasn't the right step to take. Instead, he made small talk like he had all night in the hopes that when they got to her apartment, he would get the vibes off her, and he'd know what to do. He knew he had to let her lead this, but it took all the willpower he had.

'This is me,' she said. They were standing outside a beautiful Georgian three-storey building. The wrought-iron gates blocked the basement steps from the street. The blue front door stood regal amidst its surroundings, solid, almost mocking his feeble attempts at small talk.

'Oh, great. Well, I had a great time, Karla. Thank you.'

'Me too, Matt. Thank you for asking me out.'

Unsure and out of his depth, Matt hesitated. His mind was playing tricks on him, and the confusion meant he just didn't know what to do next.

'Well, I'll wait until you're inside. Goodnight, Karla.'

'OK, OK, right so. Goodnight.' With that Karla turned and teetered up the steps to her front door turning to wave as she let herself in.

Watching her close her front door Matt shook his head feeling very disappointed in himself. He knew not going in for a kiss was going to keep him up in more ways than one tonight.

'She's blowing hot and cold on me, Harry. I'm telling you. I usually know straight off when a woman's interested. But Karla man, she's different.'

Keeping up with Matt's strides, Harry smiled at his friend. 'You know what to do, mate. What's Women 101?'

'I know, I know. But if I leave this one to too long, I think she'll move on. She's not on the hook yet. She's definitely not on the hook.' Matt looked at Harry and shook his head. 'Nobody has ever left me so tongue-tied at the end of a date like that before. I can't believe I didn't just kiss her.'

'You're overthinking this, Matt. I bet you she's already up and on the phone with one of her girlfriends talking about what a gentleman you were, and how much she thinks that you are husband material.'

They rounded the corner in the park and slowed their run to a jog in unison. Matt tapped Harry on the arm to indicate he was going to stop jogging and walked beside him catching his breath.

'I don't want to just hook her, Harry. She's everything I've ever wanted and then some.'

Harry smiled. 'Well, then my friend, you have got to play this one like you've never played before. If you want to get Karla to fall in love with you, you know what you have to do.'

'Yeah, I know. But it's going to take every ounce of reserve I have, because right now all I want to do is jump her bones the minute I see her.'

'Mate, you and I both know that's the worst thing you could do. I am going to do what best mates do in situations like this.'

'And what's that?'

'I'm going to get you laid so that you can release that pressure build-up, and then you can concentrate on hooking the woman of your dreams.'

Laughing, Matt thumped Harry playfully on the arm, 'You're a true friend. It is Saturday night after all. Dublin City may just be able to provide us with the entertainment we need. That's a mighty fine idea.'

Harry laughed and responded, 'I've always got your back mate, you know this.'

CHAPTER 21

'Fergal, we said we would take some time today to discuss our relationship.'

'No, Anna.' Fergal stood at the sink in the ensuite, the door open. 'You decided that today was the day we would talk, and I said I was busy. That hasn't changed. I have a client to see this morning.'

'You don't normally work on a Saturday.' Anna reached for her workout top.

'There are plenty of Saturdays I have worked, you just haven't noticed because you've been too busy.'

'Oh, please, don't start on me, Fergal. I just want to talk.'

'And I've said all I'm going to say on the subject, Anna.' Fergal walked into their bedroom, a towel wrapped around his waist and shaver in hand. 'My feelings have been made clear. I don't want an open marriage anymore. Unless you are planning on changing the status of said marriage, then, unfortunately, we have nothing to discuss. Anna, this isn't easy for me. All I want is you but every time you walk out of our home my mind goes crazy with thoughts of who you are with and what you are doing. More importantly, I wonder who's doing what to you, and it kills me, every, single, time. That's never going to change.' Fergal walked back into the ensuite and started to shave.

Anna sat for a moment on the edge of their bed. She rubbed the down-filled quilt and felt the soft cotton fibres under her fingers. She looked up and watched Fergal. His toned body wrapped in a white towel reminded her of the first time they slept together. The hotel room in Amsterdam hadn't been nearly as big as the master suite in their home, but they had spent hours in that room. Loving each other, satisfying each other. She knew every inch of his body and how he used it to pleasure her. He was surprisingly astute as a lover, and she had found it thrilling that it was so unexpected. She knew he adored her from the moment he saw her. Maybe that's where it had gone wrong because loving her beyond all else wasn't what she had wanted or asked for. Yet here she was, her husband telling her he wanted to love her forever, but not allowing her the freedom she knew she needed.

She stood, slowly and walked towards him.

Placing her hands on his back she gently caressed him. She could feel him tense under her touch.

'Please, Fergal, let me.'

Fergal looked at her in the mirror and their eyes locked in the reflection.

'Don't Anna, I haven't enough strength in me to refuse you. You know this.'

She traced her finger down his spine. 'I've never begged you before Fergal. But I will if you want me to?'

Fergal hung his head and shook it. 'Anna, don't.'

Reluctantly she removed her hand and gently touched his bare forearm as she walked from their room.

Fergal couldn't believe what he was about to do, but he was left with no choice. Finishing his shaving, he dressed and packed his overnight bag.

CHAPTER 22

Harry was on edge. He hadn't heard from Anna most of the weekend, just a short reply to a few of his texts on Saturday which had left him feeling frustrated and frankly pissed off. Tapping on the keys of his computer with a little more aggression than necessary, he knew he had to calm down before his next client arrived. He wished he had time to go for a run, that always cleared his head.

Damn it, the desk phone ringing interrupted his inner dialogue, and he angrily lifted it from the holder. 'Yeah?'

'Harry, I know that's not how you ordinarily answer the phone, so you better have a good reason for doing it now.'

His breath caught, 'Anna,' was all he could manage.

'We need to talk.'

'I'm waiting on my next client, Anna. It could be a few hours yet before I get finished.'

'I'll wait.' She hung up.

Harry slammed the receiver down and pushed his chair back. Having no clue what was going on wasn't a place he liked to be. He knew he needed to get his head back in the game and took a couple of deep breaths trying to push all thoughts of Anna from his mind before his client came. He'd be damned if he let her cloud his thinking while he prepped. He found himself shaking his head at how much he was affected by the whole thing and sat back down purposely. He opened the patient file to scour it for details in hopes of distracting himself from Anna. But as he read, the details in front of him jumped off the page and tugged at his heart; fiancé died, pain, loss, accident. The pit of his stomach seemed like the most unlikely place for him to feel anything right now, and yet, that's exactly where the pain felt lodged. Not his heart, not his head, but his stomach. It didn't take long for him to release the contents of his lunch into the toilet. Cursing himself and the lack of control he felt over his entire life in the current moment.

Harry looked at his reflection in the mirror. He just had enough time to brush his teeth and wash his face before he heard the knock on his office door. 'Come in,' he called out and reached the door just as she was opening it. Harry placed a welcoming smile on his face and became Dr Harry Eames. All the other stuff would have to wait.

'You must be Hilary? I'm Harry, welcome, please come in and take a seat.' Harry gestured to the seat in front of his desk and closed the office door.

'Thank you.' Hilary smiled at him and walked purposefully towards his desk. She sat, crossed her legs and gave Harry another smile as he sat down opposite her.

'It's wonderful to meet you, Hilary. We are delighted you've decided to come see us here at The Love Lab. Can I get you something to drink?'

'I'm fine, thank you. Although I'm sure I'm not the first person to wonder, could I get an alcoholic beverage?' She laughed at herself, and Harry joined in.

'No, you wouldn't be the first certainly. I get it, I'm sure you're nervous but I won't bite. I think the process, whilst tough at times, is so beneficial you'll be breathing a sigh of relief shortly, I promise.'

'I hope so.' Hilary rubbed her hands over her legs, smoothing out invisible creases.

Harry gave her a moment to settle in before he continued.

'So, Hilary, why don't we start by me giving you a little background on the Clinic and what we do, and then you can tell me what brought you here. Does that sound OK?'

She lifted her head and smiled at him. 'That sounds good, thank you, Harry.'

'Great. Well, I'm sure you know the basics, so here is the brief overview. The Love Lab was founded by Dr Anna Floesing in response to what she calls an epidemic of sexual repression. Being Swedish, but married into an Irish family, she has come from outside our upbringing and has seen first-hand the destruction our deeply held sexual beliefs have had in Ireland. She has felt for a long time that many people, not just the Irish, have relegated their sexual appetite to the scrap heap, or at the very least buried the feelings and labelled them, bold, dirty, or irrelevant. Does this make sense so far?'

'Completely, please continue.'

'Anna also believes and has based much of her life's work on the idea that sexual repression does so much harm to a person's psyche that it can become a generational issue. Anger, hurt, and resentment can all stem from this repression and permeate the very ground on which we walk.'

'Oh, I totally get that,' said Hilary.

Placing his hands together, Harry nodded in agreement. 'That's super. If you are coming from a place where you already agree with the fundamental reasoning behind the Clinic, you will have an easier time dealing with any issues and moving forward. This is very promising indeed.'

Harry rose from his chair, 'Are you sure you don't want a drink before we get started? I'm getting myself an Evian.'

'Sure. I'll take one, please. Thank you.'

'Why don't you tell me a little about yourself and what brings you here while I get these?'

'Gosh, where to start?' Hilary took a deep breath before continuing. 'I guess we could start with the fact that my fiancé died three months ago in a boating accident, that seems as good a place as any.'

'My deepest condolences.' Harry placed her water on the coaster in front of her and returned to his seat. 'It's a very traumatic time when we lose a loved one, particularly as you were setting out on your lives together.'

A little distracted, Hilary gratefully took a drink before continuing. 'Thank you. But I don't feel I deserve your condolences. You see, my fiancé,' she took another sip, 'my so-called fiancé, his name was John by the way, he, well, he was cheating on me.'

'Oh, I'm sorry to hear that too.'

'Thanks, but I certainly don't want your sympathy for that. I am so mad at him, but I can't even have it out with him. He cheated on me, and I only found out because of all the messages she left on his phone after he died. I don't know where to put all these feelings I've been having. I feel like I'm going to explode.'

Harry sat back in his chair and let out a long thoughtful sigh. 'Well, this wasn't in your bio, Hilary. For starters, that's not an easy way to find out, though it's pretty difficult to find out something like that at all. Because you found out after he passed you couldn't confront him. I get why you would be angry and trying not to, explode, as you put it.'

'I'm livid, Harry. The bastard was cheating on me for two years. Two goddamn years. During that time we were planning our wedding, telling one another that we loved each other, discussing what our children might be like and what we would call them. We were building our future lives together.' Hilary paused a moment and replaced her water. 'Do you have any idea how betrayed I feel?'

'I don't, but I can imagine. I also know that how you feel is completely normal, and you are certainly entitled to be angry and upset about the whole situation.'

'Do you know what I'm most mad about? I haven't had a chance to grieve him. It's like he took that away from me too. I know that doesn't really make sense, but that's what it feels like. It's like I need to grieve not only his actual death but the death of the man I thought I knew.'

'All very reasonable feelings, Hilary. Everything you are going through right now is valid and totally understandable. In fact, I'd say you are quite astute to understand how you are feeling.'

Harry took a large gulp of the Evian and let them sit in silence for a few moments.

Hilary spoke first, quieter this time, and he had to lean over the desk to hear her.

'Why? How could he? How could he do this to us? He made everything we had a big fat lie and I hate him for it.' A tear fell onto her lap and Hilary quickly wiped at her face.

Harry reached for the tissues and placed them in front of her. She gladly accepted them with a small smile of gratitude. He let her speak.

'I loved him for ten years. Ten years of my life wasted on him. That was pretty much all of my twenties. I'll never get those years back. And what was he planning on doing? Was he going to marry me anyway, and let me waste another ten years while he was off sleeping with some other girl and coming home to me and our children? I hate him, I hate him so much and I don't know what to do.'

Hilary was too upset to go on. She grabbed at the tissues and Harry walked around to her. He leaned against the edge of his desk and gave her some time before he spoke gently.

'I get it, Hilary, I really do. I'm very glad you chose to come to us here and trust us enough to help. I know we can.'

Hilary looked up into his blue eyes and burst out crying again. Shaking her head and waving her hand, she tried to get the words out between sobs.

'Thank you. Thanks. Oh god, I'm a mess.'

'No, you're not. You have been through so much trauma. Let it out. Use this space to just let it out and take as much time as you need. I'll be right there when you want to talk.' He smiled sweetly at her and touched her shoulder. Harry walked to the couch and sat down, watching Hilary from this vantage point he took in her appearance. Casually dressed in soft jeans that hugged her tight body, she wore a simple, but expensive tee-shirt and diamond studs in her ears. He found himself wondering about Anna and Fergal. About her cheating on him and how he might feel. Harry brought his thoughts back to the very upset woman in front of him. 'How are you feeling now, Hilary?'

She looked across at him and nodded. 'A little better, I think. Thank you. I'm so sorry and quite embarrassed that I just blubbered like that.'

'Please don't say sorry for anything. You're not here to apologise for expressing yourself. I'm delighted you were able to let it out. Would you like to come sit over here and we can continue our chat? It may be more comfortable.'

Hilary joined him on the couch and let herself relax into the velvet cushions.

'That was an interesting response, don't you think? Have you cried much since John died?'

'No, not really. Initially, when the accident happened, I was in shock, I think. I couldn't cry. It was my brother Paul who had to tell me, and I didn't quite believe it. You see, they had been out on Daddy's boat for the afternoon. They had done that plenty of times before. But John got into difficulty after diving into the water and was dead before they could reach him.' She sniffled and wiped her nose.

'It was apparently a heart attack. Nothing anyone could have done. But Paul didn't know that at the time. All he knew was that the love of my life, the man they treated like another brother, was dead. He knew my heart would be broken. I'm their only sister you see, and my four brothers have always looked out for me. They would be devasted if they found out what John had done.'

'So, you haven't told them?'

'No, I can't bring myself to intrude on their grief like that.'

'Have you told anyone?'

'No, you're the first.'

Harry let out a small whistle. 'That's a very heavy load to carry all by yourself, Hilary.'

'My family loved him like he was one of their own. Do you know how upset and angry they would be if they knew the truth? I don't want to be the one that brings that pain to them. They are all grieving John's loss and I want it to be about that, not the betrayal.'

'Whilst I admire you for not wanting to bestow any more on them, I do feel you have given yourself an extra burden to deal with by not telling them. Do you feel they wouldn't support you?'

'Oh no, it's not that. It's just that I...' she looked down at her hands. 'It's just, well, I feel like such a damn fool. How could I have been so oblivious to what was happening in front of my face? He was cheating for two years for God's sake. It wasn't just some random fling. He had a whole other relationship. He was in love with someone else.'

'You don't know that for sure, do you?'

'I do, I asked her.'

'Oh,' Harry couldn't help being surprised. 'When did you speak to her?'

'When I told her John was dead, we had coffee.'

'You had coffee? OK, how did that happen?'

'I'm not quite sure of my dates because everything was a little hazy. But a few days after he died, his belongings were returned to me, and naturally, his phone was among them. I saw all the missed calls and messages and the same name came up, Sam. Naturally, I got curious as I was the one who had called his colleagues and most of our friends, and we didn't know anyone called Sam. But it wasn't just that. It was strange because my stomach lurched as soon as I turned on the phone and the messages came flying through. It's like my subconscious knew.'

Hilary paused and looked at Harry for encouragement.

'Go on if you can.'

'I'm fine now. Thanks. You must understand our lives were very intertwined. John worked for my family business. My brothers were like his brothers. We took family vacations together a few times a year. I had no reason to believe he would ever, ever, cheat on me and yet somehow, I just knew. I knew Sam wasn't going to turn out to be a man, a colleague. I knew it was a woman.'

'So, what did you do next?'

'I read all the texts and believe me there were a lot.'

'Oh boy.'

'Yep, oh boy, is right. They were fairly graphic and left no room for wondering if I was wrong. It was very obvious that not only was my fiancé sleeping with someone else, but she was also in love with him.'

'How are you feeling right now telling me this story, Hilary?'

'Strangely, I feel a little disconnected. It's as if I'm just telling you a story about someone I know, rather than it being about my life.'

'I thought as much because you seem very calm.'

'What's the phrase? Inside I'm dying? Anyway, I'm going to continue before I lose it all here.'

'Yes, yes of course, sorry for interrupting, please continue.'

'I texted her and told her I was sorry and asked if we could meet, that we needed to talk. At this point, I wasn't quite honest with her. I may have made the text out as if it came from John.'

'Uh, OK, that's interesting.'

Smiling at Harry, she continued. 'When I arrived at the coffee shop, she was already there. She looked nervous. But she was beautiful. Early twenties and blonde. In fact, I was taken by how similar we were, except for the ten-year age gap, obviously.'

'Can I ask how you knew who she was?'

'Oh, I didn't mention the photos? He had some discreet photos of her on his phone, but once I knew what I was looking for it wasn't hard to find them and figure it out.'

'Did she know you?'

'Yes, she definitely knew me. When she saw me walk in, she started to get up to leave, but I shook my head at her. I reached her table quickly and insisted she would want to hear what I had to say. I guess curiosity got the better of her because she sat back down and was quite confident about it too.'

'Really? What did she say?'

'Funnily enough, she shrugged her shoulders and sat down and stared at me. Like a defiant child nearly. Daring me to speak.'

'Oh dear.'

Hilary laughed. 'It was perfect really because at that moment I was so nervous, and I had started to feel guilty that this was how she was going to find out he was dead. But her attitude made things so much easier for me. I started by asking her if she knew who I was, and when she said my name, I asked if she knew who my fiancé had been. She didn't miss a beat. Had been? She asked me all excited. I guess she thought she'd won him at last and I was there to tell her she could have him.'

'So, she had no clue?'

'Nope. Hadn't seen anything in the papers. I guess they aren't her jam, or whatever they say nowadays. She answered me and relaxed back into the chair at that point. I don't know if it was the way she said it, or just hearing his name on her lips, but something inside me snapped and I leaned over the table and looked her in the eyes and said, "Well, Sam, he's dead. Died three days ago in a boating accident. I guess you won't be getting your happy ever after, after all."'

Harry let out a long, slow whistle. Hilary continued.

'I felt a little sorry for her at that point because she looked so confused. So, I repeated myself and then stood to leave. At this point, she hadn't said a word. Then she blurted out, "I don't believe you." My answer? "Google it, honey. It's everywhere, and I walked out."'

Harry placed his hands together before facing Hilary. 'Wow.'

'Is that your professional opinion, Harry?'

He smiled and shrugged. 'Did it feel cathartic?'

'It most certainly did. It also felt shitty and somewhat humiliating after the fact. I got so angry with John for putting me in the position of having to confront his lover and give her that news. She was genuinely devastated and afterwards, I did feel a little guilt. Not a lot, but still.'

'Sounds to me like you did exactly what felt right for you at the time. There isn't a handbook for telling your dead fiancé's lover that he's dead.'

Hilary smiled, 'When you put it like that.'

'You know three months isn't a very long time. You're barely touching the surface of your grief in that time.'

'Oh, I jumped straight from heartbreak to anger in the grieving process, and I'm already at acceptance. Is it awful that I'm glad he's dead?'

'Well. It's not awful.'

'I don't care if it's awful. What I care about is that my anger towards him is completely consuming me. I wish he wasn't dead so I could get revenge. It's not fair he got away with it.'

'By dying?'

'Yes, by dying. He got to be with me, make promises to me and have our life together. But he also got to live this whole other life with her. In the end, he got to live both lives and be very happy and then, poof, he's gone, and everyone else is left to pick up the pieces. He goes off into his eternal rest with a big smile on his face thinking he's duped us all. That's what I'm angry about.'

'That's understandable, Hilary. It would probably be stranger if you weren't angry.'

'But I want it to stop. I don't like this version of me. I don't like who he has turned me into, and I feel stuck here. I'm angry all the time. I'm a mean person now. I was never like this before. Believe it or not, I was a loving and caring person for most of my life.'

'I believe you. Here's the thing. You still are. You've just shifted into a different space right now, and it's anger toward the unjustness of the situation you find yourself in. Until you accept that revenge isn't what you need to move on, you'll stay stuck.' Pausing, Harry smiled at her. 'And that is my professional opinion.'

'Do you mind if I tell you that opinion sucks?'

'You wouldn't be the first person to say that to me.'

'I know revenge doesn't solve anything. I'm a grown-up. But try telling my head that. My family would be broken-hearted if I told them who the real John was. Every few days I think I want to tell them, though I stop myself each time.'

'Why?'

'Like I said before, it's probably more about self-preservation. To be frank, I'm embarrassed. How could he possibly do this to me, and me not know? I feel so goddamn stupid.'

Hilary sat with her head bowed, and Harry took a moment before answering her, 'Hilary, look at me.'

She raised her head slowly.

'You are not the one that should feel stupid here. From our chat, I can see you are an intelligent, thoughtful woman. You deserved a man that treated you with respect. Unfortunately for reasons we may never know, John lost his way and stopped respecting himself, and in turn, you. That is all on him. That is not on you.'

'But it means he didn't love me enough and I didn't even see it.'

'No. You see, it meant he didn't love himself enough to trust himself that he had made the correct decision about his future. He may have had uncomfortable feelings about not being good enough for you, which made him try and prove himself by finding someone else to love him.'

Harry noticed a tear drop onto her lap and retrieved the tissue box from his desk. He handed it to her silently and continued.

'Hilary, until you accept that you will never truly know the reasons, you are going to stay stuck in this pattern of anger and wanting revenge, and you will never be able to move on.'

Between ragged breaths, Hilary responded. 'I know, I know. But I have no idea how to do that.'

'That's why you've done the right thing and come to us here. I can help you.'

'Thank you. Truly. Thank you.'

Hilary was gone and his notes were typed up, but Harry wasn't ready yet to meet Anna. He had a bad feeling and wasn't ready to face her yet.

Pouring himself a neat whiskey, Harry knocked it back feeling the burn as it sloshed against his throat, he savoured the intensity. He was about to pour another, but the knock on his door made him curse and he put the cap back on the bottle before turning.

'Don't let me stop you.' Anna sauntered in and locked the door. 'In fact, I'll join you if that's alright?'

Harry couldn't help himself. He smiled at her and nodded. 'Of course, take a seat.'

'Harry,' she said, before he realised it her hands were on his back. 'I'm sorry.'

It took every ounce of strength he had not to turn and grab her to him, instead he kept his composure, poured their drinks, and turned slowly passing Anna her glass.

'Would you like to sit?'

'I'd like an acknowledgement of my apology, please.'

Harry took a deep breath and headed to the couch. 'I don't know what you're apologising for, Anna?'

'So, you want me to beg?'

'I'm serious, Anna. Are you apologising for barely acknowledging me all weekend, or for the 'we need to talk' bullshit earlier, which left me hanging again at your beck and call?'

Anna leaned against the desk. 'I'm apologising for the lack of responses through the weekend and I'm here to talk because I want to explain myself to you. However, if you're going to act like a schoolboy I can walk straight back out that door.'

'You hold all the cards, don't you.'

'That's not fair, Harry. This isn't about one-upmanship. You know my situation. Please, just let me explain.'

'Go ahead.' He took a swig of the whiskey and savoured the taste. Trying to avoid eye contact was proving difficult with Anna staring straight at him.

'Fergal left me.'

Harry jumped up and went to her. 'What? When?'

'Yesterday evening. That's why I couldn't engage most of the weekend, I was trying to save my marriage.'

Anna took another swig and finished her drink. The irony of the situation wasn't lost on him.

'Are you OK?'

She smiled at him, and every inch of his body ached.

'Only you could ask me that, Harry. Thank you, thank you for being you.'

She reached out, touched his cheek, and held her hand there. He leaned into it and moved his face gently through her hand, feeling the softness of her against his skin, the ache grew into a deep longing.

'Anna.' It was no more than a whisper, but it was all she needed.

She pulled his face to hers and opened her mouth for him. The kiss was tender. They both savoured each other.

Coming up for air, Harry locked eyes with her and held her gaze as he reached down and put his hand under her skirt, pushing her panties aside he found her warm and welcoming. Her head fell back and exposed her neck when she moaned, he pressed hard and went deeper with his fingers. Kissing her neck, the top of her breast, any flesh he could see, he felt powerful and in control again. He needed her more than he needed to breathe, and at this moment he didn't care about her marriage, or why she hadn't contacted him, all he cared about was having her.

'Harry, please we need to stop for a moment.'

'No, we don't. Do we?' They stopped moving. His mouth was inches from her neck, his fingers buried deep inside her. 'If you want to, we can,' he mumbled, gently rubbing her clit with his thumb, a smile crossing his face. 'Are you sure it can't wait?'

She returned his gaze and murmured, 'OK, OK. Don't stop. I'd be crazy to stop you now.'

With permission granted, he didn't need anything else. Unbuckling his trousers, he grabbed her legs to wrap them around his waist and slid slowly inside her. He pulled out and in, again and again, slow and steady, mumbling her name over and over. Her hands tangled in his hair. Her nails scraped his neck. She held onto him as he drove into her, teased her, and brought her to dizzying heights. His mouth found her breasts and he held her tight, stopping all movement he felt the warmth of her surround him. She squeezed tight and held him inside her.

'Jesus Anna, I fucking adore you.' Groaning loudly, he moved inside her as his speed intensified, her head hung back and exposed her neck enough for him to devour it. He drove faster and harder into her, releasing simultaneously, they both gasped for air.

His head dropped onto her shoulder, and they stayed there to catch their breath.

Harry didn't want to move. He knew that reality was waiting for him as soon as he did. Then he remembered what Anna had said, and slowly lifted his head.

'Can we go back to the part where you said he left you?'

'Let's get ourselves more presentable first maybe?' suggested Anna.

Harry laughed and pulled back to start putting his clothes on. 'Probably best.'

Anna sat in the chair facing Harry's desk and he leaned against it surveying her. 'So, are you going to fill me in?'

'There isn't much more to tell you, Harry. Fergal decided that he couldn't be in an open marriage anymore. I told him I couldn't be in a monogamous one, and he packed a bag and left. There was obviously some discussion in between those points and throughout the weekend, but the crux of it is, he packed a bag and left.'

'I don't know what to say, Anna.'

'You said the right thing when you asked me if I was OK. I appreciate that. I do understand that my being married has been an issue for you. You must also understand that we may have to ease up for a while until I get my head sorted.'

'What? Why?'

'Because I need some time to process what has happened to my marriage, and I can't have you in my head at the same time.'

Harry reached for her hand. 'I don't need to be in your head, Anna. We can separate everything, just like we have done all along.'

'I'm sorry, Harry, we can't. I've decided.' Anna stood and brushed her skirt down. 'I'll call you when I can, and naturally, we will see each other here. But, for now, please give me the space I require.'

She leaned in, kissed his cheek, touched his jaw tenderly and said, 'Thank you for being you. I've had a great time.'

Harry was left speechless watching Anna saunter from his office.

CHAPTER 23

'Hey mate, haven't talked to you since Saturday night. What's been happening?' Matt's text went unanswered. Harry didn't know what to say to his friend and didn't feel like talking about it, though he eventually replied. 'Sorry, been a busy few days. Beer and watch the game tonight in mine?'

'Sounds good. See you around 8?' replied Matt.

'Gr8. 👍'

Harry knew he couldn't bring it up with Matt tonight or it would take over. He also knew Matt wasn't stupid. He needed to change his mood quickly if he was to keep his friend's eagle eyes out of his affairs, at least for now.

Harry gave up the pretence of working on his client reports and headed home. The stop-off to play squash didn't have the desired effect. He felt marginally better, but a long way off being able to shake the melancholy. He was looking forward to a night of banter with Matt to take his mind off things.

The evening was warm and balmy, the promise of summer not far away. Harry stood on his balcony and watched the world below. Despite having had time to cook and Johnny Cash playing in the background, he couldn't shake the disappointment. He knew he was going to miss her. There was no getting away from that.

It wasn't long before Matt arrived, and Harry was able to shake off the mood that had consumed him for the past three days. 'Mate, great you could make it. Beer?'

'Yeah, please. Are you cooking again, bro?'

'Yep, thought I'd give that new chef-at-home business a try. The one where they deliver the ingredients, and you cook the recipe?'

'Oh yeah. I heard about it. Don't see the point myself. Just order takeout and have it come to you cooked.'

'Where's the fun in that?'

'Eh, less work is my idea of fun.'

'Well, you can be the judge as to whether it was worth it, it's nearly ready. Anyway, enough shite talk. What happened Saturday after I left you and that Brazilian in 37 Dawson? You've been very quiet since then.'

'Ha, I've been a little busy since then, mate. She only left this morning.'

Harry clinked his beer bottle with Matt's. 'You're kidding me. How the hell did that go down?'

'Simple really, the Fallon charm worked its magic. Christina, that's her name by the way. Christina... I like saying it. Christina liked little Fallon so much she begged me to take Monday off work, and Harry, mate, that woman is very, very persuasive. So, I was very sick Monday, obviously.' Matt raised his bottle and smiled. 'And then, well, she waited patiently for me yesterday while I worked diligently in the office. I'll tell you something for nothing. I was a very efficient worker bee yesterday knowing Christina was keeping my bed warm.'

Harry laughed with Matt, and raising his beer, saluted his friend.

'Every, single, time, mate. Just when I think I have you sussed, you pull another one from your bag of tricks. I'm telling you that American accent works a treat for you. It can't be the looks or body anyway. So, what's the story with you and Karla? Have you asked her out again?'

'I've decided I'm not chasing her. If she wants me, she can come for me. I've made my move. Drinks were great and we had a good night, but nothing worse than a needy guy, right?'

'Do you mean nothing worse to a woman than a guy who tells her what he wants? Yeah, women hate that.'

'Hey, Dr Phil, you know what I mean. Too keen and they run a mile, right? What's with you and Anna anyway?'

'Way to deflect, mate, but we're talking about Karla now.'

'Yeah, why is that? Anna blow you off?'

Harry clicked the remote, the surround sound kicked in and the cheering and clapping signalled the start of the match. 'I'll grab our food and more beers, finish this later?' Harry threw the comment over his shoulder heading for the kitchen.

'Who's deflecting now? I'm happy to eat and drink beer, but I'll get the Anna info out of you yet.' Matt was talking to Harry's disappearing back.

He took a minute in the kitchen to regroup and shake it off. Any talk of Anna made his heart pound and head hurt; he wasn't going there tonight.

The rest of their night was spent watching football, and both men stayed away from the subjects they knew they needed to sort out.

Harry lay under the cool sheets, the window open. The street sounds from ten floors below never quite matched those of a New York City street. Tonight, Harry missed the noise, the sirens, even the stench. Dublin felt simpler, with fewer distractions and as a result, his mind could wander back to a place he didn't want to go. Despite his eyes being sore, they refused to stay closed. Soon the dawn light would creep its way through the opaque glass, and he would be expected to be awake and face another day. Cursing himself for allowing Anna to have this hold on him, he started to nod off again. As his eyes began to close, visions of a long-haired brunette, running from him in a crowded street woke him with a start.

Harry sat up and rubbed the palms of his hands over his face. It had been a while since Abigail had entered his dreams. He flicked through his phone and found the pictures he was looking for. She was smiling directly at him, the shimmering lake behind her reminding him of lazy carefree days. The memories came rushing back and along with them, the questions. He still longed to find an answer to so many what-ifs and whys.

He hadn't thought about her properly in a long time. He and Abigail had spent so much time together. Moving back to New York City with her was what led to their relationship failing and Abigail's death. The move and a lousy drunk driver. How many times had he pondered the same questions, circling back around with no satisfactory answer in the end? He just missed her was all. Things had felt easier back then. Would he ever get to understand what had happened?

Anna's face came to him then and her teasing smile brought him back to the present day. Jumping up he threw on his jogging gear and headed out to pound the eerily quiet streets. Pre-dawn runs were rare for him now, but no time like the present to get back into them.

CHAPTER 24

Before Hilary could even start the meeting Harry raised his hand slightly and cleared his throat. 'I have to apologise folks, but I've had to accommodate a client early this morning so I can't stay long.'

'No problem, Harry. Breakfast is at the back of the room, please, everyone help yourselves and we'll get moving. I know everyone's schedules are busy today.' Hilary went through the monthly figures, shared some research with the staff, and was about to hand it over to Anna when Harry rose and excused himself. *I'm not sitting through any more of that,* he thought.

By mid-morning Harry was pacing his office floor, rehearsing what he would say to Anna.

When the knock came, he ran his hand through his hair and took a deep breath before answering. 'Come in.'

'You took your time, man. You fancy an early lunch?'

'Matt, I... um. I... right, sure.'

'You OK? Expecting someone else?'

'All good, mate. Let's grab a bite.' Harry retrieved his jacket and absentmindedly looked around the office.

'You forgetting something there, Harry? You look confused.'

'No, no, all good. Let's go.' He ushered him out the door and chatted aimlessly about the best place to grab food.

On his return, Harry set his mind to complete the tasks on his desk, forcing all thoughts of Anna and any expectation out of his head. He had no more clients today, so he planned on getting home early enough to get a swim in before dinner.

'Knock, knock.' The unmistakable dulcet tones of her voice jolted him out of his reverie.

Catching a glimpse at his desk clock, he knew he wouldn't have the excuse of clients or more work to use if he wanted to get out of this.

'Come in.' He swallowed hard and stood up defiantly behind his desk, planting a smile on his face.

'Anna. Lovely of you to drop by.' Harry gestured to the chair. 'What can I do for you?'

'Harry.' Anna nodded and sat primly at the edge of the chair, her legs closed, angled sideways. He had taken in her whole look in one glance when she made her way across the room. He knew those bare lean legs and how they felt wrapped around him. He could nearly feel her nipples in his hands when he saw them press against the silk material of her lake-blue blouse. His mind was letting him down already, and she was barely in the door.

'I wanted to talk with you and was hoping to arrange a time and place that would be convenient.'

Purposely taking longer than needed to sit and respond he said, 'What do you want to talk about, Anna? If it's work, we can do it now?'

'Actually, it isn't work-related. So, if you would prefer I leave this to a more appropriate time, then I totally understand, and I apologise for interrupting your busy day.' She stood to leave.

She was at the door before he responded. 'Stay.'

She held the handle for a moment longer before turning around and facing him. He watched her turn and with it, his heart flipped.

She is so beautiful. He held her gaze until she dropped hers and walked towards him, coming round his desk.

'Please. Don't.' He gently touched her arm. 'I think it best if you stay on that side of the desk.'

'You? Oh, OK.'

'Tell me what you wanted to say, Anna. Why are you here telling me you want to talk about our personal lives?'

'I'll cut straight to it. I think we should start seeing each other again.'

Clearing his throat Harry responded, 'You do, do you? And what brought this on?'

'Are you planning on making this difficult Harry because I don't really have the energy for games right now.'

'No, Anna. I don't plan on making this,' he gestured to them both, 'difficult, as you put it. But I don't even know what this is anymore.'

Anna sat heavily into the chair opposite him and sighed. 'I think I may have handled things wrong, and you have every right to be upset and even angry with me. But, Harry, I miss you.'

He shook his head, barely hiding the satisfied smile that crossed his face. Rising slowly from his chair he made his way to her and knelt at her feet. 'Christ Anna, do you know how much I've wanted to hear you say it? I thought I'd lost you for good.'

'You gave me my space. You accepted things on my terms and I'm very grateful for that, but I've missed being with you.'

Tenderly she touched his face and said, 'I've missed this face.' She kissed his lips softly. 'I've missed these lips.' She took hold of his hand. 'I've missed these hands and what they do to me.'

Harry stared longingly into her deep brown eyes. The moment he did, his resolve disappeared. 'I've missed you too,' he murmured before devouring her mouth.

'Not here,' she whispered. 'Come home with me, share my bed.'

The seconds went by, Harry couldn't believe what he was hearing. 'Are you sure?'

'I'm sure.'

'You don't need to ask me twice.' He stood and held out his hand to her. 'It would be my pleasure.'

'It better be mine too.'

'You can bet your mighty fine ass it will be.'

'You've a beautiful home, Anna.' Harry stood on the terrace looking out at the sea. She handed him a streaming cup of black coffee which he gratefully accepted.

'Thank you. We...' she paused. 'I mean, I love it. You can't beat waking up with a morning run followed by a coffee and enjoying this view. There's something very special about the sea.'

'I agree. Did you ever think of settling in Sweden rather than Ireland?'

'It was discussed. But the clinic was a long-held dream of mine, so Ireland seemed the right place. I've always loved it here and really wanted to see the clinic open and succeed. To do that I knew we needed to live here and not just commute in or something like that.'

Harry snaked his arm around her waist and pulled her close. 'Thank you for inviting me to spend the night last night. If you couldn't tell I completely enjoyed myself.'

Anna tilted her head and laughed softly. 'I got that feeling. I enjoyed myself too, Harry.'

He kissed her lips, lingering a little. 'How about we do some of that stuff again now?'

Anna reached out and placed her mug on the table. 'What particular stuff did you have in mind?'

Her hand reached into his shorts. 'Whoa, that, em, yep, we're doing that.' Harry responded when Anna knelt in front of him and nodded, touching the tip of him with her tongue. 'Yes, we're doing this,' she said before devouring him.

'Oh god yes, Anna. Fuck.'

CHAPTER 25

Karla re-read the chapter again. Nothing was sinking in today. She usually loved research, even if it was on a weekend. She had to get to the bottom of this trauma for her client and wanted to ensure she crossed all the t's before she sought out any help from Anna. However, a chat sitting on Anna's terrace, overlooking the ocean on a beautiful warm day like today could be just what she needed to clear her head. Anna might be able to shed some light on her own Matt versus Harry dilemma too. They hadn't had much time lately to chat and Karla knew there was something up with Anna. Maybe sometime together today would help them both. Decision made, she showered and dressed covering all bases with her sundress and workout shorts combo. You never know what to expect when you go to Anna's.

She decided against calling because Karla knew Anna would try to put her off if she didn't want to talk. Some fresh croissants from that adorable bakery, The Bakers Table, in Greystones village and Anna would have no excuse but to put the coffee on and sit and chat. Karla knew Fergal was away but couldn't remember the location. She noted Anna hadn't seemed too pushed when telling her. Although to be fair, not much phased Anna. Fergal being out of town for a bit certainly would be a low priority on her worry list.

A short time later and feeling the sun on her face while strolling through Greystones, Karla wondered why she didn't think about living closer to the sea. She loved it just as much as Anna did. City living had its advantages, but it had really been Tom's choice where they lived. Karla had gone along with it as it made sense for all his gigs. Now that they were no longer together maybe a move was what she needed.

Jumping back in her car, Karla drove the short distance to Anna's and parked in her circular drive. She admired the riot of colour in the lawn and walked toward the side gate leading to Anna's enclosed back garden. That first glimpse of the ocean when you opened the gate always took her breath away, and Karla opened it calling Anna's name as she went. She knew her friend loved early mornings on her terrace, she would either be there or out for a run, and if it was the latter, Karla would happily wait in the sunshine. 'Anna, are you here?'

'Shit.'

She heard a man's voice. Definitely not Fergal's. She rounded the corner. Anna was on her knees, but Karla barely took notice. She was left staring into Harry's face. Her Harry. Naked. She'd dreamt of seeing him that way, but not here, not with her friend Anna, her boss. Actually, his boss too. 'What in the hell? Harry. Oh god, Anna.' She dropped the croissants. 'I'm so sorry, oh god, I'm...' Karla swiftly turned and grappled with the gate.

'Karla,' Anna shouted. 'Karla, don't go, sorry. Just wait a minute until we compose ourselves. Why don't you go out and come back in two minutes.'

Karla spoke to the gate, 'It's fine, honestly, I'll go. I'll call you. I should have called. I can't believe I didn't call.'

Before they could respond Karla ran from the house and sped away.

'Well, that was awkward,' exhaled Anna.

'You think?'

'Ha. It's not the end of the world. Possibly a little embarrassing, more so for Karla. I don't know why she insisted on calling round without checking it was OK anyway.'

'Maybe because she didn't expect to find you stark naked on your terrace.' Harry reached out for her, 'Which by the way, can I say, is something I'm happy about.'

'You're incorrigible, Dr Eames, stop kissing me. I have to call Karla and tell her not to be ridiculous and come back here.'

'Really? Maybe you could leave that call for a little and we could finish what we started before we were rather rudely interrupted.'

'I could be persuaded I suppose.'

'Like this?' Harry reached for her full breasts and caressed them. Leaning in he kissed the nape of her neck. 'Or this?'

'Keep going, I'm starting to be persuaded.'

Karla pulled the car in when the tears started to obstruct her view. She thumped the steering wheel. There was nothing that could have prepared her for what she had just seen. Searching her mind, she tried desperately to remember if Anna had given any hint to her that Harry was her lover. Karla knew her friend was in an open marriage, but Harry? She had not seen that one coming at all. She sat in the car contemplating what to do next and couldn't ignore the feeling that she'd been focusing her attention on someone who was clearly unavailable. The shrill ring of her phone interrupted her. She looked at the caller ID and scoffed. Wiping her face and composing herself, she hesitated but opted to answer it. 'Matt, hi. How are you?'

'Karla, hi, you busy? I can call back later.'

'No, no, sorry I was distracted but I'm all yours. What can I do for you?'

'Well, I was wondering if you wanted to do something together tonight?'

'What are you up to at the minute?'

'Me? I'm, well, I was just going to head out for a run. Why? Did you have something in mind?'

'Mind if I come over?'

'Do I mind? Eh no, not at all. Is there anything in particular you'd like to do?'

'I'll tell you when I get there.'

'OK great. I'll text you my address. See you shortly.'

'Yeah great, look forward to it." Karla checked her phone and entered the address Matt texted into her GPS. Then she removed her running shorts and panties, placed them in her glove box, and drove as fast as the speed limit would allow her so she couldn't change her mind.

She knew what she was doing was a little crazy. She also knew that the man who had just called her wanted her, and she needed someone just like him right at this minute.

Arriving at Matt's she rang the bell and knew he could see her on the camera.

'Matt, are you going to let me in?' He'd gotten lost for a few seconds. 'Sure, hi.' He released the buzzer.

'Hi.' He grinned and leaned against the doorpost as she approached him.

'Hi back,' she responded to his smile by planting a kiss on his cheek.

'Come in. It's lovely to see you, Karla. Can't say I wasn't taken back a little when you suggested coming over now.'

'Well let's just say you caught me in a moment.' Karla leaned against the hall table.

'Can I get you something to drink? Or would you like to head out somewhere to grab an early lunch?'

Matt realised Karla was still standing against the console and not following him into the kitchen. He turned slowly and faced her. 'Are you OK?'

'Matt, I'm fine, but I have something to ask you.'

'Fire ahead.'

'I need you to come back over here closer to me.'

'Karla. I'm not sure what's going on.' He stepped back into the hall and walked towards her.

'There's nothing going on, yet. Do you like me, Matt?'

'Like you? Of course, I do, Karla. You're an amazing woman.' He watched her face and it suddenly dawned on him. She didn't mean in the 'we are colleagues' way. 'Karla, if you're asking me do I fancy you, the answer is a big fat yes. I'm crazy about you. You're everything I could ever want in a woman.'

'Come closer and say that to me again.'

Matt stepped closer. His breathing was shallow, it matched Karla's. 'I... think... you... are... an amazing...' He couldn't finish his sentence because Karla's lips silenced him.

Taking his hand, she guided him from her waist to the hem of her sundress. With expert hands, she led him to the top of her thighs. Matt stopped kissing her and pulled back to look for some reassurance that this was happening, and it was OK. She smiled, a slow seductive smile that made his knees weak and his heart pound. He didn't need anything else.

Knowledgably he teased her, found her wet, wanting, and stroked her. She moaned through their kiss and her tongue found new ways of making him want her even more.

Karla writhed under his teasing hands. She begged him for more of him, and Matt felt only too happy to oblige.

'Will we take this into the bedroom?'

'Please, please,' she murmured.

What remained of their clothing was discarded moments later. They dropped to the bed in a tangle of naked limbs. Grabbing Karla's butt, he rolled over and let her sit high on him. He got to look into her eyes and watch the pleasure on her face as she rode him hard and he responded agreeably, teasing her clit with his thumb and pushing deeper inside her. Her surprised squeal of delight told him all he needed. It took everything in him to stop himself from cumming too soon and spoiling this perfect moment. Blonde hair cascaded past her bronzed shoulders. He reached to pinch and squeeze one perfectly erect nipple and used his other hand to grab her pert ass. He never wanted this to stop.

The rhythm changed between them and in unison they fucked harder and faster, moaning their appreciation to each other. Writhing in time they made each other cum in a swath of bedclothes and sweat. Karla fell onto Matt in the end, kissing his neck and shoulder before sliding off him and laying naked by his side.

Nearly afraid to believe what had just happened, Matt steeled a glance just to make sure that yes indeed it was Karla who lay naked on his bed after fucking his brains out. It seemed like an inappropriate time to high-five himself, so he gave himself a mental one and tried to hide the grin.

He reached out and touched Karla's hand and she intertwined her fingers with his. The silence only broken when she sighed and asked for water.

'I'll get us both some,' said Matt as he reached out to kiss her. She responded enthusiastically and Matt figured he better get that water before little Matt woke up again.

He stood in the kitchen and stared at the water bottle. *Karla is in my bed*. Nope, still didn't seem real when he said it out loud.

Holding two bottles of water he leaned against the bedroom door jam and looked longingly at her lean, perfect body. He told himself the mental pictures he took would last no matter what happened between them.

'Hey sleepy head, any song requests?' Matt placed the water bottle on the bedside table. Leaning up on her elbows Karla smiled in admiration at his disappearing butt rounding the end of the bed.

'Nice ass, by the way.'

'Yeah you seemed to like grabbing it at one point,' smirked Matt.

'You seemed equally fond of mine.'

'Oh, believe me, I'm fond of not just your ass.' Matt leaned over and placed a kiss on her lips, lingering just long enough to let her know he wasn't finished with her yet.

'Mm.'

'Mm, back at you. So, what music request have you got, or should I surprise you?' Matt asked.

'I'm definitely curious, so surprise away.' She heard the first line pumping through the surround sound and burst out laughing. 'Boys to Men? Really?'

'Just for you, babe. These boys taught me all I needed to know about women you know.'

'Seriously? So, they're to blame?'

'Oye! Cheeky.' Matt grabbed at the covers and pulled them off her. Stopping in his tracks he couldn't help himself. 'Jesus, Karla, you're beautiful.'

Her bronzed legs seemed to go on forever. Her taut stomach and pert breasts made him weak at the knees. He leaned in again, and this time placed a hand gently on her shoulder tracing the line of her body with his fingertips. The water was forgotten. The music somewhere in the background changed tempo slightly and still, they held each other's gaze. Matt placed himself astride her and followed his fingertips with his tongue. Coaxing, teasing, nipping.

'Karla, you are amazing.' Nothing else came out before she took his face in her hands and brought her lips to his. So soft, was all he remembered thinking before they devoured each other. Matt couldn't recall the last time he felt this comfortable and in awe of a woman all at the same time. When they had finished ravaging each other, they lay side by side, spent and panting softly. He stole a glance and caught her eye. 'Wow,' was all he could manage.

'Wow back. I'm going to start by saying, I did not expect that.'

'Gee, thanks.' Matt teased, but he knew what she meant. He had thought about this scenario for months, but at no time had he come close to knowing this was how they would be together.

'I'm very rarely speechless Matt, but I think you've gotten me this time.' The slow smile she saw creeping up his face told her how he felt.

'Don't even think about it! You had better not be doing a Carlton dance in your head.'

'How did you know?' Matt chuckled, grabbing for her and kissing her cheek. 'Only a little one. I couldn't high-five myself I thought that would be too rude.'

Slapping her forehead with her palm, Karla joined in and laughed comfortably with him.

'Oh god Matt, what have we done though, eek?'

Harry caught Anna in a smile. 'What are you smirking at?'

'I like watching you in my kitchen with your shirt off. You have an amazing body.'

'Ah shucks Anna, you'll make me blush.' Harry strode over and leaned in for a kiss. 'Now, instead of just sitting there admiring me, can you direct me to where I'd find a garlic press, please?'

'A garlic press? I have no idea what that is, but I can chop garlic if that's what you need.

'It doesn't have the same effect.'

'I may leave you and have a soak before dinner if that's alright with you?'

'Are you sure you trust me to have free reign in your kitchen?'

'I trust you.' Anna planted a kiss on his lips. 'Feel free to join me in the tub if you get lonely though.'

'Eh, you don't have to ask me twice. I'll follow you up in ten. I'll make dinner, believe me, it will hold.'

'Perfect. Hejda min alskling.

'I've no idea what you said, but damn. Feel free to speak to me in Swedish anytime you like.' Harry made a grab for Anna, which she side-stepped, as she trotted from the room. Leaving him with a smile over her shoulder, and a visible hard-on, which was going to make sorting dinner a little bit more uncomfortable.

Harry worked his way around her light-filled kitchen, trying to shake the feeling that he was an imposter in someone else's life. He was unsure how he would feel if the shoe was on the other foot.

Knowing now wasn't the time or place to think about it, he put the thought aside. This weekend was for the two of them in their bubble, and despite the inconvenience of Karla walking in on them earlier that morning, the weekend was turning into a momentous shag-fest that Harry didn't want to end. However, some sex-free sleep wouldn't go a miss. He laughed when he heard himself say it. He couldn't remember when he last wanted sex-free sleep when he had a hot woman beside him.

The pasta was cooked al dente, just how he liked it, the Bolognese sauce simmered gently, and the garlic bread was ready for the oven. It was time to join her in the bath. Dinner could wait. He smiled smugly taking the stairs two at a time.

❤❤❤

Karla lay with her eyes closed and thoughts racing through her head. She couldn't believe she'd done what she had. Matt didn't deserve to be used like that. He was a nice guy and being honest with herself, she was very surprised and thankful that the sex had been as amazing as it was, but this all started because of what she had seen earlier that morning. She was still reeling from seeing Anna and Harry naked on the terrace, with Anna performing a sex act on Harry which he was thoroughly enjoying.

She attempted in vain to dislodge the visual from her mind but to no avail. She then arrived back at the thought that she was being unfair to Matt. That thought was fleeting but made her respond instantly.

Jumping up from his bed she grabbed her discarded clothes making a dash for the bathroom. She knew Matt was busy preparing some food in the kitchen and she felt a little niggle of guilt but pushed it to the back of her mind. This isn't the time to start feeling guilty just get out and you can deal with this little mess again.

Matt was standing at the cooker, putting the final touches to the one-pot pasta dish he called his signature Fallon pasta delight. Well, in his head anyway. He heard her before he saw her, and something told him this wasn't going to be good. Turning his head slightly he looked at her, standing fully clothed in the door frame, and his heart dropped to the floor.

'Leaving?' It was all he could manage because he knew his voice would squeak out any other words. Disappointment coursed through him when he saw her half-hearted smile.

'Yeah, I forgot, I have a thing, and well, I...' She trailed off. Swinging her hand and pointing towards the door, Karla leaned down to put her trainers on and tie her laces. Matt looked at the top of her head and tried desperately to hide his disappointment.

'No worries, we can do it again sometime, maybe?"

'Sure, maybe. We'll talk at work anyway.' Karla walked towards him and placed a hand on his shoulder and a kiss on his cheek.

'Thank you. I had a great day. Sorry, I can't stay for dinner. It smells delicious, by the way.'

'Well, you'll never know now.' Matt reached out to touch her face. He had barely made contact when she coughed and said, 'OK bye. I have to go, thanks again.'

And she was gone.

He stood very still for a moment or two before switching the gas off under the pan and grabbed a fresh beer from the fridge. Plopping onto the bench he took a large swig. Not quite believing what had just happened. He felt like he was losing his touch. He turned the Sonos on and was blasted with Westlife singing, 'How do you lose the one you love?'

Hanging his head. Matt took another gulp of beer and flicked to the next song.

Karla made it back to her apartment in record time and ran inside. She needed to close out the world and think. Needed time to breathe. She couldn't believe the mess she found herself in. Feeling like a complete fool, she flung her bag across the back of the couch and opened the fridge. Staring absently at the contents she lost her train of thought. There wasn't even a glass of wine to help drown the embarrassment.

Closing the fridge she eyed the selection of bourbons and whiskeys on her drinks trolley in the lounge area. Grabbing a crystal glass and some whiskey stones from her freezer, she chose a special edition Jack Daniel's bottle that had picked up on their trip to Tennessee. Pouring two fingers of the golden liquid into a glass she held it a moment staring, remembering, then knocked it back. She poured another and another. By the third, she started to relax. Wandering over to her oatmeal L-shaped couch, she curled her legs up under her and sunk into the corner. Cradling the glass, she peered into it and let the thoughts come. She was still stunned. She had no idea how long it had been going on, or that it was even going on in the first place. And then there was Fergal, Karla wasn't sure he knew what was going on. She would be really surprised if he was OK with it. It didn't matter that their marriage was non-monogamous, Karla felt Anna was riding very close to the wind sleeping with Harry. She was his boss. Curious now as to whether Matt knew what was going on. She had more questions than answers.

She knew that going to Matt's was to release the anger and disappointment she felt after discovering Anna and Harry were having an affair. She knew fucking him was her way of trying to erase the hurt. She also knew that they had sex three times because it was enjoyable and they had a surprisingly good time. She had been taken aback at what a spectacular lover Matt was, and he was very, very attentive, which she had not expected.

Smiling a little now at the memory, Karla wondered if she had been too hasty running out on him like that.

No, I did the right thing. Staying over would have given him the wrong idea and I don't need any more complications right now.

Speaking of complications her thoughts returned to Harry, beautiful, tall, lean, intellectual Harry. Naked as the day he was born, she saw Harry receiving a blow job from his boss. Matt's best friend, Harry.

What am I going to do now? Taking a sip of the whiskey she contemplated her options, and none of them appealed to her. *No decision is the best decision right now.*

She closed her eyes in a vain attempt to shut out the world and all the problems she'd brought into her life.

CHAPTER 26

'Thank you for that information on the appointments and how the Clinic's doing, Hilary.' Anna stood and scanned the room, smiling at the faces of her employees. 'If you don't mind, I'll just interject here for just a moment.'

'Of course, Anna. No problem.'

'I want to add that everyone in this room is a valuable team member. Our clients need us to be on top of our game. We owe it to them to focus on them and give them one hundred per cent not only when they are in the room with us, but also when we are discussing case notes and researching issues they may present with. Hilary will go through details with each of you of the allotted times for this week's case study discussions. As usual, they will be held with me. Have a productive, enjoyable week everyone and let's go make a difference in our clients' lives. Thank you.' Anna strode purposely towards the door and heard Hilary take charge again to discuss schedules. Exhaling heavily after she left the room, she headed straight for her office, closed the door, and leaned against it for a moment. Composing herself she took another few breaths, placed a hand on her heart, and felt her pulse rate return to normal.

She had thought Karla and her would have been fine after the few days had passed, but after seeing her in the meeting she knew she'd have to address things with her, something she wasn't looking forward to doing.

Karla returned to her office and let out a sigh. She had felt awkward and embarrassed throughout the meeting. She couldn't look in Anna's direction because all she saw was Anna on her knees in front of Harry with his manhood in her mouth. She couldn't look at Harry because not only was she thinking of Anna and him together, but the thought of them meant there was no hope for her. She also felt embarrassed when she saw Matt, because she felt like a prize idiot for racing to his house to try to fuck the memory away, only to spend the afternoon having mind-blowing sex with him which left her even more confused. She was tired already and it was only Monday morning.

Matt sat behind his desk and tried to put all thoughts of Karla aside so he could prep for his first client of the week. It wasn't working. She'd all but ignored him in the meeting, which had pissed him off, but it didn't take away from the fact that now he knew how mind-blowing sex between them was, and it made him want her even more.

Watching Anna command the room, and then stroll so elegantly from it, her hips swaying, bronzed lean legs wrapped in a satin skirt that clung to her curves, Harry knew he was in trouble. He knew the hard-on he had for her wasn't going to go away with a fleeting thought. His new client would be here any minute and he needed to concentrate. Leaving Anna last night and waking up without her beside him this morning had proven more difficult than he had imagined. Concentrating on the work in front of him was all he could do right now. The rest would have to wait.

CHAPTER 27

'Good morning.' Karla welcomed her client with a bright smile and a firm handshake. 'My name is Karla; you must be Karl?'

Karl shook her hand vigorously. He kept repeating his name until she smiled again and added in a little laugh. 'You can let go now, Karl.' He released her hand, and she guided him to the chair in front of her desk. 'Can I get you some Evian perhaps? Or some tea or coffee?'

'Eh, water would be grand missus, thanks. Real nice setup here, Karla. Real nice.'

Her client was scanning the room and Karla was very conscious of his eyes following her every move.

Not another one. I'm not tolerating any bullshit with this one. The first sign of an issue and I'm calling Anna in here. I don't care how we left things on Saturday. 'Thank you, Karl. Although technically, it's not my setup. My boss has very fine taste.'

'That's an accent I can hear off ya. Where you from 'cause yer not from round 'ere?'

'Very astute, Karl. I'm originally from Sweden, went to secondary school here though and spent a lot of time travelling, so I guess my accent has become indistinguishable. I'm from everywhere and nowhere.'

'Well, I like it Karla, have to tell ya. I like it a lot. Suits ya.'

'Thank you for saying that. But enough about me. Why don't we talk about you and why you have come to us here in The Love Lab today?'

'I'd much prefer to talk about you.'

'Nothing much to talk about from my end.' *If only he knew*.

'Tell me a little about yourself, Karl?'

'Well, I heard about you from a fella in the gym, Paulie, friend of a friend kinda. See, I heard he was havin' a bit of trouble keeping it up if you know wha' I mean?"

'Yes Karl, I know what you mean, go on.'

'Well, I heard one session with you, and he was cured. Real cagey about it doh. Never mentioned you were smokin' either. Sneaky bastard. Oh, sorry, didn't mean tha'. But Jaysus, he could've warned me like 'cause yer shit hot.'

She couldn't help herself; Karla laughed a little.

'Well, I'll take the compliment and now that's out of the way. I'm glad your friend of a friend was helped when he came here. Everyone's story and problems are different so why don't we focus on yours? Why are you here?'

'Same problem as Paulie had, Karla, can't get me johnson to rise to the occasion and it's pissin' me bird off somethin' rotten. If I'm not careful she'll start to suspect me bit on the side.'

'OK, so let's roll back a little if you don't mind. Can you clarify if your bird is your wife or your girlfriend?'

'Oh, me bird is me girlfriend, mother of four of me babies.'

'OK, and your bit on the side is...?'

'Charlene, she's me mate Tosser's bird. I've been bangin' her for a few months while he's on holiday. Wouldn't ordinarily do it ya know, but gotta keep her happy or she'd be off with all bleedin' sorts and Tosser would go mental.'

'So, just to be clear, your friend Tosser, where is he on holiday and for how long?'

'Holiday? Oh, eh, well, when I say holiday, I mean he's inside like?'

'Inside? As in, he's in jail and you're sleeping with his girlfriend to stop her from sleeping with anyone else because that would make Tosser very angry?'

'Yep, that's the gist, Karla. Not doin' much sleepin' if ya get me drift.'

She couldn't help herself and laughed with him.

'I get your drift, Karl. Now, your girlfriend, mother of four of your children, what's her name?'

'Tracy.'

'OK, and when you say mother of four of your children it implies you have more?'

'Yeah well, I've six. Two o' dem are grown demselves, don't really see much of 'em. Their ma, Trish, died of a heroin overdose few years back. Love of me life Trish, but she fucked herself, sorry, Karla.' Karl held up his hands. 'Messed herself up a few years after the kids were born, nothing anyone could do to sort her out like.'

'I'm sorry to hear that, Karl. That must have been very tough for you when she passed away.'

'Ah, she was long past bein' my Trish when she died to be honest with ya, Karla. But it messed with the kids' heads for a while. Probably still does. Think they blame me 'cause I'd fecked off and left them with her. Their junkie ma, as they called her. Weren't too impressed with me. But sure, what could I fuckin...' He held his hand up again, 'Sorry, sorry Karla, not use to bein' in company such as yourself. Hard to remember not to use the language like.'

'It's fine, I appreciate your effort, Karl. Go on. The kids found it hard to forgive you?'

'Yeah, ya see I met Tracy and shacked up with her. She'd a lovely council house, done up real nice. Kept herself real pretty. Not a looker like you, but she did her best with what she had and Jaysus could she ride.'

Holding up his hand again. 'Sorry, sorry, but eh the other word I know for it is worse.'

'That's OK. So, you and she were very compatible?'

'Yeah, that's one way of saying it. We were at it like rabbits in the beginnin'. Then the usual, she had a few sprogs, started letting herself go, and one night I'm down the pub with me mates, just had a big win on the gg's and Charlene caught me eye. Hadn't been around Tosser for a few years before he went inside so I hadn't met Charlene. Jonno said, "Look at yer one, Tosser's moth." He'd only gone inside a few days before. In for murder. Fifteen years the poor bastard got, bleedin' disgrace if ya ask me. Anyways, Jaysus, when I saw her me pecker stood ramrod straight, knew I had to have her. Bought her a couple drinks that night and then back to her place. Her and her flatmate were mad for it. I'll be honest with ya now, Karla, I took a bit of smack that night. Don't do it often, but there were two of them and they were all over me. What man could refuse?'

'What man indeed?'

'So, there I was banging away all night, no bother and Charlene, Jaysus, she just wanted more and more, and I was like OK, sure why not? Didn't get home for two days. Me pecker was in bits. Tracy was goin' bleedin' bananas and me Ma had been left with the three kids 'cause Tracy was out lookin' for me.'

Karla took a sip of water and listened to Karl re-tell a story he no doubt had told a few times to friends down the pub, and no matter what, she was sure he had come out the hero every time.

'Did Tracy find you?'

'Ah yeah, she did. Beat the shite outta me and made me ride her. Made me promise there was nobody else. Told her I'd fallin' asleep at a party and me phone went dead, and I didn't know where I was.'

'Did she believe you?'

'Yep, fell for it no bother. Gave her another rattle the next morning. She was happy as Larry, and then I gave Charlene a buzz and hooked up with her. Lucky thing I did anyways 'cause Tracy got preggers again and she hates havin' sex when she's havin' a sprog. Says it's not good for the baby. I know that's a lie, but sure I didn't give a shit. Me and Charlene were goin' at it like the clappers. Couldn't get enough of me. Let me bang her flatmate again and watched and all, she's a real woman that there Charlene is.'

Karla was trying to keep up and held her hand up to get him to pause for a moment.

'Karl, can I ask you something?'

'Fire away, love.'

'Do you love any of these women?'

'Love's a strong word. I loved Trish, that's for certain. Tracy? Well, Tracy's me girlfriend, like. I love her I guess cause of all the kids, and yeah maybe I did love her a bit when we first started doin' it. But she's really let herself go now, and no matter what she does to me the little guy won't stand to attention anymore.' He gestured towards his crotch in case there was any doubt in Karla's mind as to what he was referring to.

'What about Charlene? Do you love her?'

'Ah, she's a feckin' babe. Like hot, not classy hot like you Karla, but can wear short skirts 'cause she's got bleedin' deadly legs, all long and sexy like. She's a pair of knockers on her.' Karl gestured with his hands. 'She lets me do anything, and I mean anything to her.' Karl emphasised his point by raising his eyebrows and opening his eyes wide. 'That's why I have to get me langer, sorry me penis workin' again. I'll lose everythin' if he can't work.' Karla let the story sit in the air and took a moment to compose herself before responding.

'Karl, I think I can help you, but you are going to have to trust me and do what I ask even if your first instinct is to say no. Does that sound like something you could do?'

Karl nodded furiously.

'Yes, yes, I'll do whatever you say as long as you can promise me me langer 'll be workin' by the weekend?'

'Well, I can't promise anything, but I can say I'll do my very best to help. Although by the weekend? That definitely won't happen.'

'Ah, Karla, please. I've planned two nights down in me mates in Wexford with Charlene and if I can't get it up, she's leavin' me I know it. That fecker Charlie from down The Parrot has been sniffin' 'round an' I know he'd gladly take her off me hands.'

'As I said, Karl, no promises, but let's get started and we'll see what we can do?'

'Great where'd you want me?' asked Karl.

'Sorry?'

'Where'd you want me? Do I lie on the couch, and you ask me questions? Isn't that what they do in the films?'

'Well, we don't quite do it like that. The session started as soon as you walked in the door and you began telling me about your life. From that, I can make some professional deductions, but I do need more information.'

'Go for it, I'll tell ya whatever ya need to know.'

'Well, for starters, when did you start experiencing problems getting a hard-on?'

'Eh, Jaysus, about a month ago maybe, I'm not sure.'

'Right. Who were you with at the time?'

'Jonno's bird at the back of The Parrot. She was givin' me a blow job, well she was goin' to and the fuckin' thing.' He held up his hand, 'Again sorry, but he wouldn't work, and she's known for her blow jobs. Still couldn't get him to stand up. Morto I was. Told her I'd too much to drink and it 'ad never happened before, but I'd only 'ad two pints. I bet she's told loads of the birds in the pub now as well.'

'OK, so Jonno's bird, does she have a name?'

'Eh, yeah, it's...' He ran his hand through his hair, 'Jaysus, let me think a minute now.' Karl scratched his head. 'Yeah, it's Denise.'

'OK, so Denise. And were you attracted to Denise? Was this why you were out the back of the pub getting oral sex from her?'

'Eh, not really, bit of a rough one if I'm honest. But Paulie had bet me a score I couldn't get one from her, so who am I to turn down that right?'

'Right. OK, so was there any conversation before you went outside?'

'Well, yeah, I met her at the jacks and said I'd give her a tenner if she gave me a blowie out the back and came back and told Paulie. She agreed, I thought deadly, I'm in there and I'll have a tenner meself when I collect from Paulie. Bleedin' thing cost me thirty quid. Still owed her a tenner and owed Paulie a score for losin' the bet. I tried pleadin' me case but wasn't much I could say without Paulie knowing me langer stopped workin'.'

'So, this was the first time. What about with Tracy?'

'Ahh, I can't remember the last time we did it. She just had the new baby like so outta respect I stay away and all. Me ma says I need to give me woman time to sort herself out down there before bangin' her again. It's grand Charlene sorts me out but that's where I'm havin' awful trouble now. Only so much fingerin' and all that stuff you can do. She's started to notice. Went to me doctor and got those Viagra thingys. Nothin', like I mean nothin'. What's the craic there?'

'It's hard to say for sure, Karl. But I think that your issue might be psychological rather than mechanical.'

'What's that mean in English like?'

'It means that no amount of tablets will help because your problem isn't in the up and down of your penis, rather it's coming from your head.'

'Me bleedin' head? Are ya havin' a laugh? Sure me head is tellin' me langer to get up. I'm gaggin' for it; me bird is gaggin' for it. Nothin' wrong with me head.'

'Well, let me explain it a different way.' Karla stood up and walked around from her desk. Leaning against the edge, her leg grazed Karls's as she placed her hands on either side of her thighs and leaned back a little. Her silk blouse strained at the peak of her breasts, and she saw Karl starting to react. He licked his lips, rubbed his hands together and stared at her chest area.

'Karl, if I was to ask you, oh sorry…' She paused and bent over, exposing the lace of her bra directly in his eyeline. Reaching over she rubbed her thigh at the hem of her skirt drawing it up slightly. 'Apologies for that. What I was saying is, if I were to ask you how you are feeling right now, what would you say?'

Clearing his throat and averting his eyes, he stared at the ceiling, out the window, and anywhere but at her. Karl responded, 'Eh, I'd say the up and down is working grand.'

'Yes, you see this is what I meant. The mechanics are fine, the up and down part, but there is a deeper reason why when you are with a woman you say you clearly want to have sex with, in all its forms, you can't seem to perform as you want.'

'OK, I kinda get it. But, whatever about Tracy or even that Denise one, I really want Charlene, like really want her. Why won't it work for her?'

'Well, that's what we are going to find out. But for now, this session is coming to a close, but before it does, can I make a suggestion?'

'Yeah, go on so.'

'Would you consider not going away with Charlene this weekend and focusing instead on Tracy and the baby, and giving the kids and her some of your time and attention?'

'Really, that's goin' help me langer?'

'Believe me, it will help more than you know, but only if you have patience and trust me?'

'Ah Jaysus, wha' am I gonna tell Charlene? She'll start riding that Charlie fella I know it.'

'Would that be the worst thing? You might be better off if Tosser doesn't know you've been doing that with his girlfriend.'

'Yeah, yeah. I'm not promisin' anythin' but I'll give it a lash. No bleedin' ridin' all weekend. Jaysus, I thought you'd have me sorted.'

'Well, I did prove a point to you that your manhood is not physically broken, and that I can help you if you allow me to.'

'Yeah, yeah, fair enough. Jaysus, you're something else, suppose there's no chance of ...' Before he could finish, Karla put her hand up and stood tall. 'Don't even go there Karl, or you and I won't be working together again.'

'Fair enough, fair enough, just figure you know.' He saw her warning look, 'Yeah, yeah, OK. Ta Karla, you're a bleedin' rockstar anyways.' Karl held out his hand and she accepted his handshake politely.

'Until next week, Karl. Now don't forget what I said.'

'Yeah, yeah, I know. See ye.'

Karla stood in the room and let the energy simmer and dissipate. She poured a long, stiff whiskey and knocked it back before retreating to her desk. Rehashing the session as she wrote up her notes, Karla couldn't help but giggle. She had never come across a man like Karl before. His take on the world, and in particular, the role of sex and women was quite interesting. She would discuss it further with Anna in the weekly de-briefing but, maybe Harry would have a better take on it as he was from Dublin. Harry was clearly not from where Karl was from, and they obviously had different upbringings, but his viewpoint would be welcome and maybe it would be a way to break the ice between them.

Matt just wanted the session to be over. He was listening to his client and giving her attention, but his heart wasn't in it. He needed to talk to Harry, and soon. Lunchtime was coming up and maybe he could persuade him to grab a bite in Bakery Zero down the road. As soon as he had said goodbye to his client, he dialled Harry's extension.

Surprisingly, he answered on the second ring.

'Harry. You free for lunch?' Not waiting for an answer, he continued. 'One o'clock in Bakery Zero? Come on man, my shout. I want to ask your opinion.'

'Doesn't look like I've much choice. I'll have the BLT with avo if you're there before me.'

'Cheers, see you there. I'm finishing up shortly here.' Matt sat back in his chair and thought about what he would say to Harry. He had pretty much told him Karla had stayed in his texts, but he hadn't gotten around to saying she'd run off the way she did. Harry's take on these things was usually good, and he trusted his friend, so he would open up and tell him, and take it from there.

All he had to do was avoid Karla between now and then. He wasn't ready to see her again after the awkwardness of this morning's meeting. They'd nodded politely at each other and sat on opposite sides of the table. Nobody would have guessed they'd spent Saturday in bed together fucking each other the way they had.

Matt sat staring into space for a few more minutes, wondering how they'd gone from the best sex of his life to barely acknowledging each other in less than forty-eight hours.

Harry contemplated whether to contact Anna before lunch to let her know he was meeting Matt. He dialled her extension 'Hey.'

'Hey back. How was your morning?'

'Busy. Yours?'

'Yes, very busy but good, thanks.'

'Just letting you know Matt has asked me to go for lunch. I was checking in case you had plans for us?'

'Do you mean sexual plans, Mr Eames?'

'I may mean sexual plans. If you had those plans, I could blow off Matt in a heartbeat,' he laughed.

'You go ahead and meet Matt. I've plenty to be getting on with. In fact, I was going to see if Karla and I could have a chat. I really need to discuss the incident with her.'

'Oh right, probably best I'm not there. I'll leave you to it so. You fancy getting together tomorrow night?"

'Tomorrow's not good for me. I'll come back to you.'

Harry hesitated a beat before replying. 'OK, no problem. Chat later.' Hanging up the receiver he wondered at the tone. Then reminded himself it was Anna, she was a woman who said what she meant, and he just wasn't used to that.

Grabbing his jacket, he headed out to meet Matt.

Karla's desk phone rang and noticing it was Anna calling, she wondered if she should answer it. Figuring she had to deal with the embarrassment and upset sooner rather than later, she picked it up.

'Hi, Anna. How are you?'

'Great thanks, Karla. Can you come into my office for a quick chat if you have a moment?'

'Sure, I'll be right there.'

The light knock on the door signalled Karla had indeed come straight away.

'Come in,' called out Anna, not lifting her head from her computer. 'Take a seat. I'll be two more minutes.'

Karla sat quietly and patiently waited.

'Now.' Anna looked up.

But before she could speak Karla cut her off. 'I'm so sorry about Saturday, Anna. Really, I'm mortified. I had no right to just pop in like that.'

Anna sat forward in her chair and smiled at Karla. 'Oh, Karla, please don't apologise. Ordinarily, I wouldn't be on my terrace on a Saturday morning giving head to one of my employees. So, let's just call it as it is. An embarrassing moment that's done and over with now?'

'That sounds like a deal to me. Can I ask what the deal is or is that pushing it?'

'Are you asking as my friend or my employee?'

'Your friend obviously.'

'Well then, I shall tell you. Fergal and I are, let's just say, taking a break, and Harry and I have been seeing each other for a little while. There isn't much more to tell really.'

'Oh please, there's a whole lot in between those lines, but that might be for another time when we have some wine in our hands and certainly a different setting.'

'Why don't you come round this Friday? We're well overdue a catchup and I can fill in a few more details. Although really, it's very simple.'

'Anna. Your idea of simple and mine are definitely different. Friday would be great. It's been way too long since we had a proper catch-up.'

'Why don't you stay over, and we can make a proper evening of it? Maybe catch the market in Dalkey on Saturday morning, or take the boat out if the weather is good?'

'Sounds wonderful. Why not. Are you sure we're OK? I am sorry I walked in on you like that.'

'It's forgotten.' Anna waved her hand in the air and Karla took it as her signal to go.

'I'll look forward to Friday, Anna.'

'Me too, Kaya.'

Once Karla heard her college nickname, she understood all was back on track and she left Anna's office satisfied that they were OK. Back in the security of her own office, she locked the door behind her, took a sparkling water and chilled glass from her mini fridge, and sat on her sofa. Her head was filled with the devastating news Anna had imparted, without her even realising she had. Harry and Anna, together. It wasn't just a fling. They are together and Fergal and Anna have broken up. Fergal and Anna, she couldn't believe it. She thought they were impenetrable. Karla was aware of Anna's non-monogamy and understood Fergal was also agreeable to it. Why else would they have married? Had Anna fallen so hard for Harry that Fergal couldn't do it anymore? Did Harry know about the marriage, the arrangement?

So many questions and not nearly enough answers. All she knew was that Harry, the focus of her attention since the day they met was now in a full-on relationship, certainly a full-on sexual relationship, with Anna, and Karla felt devastated beyond words.

How had she not seen it happening? Maybe it hadn't been going on for that long. Surely, she would have noticed the subtle exchanges that lovers have? She was sure something would have been given away at staff meetings over the past few months. Maybe it's just a passing thing and she just needed to bide her time and wait it out. But then there's Matt. Matt's a nice guy. She felt like she was messing things up at lightning speed right now. Dissatisfied with the lack of answers and her own feelings on the subject, she gave up on the idea of eating any lunch. Instead, Karla decided to focus on client notes to see if she could draw her attention away from a loss she had no entitlement to feel sadness over.

CHAPTER 28

Matt raised his hand in greeting when he saw Harry enter Bakery Zero.

Harry gestured his intention to order a coffee at the counter, Matt nodded and he continued eating his sandwich and scrolling through his phone. Twitter was a fascinating insight into people's psyche for him and he loved looking at responses to posts. He didn't like posting much himself, as he preferred face-to-face with people rather than anonymous chats online. He had never gotten into the online thing like his peers and saw no reason to change now. As far as he was concerned though, once Harry joined the table, the phone was put away and he had that face-to-face with no distractions. If his mother had taught him anything growing up it was manners. She was a Southern girl with old-school ideas, and bad manners were never tolerated in the Fallon household.

'Hey.' Harry placed his coffee on the table. 'How was your weekend mate, or should I ask? You got it together with Karla at last? Nice one. How was it?'

'Good, yeah. Real good.'

'Good? Come on, man, I know it was better than good.'

Matt took a bite of his sandwich to give himself time to respond. He knew it was much better than good, but Karla running out on him had soured the experience.

'It was great, yeah. But hey, how'd you end up spending the weekend at Anna's? No husband around?'

'They're taking a break, according to her, so I didn't ask any more questions. None of my business. I benefited to the tune of a weekend of sex, who am I to complain?'

'True.'

'Nice one on the Karla thing, mate. You've worked for that. If I wasn't otherwise engaged, I'd be fighting you for her.'

'Well, I'm glad you aren't 'cause she's it for me, Harry. Seriously, she's everything, but…'

'No, buts, Matt. She came over to yours, you had a great time, why is there a but?'

'She left Saturday evening. I was making us a bite to eat, as we'd been at it all day, and then she just appeared in the kitchen and said she had to go.'

'OK, I'm confused. You had great sex all afternoon and then she left you in peace to enjoy your Saturday night, and you find there's a problem in that?'

'She's not like the others, I just wanted to hang out with her, have some amazing sex and chill. For once, I wanted to wake up beside the woman I slept with.'

'Christ on a bike you are smitten. Did you say it to her like that? That could have scared her off.'

'Of course I didn't. I didn't get a chance to say anything. She just arrived down to the kitchen, already dressed, and left. I couldn't have read it so wrong. We had a fucking amazing afternoon. I was pretty darn sensational.'

'I've been the other side of the wall plenty of times to know you can satisfy the fussiest of them. So, what you reckon happened?'

'That's what I don't know. Radio silence since she left.' He held up his hand before Harry interjected. 'No, I didn't bombard her with texts. Just the one, it's nice to be nice. I told her I'd enjoyed spending time together and hoped we could do it again outside of work.'

'OK, OK, that's allowed. Ma Fallon would be proud.'

'Yeah, but she didn't even respond. Nothing, nada, zilch! Then, no eye contact at the meeting this morning. Despite me sitting directly across from her. Like what the actual!? Give me something.'

'Sounds like she doesn't want to give you anything Matt. Karla's a very independent woman. My advice, bro? For what it's worth? Leave her be. She'll come round. Give her time, and if she doesn't then you haven't made a complete ass of yourself chasing her.'

'What if she wants me to chase her? What if she wants romance and her prince charming to fight for her?'

'Really? Is that the vibe you're getting? I'm thinking cold shoulder is what it is, and you can figure out why in time. But, right now, if you push, you may push her so far away she'll never come close again. You're too damn charming for this to be long-term. She'll figure it out soon enough. The sex was amazing, you get on great, yeah, she'll come round. It sounds like she's a little confused and pressure from you right now might not be the wisest thing.'

'Shit.'

'Well thank you for your insightful response to my analysis, Mr Fallon.' Harry jibed, making Matt laugh.

'Yeah, yeah. I bought you lunch, that's my response. You may have a point, doesn't mean it doesn't suck though.'

'Yeah, I know. Haven't seen you like this over a woman before. Nice to see you have feelings after all.'

'Yeah, yeah. Here, let's get back to you. What the hell's going on with Anna? All weekend? In hers? Was that not weird?'

'Nope, well, mostly no. Felt a bit like I was being watched when I was in her kitchen and shit. Surprisingly, the bedroom was grand. No problems there. Speaking of being watched. Wasn't the husband who walked in, but your missus, Karla.'

'What you mean?'

'Karla. She popped in Saturday morning to Anna's and got more than she bargained for.'

'She walked in on you?'

'Anna and I were on her terrace you know, getting it on, and who walks through the side gate, only your Karla. Anna had a mouthful if you get my drift! I look up, and Karla is standing there gawping. Got a shock she did for sure. I'm surprised she didn't mention it to you.'

'Ah, we got kinda' busy as soon as she arrived in mine. She had other things on her mind.'

'Yeah, sure. Well, Anna was going to have a chat with her today. She was very embarrassed. Anna and I laughed it off and she finished the job as well. Barely lost her rhythm, some woman.'

Shaking his head Matt couldn't help smiling, but his stomach had turned a little. 'Some woman alright. Hey, let's get out of here, my next client arrives at two thirty and I need to prep.'

'Yeah, I've nobody for the afternoon but a shit-ton of paperwork to catch up on before I finish early. Fancy catching the game tonight?'

'Yeah, sure. Over at yours?'

'Yeah, great. Good plan.'

Matt reluctantly got through the afternoon and spent the trip home thinking about what Harry had said at lunchtime. Karla must have come to his straight after seeing them in Anna's. *But what difference did it make if I benefitted?* He thought. *Maybe seeing them and getting the phone call from me was just good timing? Maybe she was embarrassed but also horny, and seeing work colleagues together made her think it was OK to do it with me? You're overanalysing again. You lucked out. Leave it at that.*

Karla held her hand over the send key, paused, thought better of it, and deleted the text. *Wimp. The least you can do is say it to his face. You've to work with him every day, at least in the same building. Just put on your big girl pants and have a conversation with him. He's a nice guy, he'll understand.* Karla wasn't sure she had convinced herself. But satisfied a conversation was the better option, she changed into her running gear and headed out. She needed a long run to clear her head.

Anna sat on her terrace, enjoying the evening sun, savouring her favourite Sancerre in a wine goblet that had been a wedding gift from one of Fergal's work colleagues. She played with her salad. She had no real appetite and found herself forcing some food down to stave off any hunger pangs that might appear. Watching the waves crash further up the beach against the cliff, she contemplated her life. Fergal had called earlier but she had ignored the call and let it go to voicemail. *What was he going to say? Am I ready to hear whatever it is?* Work was tremendously busy. She was very proud of the Clinic and how far it had come in a few short months. But at what cost? It may have been her dream to open it, but it was both of them who had decided to relocate to Fergal's hometown. She loved him dearly and missed him now that he had been gone from her life for over a week. He had waited a whole week to make contact. She wasn't sure if that was because he had been so angry or if that was to give her time to miss him. She definitely missed him. But she also had an amazing weekend with Harry and found it difficult to imagine not having him available to her when she needed him. If only Fergal could accept that she could enjoy the company of more than one man and that her love was not diminished for him by doing so. In fact, Anna felt that her capacity for love and her sensuality had increased the more she was allowed to be herself. *No, I'm not ready to speak with Fergal, because my feelings on the issue haven't changed. I'm still annoyed that he has changed the rules and just expects me to follow suit. Damn him.*

Harry sat watching the pre-game interviews and discussions, not hearing anything they were saying. His thoughts couldn't help themselves. They returned to moments from the weekend, moments of her face, her body, her smile, those eyes. Snippets of pleasure that made him smile smugly and nod his head in approval. Toasting himself silently with his bottle of beer he took a long drink, closing his eyes so he could feel the sensation of his hands exploring Anna's lithe body. *Goddamn it. I could do with her being here right now.* Instead, the doorbell ringing signalled Matt's arrival to watch the game. *Put those thoughts away till later,* he told himself.

CHAPTER 29

Matt's last client of the week was certainly going to demand his full attention, which didn't bother him. Having not heard anything from Karla all week, he was feeling a little despondent and needed a distraction.

'Welcome, Maeve. Please make yourself comfortable and we can get started.'

'Thanks, Matt. Honestly, I'm not sure you can help. To be perfectly honest, I don't know why I'm here. My friend convinced me to come but now I'm not so sure.'

'How about we have a chat, and if you decide that it's not for you after that we can cut the session short and finish up. But you may be surprised. Let me ask you to keep an open mind. Try to relax and I promise it will be as painless as possible.'

'I'll trust you for now, I like you.'

'Thank you. I'm not an ogre I promise. Would you like a drink? Some coffee, tea, or water maybe?'

'I'd love a water, please. I won't lie, my mouth's a little dry.'

Matt made his way to the mini bar and gathered two chilled glasses for them both.

'Why don't you tell me a little about yourself while I do this? Maybe start with why your friend thought it would be a good idea for you to come here?'

'OK, well I'll just dive straight in. Unlike what I do with sex,' laughed Maeve. 'I haven't been in a relationship for a long time, and I think my friend, well a few of them really, thought this place would be a good idea. She read about it in the Times on the weekend, and instantly sent me a screenshot of the article. Insisted it was just what I needed.'

'Well, you're here, so do you agree with them?' Matt handed her a tall glass of ice-cold water and placed his glass on the desk. Sitting down to face her he waited for her reply. Maeve took a sip of water and contemplated the question.

'Sure, if they think I need therapy, who am I to argue? Right?'

'Well, not exactly. When you read the article what did you think about it?'

'Honestly? I'm very happy with my sexless life. It's been so long I don't think I'd know what to do, anyway.'

'Is that really true?'

'Well, no. I think I'd remember. I loved having sex when it was available to me. But the pleasure usually got outweighed by the intense pain of being hurt over and over. No offence to you or to the men I know that don't fit this category, but in my experience, men are thoughtless, selfish, liars, and it's just too much effort to wade through the crap to try and find a half-decent one.'

'OK, now that's a statement we can work with. Tell me a little more.'

'More? Sure. Well, any man I've been remotely interested in since my first serious boyfriend cheated on me with my so-called best friend, has also been a complete asshole. Now as I hear myself say it, I wonder what it is about me that attracts complete assholes, all the time?'

Maeve shrugged her shoulders. 'I have a very strong asshole attraction magnetism, obviously.'

'I know you are laughing, but I see a lot of pain, Maeve. You don't have to cover it up here.'

'I didn't realise I was. Sorry... gosh...I just tend to laugh it off most of the time, because if I didn't, I'd probably cry, like, a lot. I really do miss being intimate with someone. I do wish at times I could just be normal and have a normal relationship. But then I just think it's not on the cards for me.'

'I can understand that. Why do you think you keep meeting assholes?'

'Your guess is as good as mine. I was kinda thinking you might be able to decipher that for me?'

'Let's do it together. Go back a little to your serious boyfriend, tell me a little about that relationship.'

'There's really nothing much to tell. We were together for about five years. He cheated on me throughout that time, and each time I forgave him because he begged me too and insisted it would be the last. The last time was when he met someone else and told me he was moving on just before we were supposed to go on a holiday that I had paid for.'

'Ouch.'

Maeve shrugged. 'Sure, what could I do?'

'What was your reaction?'

'I screamed at him that he was a selfish horrible man and bawled crying in front of him. I made a complete show of myself in a public park, and he walked away anyway. Left me there crying, alone, sitting on the park bench feeling terribly sorry myself.'

'That must have hurt a lot, Maeve.'

'I was sad, no doubt about it. But as I said, what could I do except cry my tears, dust myself off and move on?'

'You could have been very angry about how he treated you and told him so?'

'What good would that have done?'

'It may have given you some closure and released some of the anger. Do you think you may have internalised some of it?'

'Like do you mean stayed angry for a long time?'

'I was thinking more that you may have blamed yourself.'

'Well... maybe... a little,' she chuckled. 'There I go again, trying to laugh about it. How else should I react?'

'You shouldn't do anything. Should is a word I tend not to use a lot. It implies there are right and wrong ways to do things, and when we are talking about feelings it's really about, could do, or am doing, not should. Does that make sense?'

'Yeah, I guess.'

'So, going back a little. Do you think you laid any blame on yourself?'

'There's a slight possibility. OK, maybe there's a great possibility that I blamed myself. I had nobody else to blame.'

'And do you think that laying blame at your own feet has served you well?'

'Well, I think that I had nobody else to blame, and each time it happened to me, so, yes.' She nodded her head. 'Yes, I blamed myself.'

'With hindsight do you think that was appropriate?'

'I didn't have the luxury of hindsight. But, at the time I felt I had to lay blame somewhere and I was the common denominator with all the breakups, so it made sense to lay blame at my door.'

Matt nodded and took a sip of water letting Maeve continue.

'If I add hindsight into the equation and look at where I find myself now, I feel that maybe some of them were just assholes, and I probably didn't need to blame myself for some of the breakups.'

'What would you think if I said you didn't have to blame yourself for any of them?'

'I'd say you're just trying to make me feel better, and that's not true.'

'Let me put it a different way. What if I said that it's OK not to blame anyone, but rather to look at the relationships as learning opportunities? If you don't repeat mistakes, they become lessons learnt. If you do repeat them, it means you still have lessons to learn.'

'But why can't I blame someone? Me, him, the other woman, whoever. My anger has to go somewhere.'

'And why do you think your anger has to go somewhere? What if you dealt with your anger at the time of the breakup, and then let it go? Move on, and then the blame is irrelevant because at that point there's nobody to blame.'

'You may be blowing my mind here a little, Matt. I'm not going to lie.'

Laughing Matt nodded, 'I think sometimes when you hear it, the idea of removing blame and dealing with anger to move on makes plenty of sense, but you have to actually hear it first.'

'I'll admit I have never really looked at it like that. I have spent years analysing what I did wrong each time. I have questioned everything I've said, how I've acted, and I suppose ultimately, I've wondered why I was never good enough for any of them.'

Maeve swallowed and took a deep breath. Matt could see the tears start to pool. He grabbed the tissue box and placed it in front of her. The silence hung in the room and yet Maeve couldn't speak. The tears that had started to form flowed freely now. He said nothing. Time slipped by and Maeve's tears dried.

'There's a lot of pain there.' She knew he understood and that was enough to open the floodgates again.

'It's alright you know,' Matt spoke softly. He walked around the desk and laid his hand on her shoulder. 'It's OK to let it out.'

Maeve couldn't help it. The tears wouldn't stop. She gratefully accepted the bunch of tissues he handed her and the comfort he gave with his light touch.

'I'm so tired of being strong,' she murmured through the tears.

'I get it. I do let it out.'

'I just want to meet someone who loves me when I am one hundred per cent me. Someone who'll hold me when I need comfort, who'll make me laugh at silly jokes. I'm tired of always having to have my own back. I know I can be independent and strong and all those things I'm meant to be, but sometimes I just want to be held and told that everything will be OK. Matt, I want a man to want me as a woman, to fulfil my desires. Dammit, I miss being intimate with someone. I miss being kissed and stroked and told I'm beautiful even on my worst days.' Maeve's shoulders sank and Matt nodded.

'All of which is completely normal and rational, Maeve, and you deserve to have it all.'

She looked up at him with a tear-stained face and pleaded. 'Then why don't I?'

'That's why you're here, Maeve. We can figure this out together.'

'Thank you.'

'Does that mean you'd like to stay? Do you think I can help you?'

'I think that's what I mean.'

'Well, if you're up for it why don't we explore the 'assholes' a little?' Matt smiled warmly and Maeve returned the simple gesture with one of her own.

'Do we have to? I've tried to forget them to be perfectly honest. There also haven't been that many, but even the one-night stands were horrible to me.'

'Give me an example?'

'Well, there was this one guy, we'd been together before, kissed and stuff. So, it was a big deal that night I went back to his place, and well, we were doing stuff and then he just stopped, said he wasn't feeling it anymore and suggested I leave. I was still naked in his bed, kind of in the middle of giving him oral sex.' Maeve was mortified and tried looking anywhere but at Matt.

The low whistle caught her off guard and she looked questioningly at him.

'See, even you think that's awful, right?'

'It's not the nicest for sure. So, what did you do?'

'I wasn't going to pay for a taxi all the way home when I could get a bus in a few hours, so I stayed.'

'You stayed at his place? On the couch?'

'Well, actually, I stayed in his bed.'

'Oh, Maeve.'

'What?'

'You didn't have to stay. I'm sure that wasn't pleasant for either of you.'

'Well, no, it wasn't. But if I'm honest, I thought he might change his mind if I was just there and...'

Matt held up his hand. 'Stop, you were still going to be with him after that?'

'Well, what if he changed his mind? You know, decided he'd been too rash in his decision, and we could sort it out?'

Taking a deep breath, Matt shook his head and smiled sweetly to try to take the sting out of what he was about to say.

'Maeve, I'm going to say this not to hurt you but to help you, OK?'

'OK. What do you want to say?'

'A desperate woman is one of the most unattractive women in the world. And I hate to say it, but you sound like you were desperate.'

She shrunk into the chair and dabbed at her eyes. Matt felt awful. 'Please don't get upset. Look, this is powerful stuff.'

'Really? My humiliation is powerful, are you serious?'

'No, no, it's not humiliation. It's me understanding what's going on with you, and now that we know, I can help, and things will change for you I promise. If I gently step around this you won't get what you need from this session, so we can either tiptoe around the issues or dive straight in. If you choose the former, I'm telling you now, it's going to be some very expensive weeks, maybe months of sessions. If you choose the latter, we could do this in one or two sessions. What do you say? Do you think you can plough straight in and rip the band-aid off?'

'I can't tell you how mortified I am right now.'

'Look there's no reason for mortification. I promise. I have seen and heard many, many things, and believe me when I say this doesn't need to be up there on the mortification scale. Let's just look at it as lessons learnt and figure out how not to repeat the same lessons. Does that seem fair?'

'OK, but you telling me not to be mortified doesn't change the fact that I am, so can we just get on with it? Tell me what to do differently, please.'

'Let's start with a coffee. I need a coffee; would you like one? Or water maybe?'

'Any chance of a cuppa? I'd love a tea.'

'Sure, a cup of tea coming up. Now while I sort that out, why don't you tell me a little more about yourself? What long-term relationships have you been in?'

Maeve uncrossed her legs and sat looking at Matt preparing the drinks.

'Well, there's not really that many. Probably like five longish-term, one or two for a few months, and then a few drunken nights out, one of which you now know about, mortification.' Ignoring the embarrassment she felt, Matt tried to steer her clear of the last story.

'What about the long-term ones, tell me briefly how they were and how they ended?'

'Oh, that's simple really. One was the guy I nearly lost my virginity to. Teenage love on my part, teenage lust on his. We were too young to be at it so we never quite got there. But, a few years later we got together, and he ended up back in my flat. We had what I thought was a great night until I picked up the phone extension to make a call a week later and heard my flatmate and him having phone sex.'

'Oh, wow.'

'Yep, and that's not the worst. A few years later I saw him again in a bar, and obviously, I didn't feel humiliated enough, so I started flirting with him and I'm thinking he was reciprocating, but then he just walked away, like, mid-sentence walked away. I thought he was getting me a drink. He didn't come back.'

'Oh, Maeve.'

'The next one was the one I lost my virginity to. Crazy about him I was. He flirted with any woman he could, slept with one of my best friends, and still, I didn't break up with him.'

'Really? So, what happened?"

'Oh, he met someone else and broke up with me. But then whenever she was back down home, he'd ring me and say he missed me. I'd fall for it, we'd sleep together, and then surprise, they'd be back together and good ol' Maeve would be left with her heart shattered into a million little pieces.'

'Did you love him?' Matt knew the answer but wanted her to say it anyway.

'Love him? I adored him. I've never again felt the way I felt when I was with him. He has this ability to make me feel like the only woman in the world one moment, and completely broken the next when he takes his attention away.'

'You said, he has the ability. Do you mean he still can?'

'Matt, I hear how pathetic I sound, but what can I do? I adore him. I love him like nobody else, ever. I've had other long-term boyfriends in the last few years, and nobody can make me feel how he can.'

'Do you mean? Make you feel like shit?'

'No, I mean make me feel like I don't want anyone else in my life other than him. I'd walk on hot coals for him. I'd do absolutely anything he asked of me just to please him and try to make him happy.' She shook her head and held up her hand. 'And yes, before you say it, I know how pathetic, oh god, and how desperate that sounds. You were right, I stink of desperation.' Maeve dropped her head into her hands.

'Maeve, you may have just given me an excellent insight into what's going on in your relationships.'

'Yeah, well, if that's the case, please tell me.'

'It's clear to me that you have spoken about these men in terms of how you can make them happy. How you want to flirt with them, satisfy them. What about you? What makes you happy? Did any of these guys try to make you happy?'

'Making them happy is what makes me happy, Matt.'

'Maeve, you do understand that you are worthy of being loved? You are enough as you are and deserve affection and love, don't you?'

Maeve hung her head. Tears glistened in her eyes, and she tried to answer but her voice caught. Her sad eyes looked at Matt, shaking her head, he watched the tears slide down her cheeks.

'I can't…' She paused and whispered, 'I can't go there, it's too painful.'

'It's OK, Maeve. But I'm going to say it again. You deserve to be loved. You are worthy. You deserve to be wanted for who you are, not just how happy you make someone else.'

She couldn't stop them now, heaving sobs flooded through her. He'd never heard someone cry as hard as she did. He came around the desk and handed her the box of tissues.

'Here. Let it all go.' Sitting beside her he let her cry. He waited. Maeve tried to speak, but the heavy, heaving sobs wouldn't stop.

Matt sat in silence and waited.

Eventually, Maeve spoke through the tears.
'How do I stop hurting, Matt?'
His heart felt for her. The pain was palpable.
'This is the first step. I've got you. I'll help, I promise.'
His kindness was too much for her and set her off crying again.

CHAPTER 30

Karla was raging with herself because she hadn't managed to talk to Matt before the week was out. The work crew were heading into 37 Dawson, and she wanted to go but she wasn't sure how Matt would react if she turned up. Applying her lipstick and taking one last look in the full-length mirror she decided that it didn't matter, they were both adults and could chat if they wanted to, or not.

She wondered if Anna and Harry were going to be there. Would they flaunt their affair in front of everyone? She doubted it. Despite knowing it made no sense and was probably a little crazy, she was still looking forward to seeing Harry. Maybe more than a little crazy. Harry was involved with Anna, Karla had slept with his best friend, and here she was hoping he was going to be there tonight.

She knew she needed to let Matt know that what happened between them was just a blip, that would at least clear things up with him. Then she could sit and wait to see what, if anything, Harry and Anna turned into. At least that way she knew she'd done what she could to limit the damage done by sleeping with Matt in the first place.

Walking into the bar Karla put her shoulders back and her head up. She wasn't going to let anyone dictate how she would feel, or what she would do. Noticing the work crew in the far corner of the bar she made her way over gave them a big smile, waved and said a collective hello, which stopped the need for any individual air kisses or contact.

Luckily the music was loud so there was very little opportunity for much conversation other than the pre-requisite, 'Hi' or, 'How are you?' She took an offer of a drink from Hilary and mouthed her order finding a seat beside Tom, the cute, intellectual therapist who had amazing talents when it came to therapy but had zero social skills. Karla knew he would be feeling even more awkward than she was right now, and a friendly face and a nudge of the shoulder was the least she could do for him. She smiled and tried to start a stunted conversation over the music. She spotted Matt at the bar and tried her best to engage in conversation with Tom, drawing anything she could out of him. There was no sign of Harry, but Anna was chatting amicably to the group Matt was in, and Karla tried her best to divert her attention away from them.

Hilary returned with the drinks, and once settled, Karla got into the swing of the night, dragging people to the dance floor at every opportunity. She managed to avoid talking to Matt for the entire evening. Keeping eye contact to a minimum, and on the odd occasion she felt him trying to vie for her attention, she grabbed another unsuspecting soul to dance with her. Despite her reservations and the awkwardness of trying to avoid any messy conversations with Matt, Karla ended up having a relatively good night. Yet, she couldn't shake the feeling that she was being intentionally obtuse with Matt, and having managed to avoid him all evening she went home feeling less than pleased with herself. She knew she'd been juvenile and had hurt Matt's feelings. After all, he'd done nothing wrong. If anything, he'd been very attentive, caring, and thoughtful, and they'd had a really good time together at his place. The feeling wasn't going to go away any time soon. She knew she'd played it wrong and walked home disappointed with herself.

❤❤❤

The following Monday Karla sat in her office wondering whether the best thing to do was walk straight down the hall and apologise to Matt, or just leave it be. She wanted to say sorry. She really did.

But the embarrassment had taken hold, and she wasn't sure she could face him.

Shaking her head, she relived the previous Friday night's antics and admonished herself. Feeling like a complete fool she'd spent the weekend wondering why, not for the first time, she had focused her attention on a guy who was clearly not available, over a guy who clearly was. She didn't need to answer the question. She had decided what she needed to do, and it went against all her instincts, which told her she was onto something. She knew she just needed to walk down the corridor to Matt's office. Gathering herself, she stole a glance in the mirror and slowly made her way down the hallway. Tentatively knocking on his office door, she waited patiently for the 'Come in,' she kind of hoped she wouldn't hear.

'Come in.' Karla took a deep breath, opened the door and walked in.

'Matt?'

He looked up, no smile, a slight nod of acknowledgement.

'What can I do for you, Karla?'

'I, well, to be honest, I wanted to have a quick word with you about Friday night if you have a moment?'

'Sure, fire ahead.'

Karla had never felt so uncomfortable in her life, she certainly wasn't used to having to apologise to a man or explain her position. It was usually the other way around, and once he was done grovelling, she'd be walking away anyway. That was old Karla. But being new Karla was much harder than she anticipated.

Matt looked up from his paperwork and angled his head. 'You wanted to say something?'

'Eh. Yes. I'm sorry.' She paused for effect but when she was met with silence and his stony face she continued. 'I acted like a complete idiot. I was rude and obnoxious, you didn't deserve that, and I feel awful about it and wanted to apologise.' The words fell out of her, and she kept speaking waiting for a reaction, any reaction from Matt. His face gave nothing away. She stood waiting, hoping he'd speak. When it was obvious he wasn't going to reply, she made to leave. Turning at the door she whispered, 'I'm really sorry, Matt. You didn't deserve that.'

'Karla, wait.'

Holding the door handle she turned.

'Come here.' It wasn't a request.

Yet, she didn't hesitate. She strode towards him.

Matt leaned against his desk and watched her.

She reached him and stood demurely in front of him.

He reached out and took her hair in his hands drawing her in and devouring her mouth with his. There was no protest. Karla's lips parted willingly and if she was surprised, she didn't show it, instead he felt the compliance, the way her lips parted, the way her tongue reached for his.

After a few moments, he pulled away, untangled her hair from his hands and spoke. 'I accept your apology. I'm not sure what you're searching for, and I wish you well in finding it. But don't ever treat me like a piece of shit again. I did nothing but want you.' He turned and sat back behind his desk. 'Close the door on your way out.'

Completely shocked and unsure if her legs would take her, Karla headed for the door, just making it to her office before collapsing on the couch. Thumping the cushions she shouted into the empty room, 'Fuck'.

CHAPTER 31

Alice knocked and tentatively walked into Harry's office. 'Hi.'

'Alice. Lovely to see you again. Come in. Take the weight off. Can I get you something to drink?' He smiled watching her place her bag at her feet as she sat in the bucket chair in front of his desk.

'Yes, please, I'd love a still water if you have one.'

'No problem. So, tell me, how have you been?'

'I've actually been quite good all things considered.'

'Really? That's great. You seem surprised that you are feeling good?'

'I guess I wasn't sure what to expect when I came the last time. I was also so nervous and couldn't think beyond coming here. You see, what I figured out was that I had no expectations of an outcome, which is so unlike me.'

Harry nodded knowingly.

'I get that. But tell me a little bit more about how you felt after our session?'

'Well,' Alice took a sip of water. 'I guess I just felt lighter. A lot lighter, and what you said about me not being broken struck home with me. I think I had labelled myself as broken and it had stuck. But then, when you spoke about the loved ones in my life and the love Brian and I had shared, it dawned on me that I was doing his memory a disservice by believing that I was broken. I know I'll never find the type of love Brian and I shared, ever again. It wouldn't be possible, and quite frankly, I'm not interested. I was very lucky to have found my true love so early in my life and that we had so many wonderful years together.' Alice smiled softly at Harry. 'I know not everyone has that opportunity in their lifetime and I feel sad for them, but I feel happy for us, for what we had, for the time we did have, despite it being cut far too short. I really do feel grateful.'

Harry nodded, returning Alice's smile.

'That's wonderful, Alice. Truly wonderful. What brings you back here to us? How can I help you today?'

Alice looked a little sheepish. 'I'm ready to meet someone, in a kind of romantic way but when I started thinking about it, I got quite panicky and, well…' She twirled her skirt around and looked away. 'I'm not sure how to do it. I was hoping you could help.'

'Do you mean sex?'

Laughing nervously Alice replied, 'Well, I know how to do sex, but…' She stumbled over her words, 'I don't know how to do it with anyone except Brian, and that's so scary. But it's even more scary thinking about being on my own for the rest of my life.' Exhaling slowly, Alice lifted her head and Harry was touched by her honesty.

'Alice, do you know what? I think you're more ready than you think you are. Can I make a suggestion to help with the panicky feeling?'

'Anything, please.'

'Stop thinking.'

'Sorry?'

'Stop thinking. Stop wondering what you will say or do on a date. Stop thinking about how you will kiss a man if you get to that point, or even how the sex will happen if you get there. Let it go.'

'I don't understand. How will it happen if I don't think about it? How will I know what to do if I don't think about it? If I don't figure it out?'

'Let me put it another way. Let's think of it like an exercise class.'

'An exercise class? Now you have me all confused. Are you saying I should go to an exercise class to find a man?'

'No, no. Just go with me. I bet you've taken up a new exercise routine since Brian died, right?'

'Well, yes, but not to find a man. Sheila was on at me to join her yoga class for months and I eventually gave in and joined her. She's gotten very flexible lately you know, and I thought it would be a nice way to get fit and maybe get back a little of my flexibility. I used to be able to do the splits you know.'

'Very good.' Harry leaned forward on his desk, joining his hands together. 'What I mean is, when Sheila asked you to join her yoga class, what did you feel?'

'Feel? Well, I guess, I was a little nervous if I'm honest. I knew Sheila and the bridge girls had been doing it for a long time and I didn't want to embarrass myself, you know, not knowing all the fancy moves or anything. But the teacher was good, and she let me go at my own pace. Yes, very good actually.'

'Really? Let's look at that. You'd never done yoga before, decided to give it a try, and didn't overthink it. Even though you were nervous, you went along and found a teacher who was patient, kind, and helpful, and now you go every week and aren't the new girl in the class anymore.'

'Well, yes. Can I ask what that has to do with me finding a relationship?'

'Remember when I said stop thinking? What did you do with yoga?'

Alice looked at Harry and he could see her face change when it sunk in. 'Well, Harry, you are a genius! I never even saw that similarity. But you're right. You're so right. My goodness. Do you really think I can approach relationships the same way?'

'I think you've no choice. If you approach them the way you were, you'll continue to be so scared of what may or may not happen, and you'll never even go on a first date. But, if you approach it like your yoga class, well, then who knows what might happen?'

'Well, I must say. I wasn't expecting this to be such a sensible solution. So, what you're saying is I should stop overthinking everything?'

Harry chuckled. 'Well now, that's your word, not mine. I don't think it was necessarily overthinking, more a case of letting the mind wander a little and then the panic would set in. Alice, if I let my mind wander to all the what-ifs when I go to do something, I'd also be paralysed with the fear of doing anything. Everyone can overthink, but equally, we all have the potential to just get on with it and put the worries and what-ifs into a little box when they jump up at us. Do you understand that?'

'Yes, yes, I do. It makes perfect sense when you describe it like that. Why in god's name has nobody ever explained it to me that way before? Not just relationships but everything. My goodness, the ladies are going to have a field day with this one. Now some of them, like that Mags Smith and maybe even Cynthia Byrne, they will probably scoff at the very idea. But my goodness, Sheila is going to love this. And as for Majella, well, her youngest daughter Amanda is all about your energy and the universe stuff all the time, and she's tried to get us all to meditate and everything to help when the panic sets in, but she's never even come up with this. It's so simple really. Just stop forward-worrying, isn't that it?'

'In a nutshell, yes. You can welcome the idea of being nervous and then just choose to let it go. Park it, as such.'

'And you think I'll be able to use this to find myself a relationship?'

'I think you'll be able to use it for more than that, but that too, yes.'

'Honestly, Harry, you're a genius, and it's been really lovely having you to talk to about all this stuff. It isn't an easy subject for me, but somehow, I can talk to you. It's lovely.'

'Alice, it's been a pleasure. I do hope you get out there now and find yourself a companion.'

'Oh, I will. But to be honest with you, I'm not desperately looking or anything. I feel good on my own, I like the independence, but if he turns up, I won't be too scared to give it a whirl.'

Alice stood and reached for Harry's outstretched hand. 'Thank you so much. For everything.'

'It's been my pleasure, Alice. You take care now.' Harry watched her leave.

The door closed softly behind her, and Harry sat down reflecting on the session.

What a lovely lady. Whoever is fortunate enough to meet her will be a lucky man indeed. I think I should probably take my own advice. I hate when that happens, thought Harry shaking his head.

CHAPTER 32

Karla was grateful it was Friday and standing with a glass of wine in her hand watching the moon sparkle off the sea, she started to feel the weight of the week dissipate a little. She turned to Anna. 'It is quite spectacular here, isn't it? I'd never tire of these views.'

'I know, I pinch myself sometimes. That's my favourite view from the house. I don't know what I'll do if Ferg and I can't work things out and we have to sell this place.'

'Oh, so there's hope of a reconciliation?'

'I don't know if there is. But I also don't know that there's not. We haven't talked about anything since he left. I'm still too angry with him to discuss it yet.'

'Oh, you're mad at him?'

'Yes, of course, I am. He's changed the goalposts and expects me to be the one to change. Why should I?'

Karla nodded. Unsure if Anna was looking for a response, she aired on the side of caution. Taking a sip of her wine she joined Anna at the table and nibbled on an olive.

Anna continued, 'I haven't changed since we met. He knew the situation and we married on that basis. I wasn't the one who wanted to marry. I did it for him. I was happy for our commitment to each other to be valid without the need for marriage, a wedding, and all that. I did that for him. Wasn't that enough to show him how much I love him?' Anna sipped her wine and shook her head.

Karla turned toward Anna. 'Dare I ask about you and Harry?'

'Sure.' Anna's demeanour changed and her shoulders relaxed. 'He's an extremely talented lover. I knew the moment I saw him he would be good, and he hasn't disappointed me yet. It's been a lot of fun.'

Karla drained her glass and retrieved the remaining wine from the fridge, topping up both their glasses and mumbling a little as she spoke. 'I'm happy for you if it makes you happy, Anna.'

'It does, or at least it did when everything was in its place. Fergal being the way he is hasn't changed that, just dampened it a little.'

'Can I ask your advice, Anna?'

'Sure, of course. What about?'

'Well...' Karla wasn't ordinarily shy about discussing men, particularly with Anna, but for some reason, she felt it now. Anna was one of her oldest friends. This is ridiculous. Just ask her.

'I slept with Matt.'

'And? What's the question?'

'And? That's all you have to say?'

'Well, did you want me to act surprised when I already figured one or other of you would go for it sooner or later? I mean really, Karla, the man is adorable and my god his body is H. O. T.'

'Anna. You're incorrigible.'

'Oh, don't act all prissy on me, Karla Gutenberg. No woman in her right mind could resist that charm. He's adorable. So, did you say you're sleeping with him or slept with him?'

'Well, I slept with him and then I walked out. I kind of left him high and dry and ignored him.'

'Oh no, you didn't?'

'Well, yes. I didn't know how I felt. I needed time to process.'

'Was the sex not good?'

'The sex was spectacular.'

'And you like him? Are you still in love with Tom? Is that the issue?'

'Gosh no, nothing like that,' replied Karla. She hesitated. Thinking about her crush on Harry now just made her feel disappointed in herself, and she couldn't believe she messed things up with Matt so much.

'I, well, I ignored him and didn't address it, and then I saw him today and he kissed me, Anna. I swear I've never had a man kiss me like that.'

'Oh very nice indeed.' Anna raised her glass. 'Continue.'

'But, it was a goodbye kiss. He told me he hoped I find what I'm looking for and never to treat him like that again. He told me he had only ever wanted me.'

'Well, I am impressed. Maybe that baby face is a little deceptive so.'

'Don't high-five him for chrissake, he humiliated me.'

'Bullshit. He was humiliated first, and he wanted you to know how it felt. But by the sounds of things, he also wanted you to know what you were missing. Seems to have worked from where I'm sitting.'

'Damn him.' Karla took a long swig of wine. 'Damn him. Now all I'm thinking is how I fix this.'

'You want my advice, sotnos?'

'Yes, yes, I do.'

'Well then, my advice is to stay away from him. Make him come to you.'

'He came to me. I shunned him, and now he's made it very clear he's done.'

'Karla, I know for a fact you're not this naive. Look at this as if it's a client coming to you with the same problem you just presented here to me?'

'Well, I guess I'd ask her how she felt?'

'Sure, maybe you'd ask her that. Well, what's the answer?'

'I can't believe how stupid I've been and that I didn't see what was right in front of me before it was too late.'

'No, that doesn't tell me how you feel, sotnos.'

'Damn, Anna, I feel foolish. I feel like I really like him, and I feel like I just messed everything up.'

'Better. Now at least you've something to work with. We both know that Matt is a hot-blooded male, and you have a certain effect on those creatures. You've obviously had that effect on Matt already, so what do you reckon is the solution?'

Laughing, Karla swallowed the last of her wine. 'Make him want me again?'

Anna was already retrieving the bottle from the fridge. 'Oh, you can do better than that.'

Karla stood for emphasis. 'Make him see what he's missing?'

'Absolutely. Karla, you will have him begging for another chance in no time, but you have to be sure that's what you want.'

'It is, I swear. When he kissed me today, I could barely make it back to my office my legs were so weak. I didn't want him to stop.'

'I think you have your answer. Now all you have to do is let him know how you feel.'

'Easier said than done when he's so mad at me.'

'I have every faith in you, my dear friend.'

In 37 Dawson Harry was listening to Matt recount that same kiss, following it with a few back slaps. 'You're inner me? Really? I'm flattered, mate. So, what did she do?'

'I didn't give her much choice, I told her to close the door on her way out.'

'Ouch.'

'What? Bit harsh you reckon?'

'Nope. But ouch. Karla isn't going to take that lying down, Matt.'

'Kinda wish she would.'

'Ha. It should be certainly interesting to see. Don't think it's the last of it though.'

'I hope not, Harry. Still, the hottest piece of ass I've ever had. But I don't care how damn hot she is, there's no way she's going to walk all over me.'

'Good for you. Now it's a balmy Friday night in Dublin, what's say you and I take advantage of these fine Irish women?'

'Be rude not to.' Matt caught the bartender's attention. 'Two more pints and a couple of whiskey chasers, please.' He ordered while simultaneously scanning the bar. 'Nine o'clock, Harry. Check it out, looks like we've found ourselves a couple of enthusiastic women.' Matt nodded in the direction of two blondes doing shots and whooping with delight as they slammed their glasses at the bar, giggling at the flirtatious bartender.

With his megawatt smile, Matt held his glass aloft and toasted them both, walking towards them. Harry coming up the rear ordered a round for the group as introductions were made, flirty glances exchanged, and the girls giggled some more.

Matt woke with a sore head and a dead arm. Turning his pounding head very slowly, he opened one eye hoping that the reason for his dead arm wasn't what he thought it was. Sure enough, he glimpsed the blonde hair and felt the rise and fall of her chest.

The memories of the night before started to come back and with it a whole string of other feelings he hadn't felt in a while.

Pleasure coursed through him as he thought back to the night before and looked at the beauty beside him. He felt himself stir and harden. Despite his body's response, his thoughts lead him to Karla, wishing it was her in his arms. But he wasn't a complete idiot, and he knew exactly how to solve that. Reaching for the soft warm body beside him he set aside his anger, smiled as a sleepy woman stirred under his expert hands and responded eagerly to his caresses. 'Good morning sleepy head,' he mumbled before kissing her breasts and feeling her nipples harden under his expert tongue.

Her groan gave him the permission he needed, and he focused his attention on the taunt eager body under his. 'This is what Saturday mornings were made for,' he whispered. If only he could remember her name.

Karla and Anna finished their beach jog together leaning on the steps up to Anna's home.

'I need to do more of this.' Karla paused to catch her breath. 'I didn't realise how out of shape I'd become.'

'You're not out of shape, Karla, a few runs and you'll be back to where you were no problem. Life has been very busy since the clinic opened,' Anna reminded her.

'I know, but you're barely out of breath and we did the same pace and distance.'

'I've managed to keep it up despite everything. I suppose I find my runs therapeutic.'

'I hear you. I'm adding them to my schedule effective immediately. Now, how about the market you promised we could go to? Can we get that gorgeous sourdough bread, avocado and tomato you've been raving about?'

'Absolutely.' Anna started to run up the steps to her back door, shouting behind her as she went, 'We'll shower and meet back downstairs in twenty. The towels are in the guest bathroom, and you should find everything else you need there too.'

Karla smiled at Anna's retreating back. 'I'll walk thanks, but great, see you in twenty, maybe thirty minutes.' She shook her head, and smiling she held onto the banister to make her way into the house.

An hour later they were sitting eating brunch outdoors. 'Oh my god, you were so right.' Karla munched on another delicious bite of her open sandwich. 'What do they put on the tomatoes and avo to make it taste so good?'

'I'm not sure, but I think it's just a really good olive oil or some sort of oil. The flavours are delicious, aren't they?'

Karla's mumbled reply sounded as enthusiastic as it could with a mouthful of food.

'Well, have you thought more about how you plan on letting Matt see what he's missing?' Anna asked.

Karla sat back and placed her hands on the side of the table. 'Oh, I think I have a plan alright.'

'Care to share?'

'I'm going to keep this one a little close to my chest for now.'

'The poor guy isn't going to stand a chance, Karla.'

'That's part of the plan.'

'What about you? Any clarity in your situation?'

'None needed on my side really. I plan on being with Harry for as long as we both enjoy it. If Fergal can't see past this, then we can't move forward. It's very simple in my eyes.' Anna finished the last of her sandwich.

'You know I love Fergal and I think you make a great couple, but I also feel you have a right to be angry at him for changing the goalposts.' Karla took a sip of her coffee. 'I will say something you may not want to hear though.' She eyed Anna over her cup.

'Go on.'

'Well, the way I see it is, despite Fergal knowing that you wanted an open marriage, and agreeing to it before the deed was done, I do feel he has the right to change his mind, we all do. Particularly with something so important.' Karla waited to see Anna's response. When nothing came, she continued. 'I know you are very clear and precise about everything you do, but you chose a mate that isn't like that in all areas. He's clinical and factual in his work, but he's not like you Anna in his day-to-day life. That's why you have worked so well. I do think you need to look at what you may be giving up on because of long-held beliefs that may need to be questioned in light of where you find yourself now.'

Anna smiled softly and sipped her cappuccino, 'The student becomes the teacher.' She paused and looked at Karla. 'You make some valid points, Karla, but it's not like I haven't thought about them already. I have looked at all the scenarios. I agree with you. Fergal has a right to change his mind. But I also have a right to stick to my beliefs. I can't suddenly change them because he's changed his mind.'

Anna paused, twirling the last of the salad around her plate. 'And he can't expect me to.'

'What if you looked at it from a different point of view?'

'Who's?'

'Future you.'

'Future me? I don't get it?'

'Let's move forward a year. You and Fergal never got back together. How do you feel now that he's not in your life anymore?'

'Well, I, em…' Karla had rarely seen Anna lost for words. 'I would have to say I would miss him terribly. I already am missing him, and it's only been a few weeks.'

'What do you miss?'

'Everything. Him. Us. How we are when we are together. How we are when we are apart. We just work. Mostly.'

'And don't you think you should take all of that and see what's the most important part for you?'

'But I like being intimate with other men. I adore men. I adore the opportunity and excitement and the control I can exert over them, over my life through it.'

'What if, and I'm not saying it's possible, but what if you could somehow find that control and excitement with just Fergal? Do you think it's worth exploring the possibility at least?'

'You know I've never believed in monogamy, Karla, it's just not something I fundamentally believe in. No matter how much I love Fergal, I can't compromise my beliefs to the extent that I cave on something so intrinsically important to me.'

'Anna, your language is so strong around the subject. I wonder if you relooked at your beliefs and why you hold them in the first place, perhaps your attitude would change?'

'Wow, Karla, you seem really intent on getting me to change my mind.'

'No, no, not at all. I'm only concerned with making sure that whatever decision you come to is one you won't regret in the future. That's all, Anna.'

'I never regret my decisions, you know that. I never look back. A decision is made at the time with the information to hand, and looking back with regret is completely futile. You know this about me, Karla.'

Sighing, Karla agreed. 'I do, Anna. But I also know that a long-held conviction, over time, can become a noose around someone's neck, inadvertently tying them to something they no longer believe in and that doesn't serve them.'

'OK, OK, I get it. I will take a look at my core beliefs and see if I should change them just because my husband has decided they no longer serve him.'

Before Karla could comment Anna held up her hand and continued. 'Yes OK, sorry. Before you say anything and point out the obvious, I am being facetious, and I'll stop now. I do promise to spend some time looking at it though. Thank you. I do appreciate your concern and your insights.'

'Good, I think it's a wise thing to do. And we all know how wise you are.'

'Ha, ha. We do actually.'

'Let's get the bill and have a look at the rest of the market.'

'Sounds good to me.' Anna raised her hand to call for the check.

CHAPTER 33

Fergal's conversation with his brother wasn't going as planned. 'I get what you're saying, Seán, but aren't I allowed to change my mind?'

'Sure you are, Ferg. But she's also allowed not to. Man, you knew what you were signing up for when you married, heck we all told you. Well, all except Lizzy, but she's the family weirdo anyway. You know we expressed a lot of concern, but it was you who convinced us you were very happy with your decision and could handle it. In fact, to quote you, 'I'm marrying the woman of my dreams and there is nothing we can't deal with or get through.' End quote, I believe.'

Hearing his own words spoken back to him made Fergal feel desperately sad knowing what he was going to have to give up.

'I truly believed it at the time, Seán. Don't you think if I could deal with this any other way I would?' He couldn't hide the pain in his voice.

'I know, Ferg. I wish there was something we could do. All we want is for you and Anna to be happy. It's why, despite our better judgment, we accepted what you said when you floated the whole non-monogamy thing in the first place with you and Anna. But you're not happy, I get that. There's a woman out there for you who will want what you want. It just seems Anna's not it. I'm really sorry, Ferg. We all love Anna, but it's hard seeing what her choices are doing to you.'

'I appreciate you're all only looking out for me, but it's not Anna's choices that's doing it as such. I agreed to non-monogamy. I just don't think I can do it anymore. It's kind of ironic, I love her more than I ever did, and that's what's going to break us up. Thanks, Seán. I'll let you go. I'll see you at Mum and Dad's next weekend.'

'OK, mind yourself. You know where I am, see ya.'

'See ya.' Fergal hung up and slumped against the back of the bench. The powerful crashing of the waves against the rocks below was the only sound he could hear. It was enough. The thoughts in his head filled whatever space remained. It wasn't that he didn't know this time would come, perhaps instead it was that he hoped it never would. But any intelligent man, and he considered himself to be one, knew that when two people fell in love and only one believed in monogamy, it wasn't going to end well, no matter how much you tried to convince yourself otherwise.

He'd spent weeks questioning how he'd let himself believe it would be different for them. Each time he came to just one answer. He loved her. It was that simple and that complicated all at the same time. His life wasn't the same without her. But being married when she was sleeping with other men? He couldn't do that to himself anymore. It was eating him up, yet being without her the past month made him feel like half of him was missing. Everything seemed so dull without her, life's colour had been drained. He knew he'd made his decision, but questioned whether he could bring himself to say it out loud.

CHAPTER 34

Matt was ready for the Monday meeting. He wanted to see Karla. The weekend had turned out better than he'd expected, and Friday night had run into Saturday night, but despite great sex, she was no Karla. He had no plans to let Karla know that, but still, he needed to see her and wanted to hear her voice.

He didn't have to wait for long.

She sauntered in and sat directly across from him, smiled brightly, and before he could react turned her attention to Rob sitting next to her. Not quite sure what he was seeing at first, it started to dawn on him when he saw her toss her hair to the side and laugh at something Rob said while simultaneously touching his arm. Shaking his head, he felt Harry's hand on his shoulder and looked up to his mate's knowing nod and saw him shake his head too. They both knew he was a goner.

Matt listened to Hilary talk about rotas, training, and patient files. He even managed to answer questions put to him when appropriate. He had no idea how, because every time he tried to concentrate on what was going on, he had visions of Rob's grubby hands all over Karla's body. OK, maybe he was being a little harsh. Rob had quite lean hands for a man, a fact he'd never noticed before, and really, why would he? Why the hell would he need to look at Rob's hands at any point in his life? He caught Karla's eye. Her enigmatic smile and tilted head didn't help matters for him whatsoever, and he wished the meeting would end very soon. He heard Hilary draw proceedings to a close.

'I'm outta here.' He stood abruptly, not realising he'd spoken out loud.

'Thanks for sharing that insight with us, Matt,' replied Hilary curtly. 'Sorry if our meeting interrupted your day too much.'

'Oh gosh, Hilary, no, not at all. I didn't mean that the way it sounded. Not at all. I'm sorry, really. That came out wrong.' Matt stumbled over his words gathering up his paperwork, and left shaking his head and muttering under his breath.

Harry caught up with him outside and followed him into his office.

'Matt, what the actual?'

'Leave it, Harry.'

'You sure?'

'Yep. I've a busy day ahead. Just leave it.'

'Good enough. Chat later.' Harry left Matt's office, and closing the door behind him he bumped straight into Karla.

'I wouldn't attempt to go in there if I were you. The mood's not the best.'

'Really? You sure? I was just going to check and make sure he was OK?'

'He's good. But if I were you, I'd leave it be, Karla. You're probably the last person he needs to see right now.'

'Oh, right. OK so.'

Karla walked away, Harry's words ringing in her ears. *That didn't quite go as planned*, she thought to herself. She was sure once she acted normal around Matt and showed him what he was missing, he'd be putty in her hands.

Damn it, anyway. She closed her office door. *New strategy needed*.

Matt didn't have much time to deal with the Karla situation, as he was now calling it. His clients were demanding and by 7 p.m. he was still working. The knock on his office door brought him back to the room and he called out, 'Come in,' without really thinking. Standing at the door, Karla seemed to hesitate, unsure whether to stay where she was or move towards him. She stayed by the door.

Matt took his time. Her scent filled the room. Taking a deep breath, he looked at her, stood, and holding her gaze, walked toward her. He wasn't giving her a chance to assess the situation. He took all of her in and she seemed a little unnerved. He reached her in a few long strides and stood inches from her face. 'You did that on purpose today, didn't you?'

'Yes,' she said, and her breath caught. He was so close now, she could feel his breath on her face. 'I'm sorry. I didn't know any other way to try to get your attention.'

'Really? And why would you want my attention?'

'Isn't it obvious?'

'Not to me, no. What is obvious is that we had an amazing time together and you up and left suddenly, and then proceeded to treat me like a conquest from your twenties when we were out with our work colleagues. You didn't so much as say hello that night in 37.' Matt reached his arm over Karla's head and leaned against the post. His face was so close to hers now if she moved at all he could kiss her.

'Matt, I'm sorry, I'm not willing to apologise anymore though. I've said I'm sorry and meant it. I treated you appallingly and I shouldn't have. But I'm ready to admit that what happened between us was something so good that I want it to happen again. I need it to.'

Matt sighed and placed his hand on the side of her face, tracing the line of her cheek with his finger, following the line to her bottom lip, he stopped.

'You need it to?'

'Yes.'

'Show me how much you want it.'

'What? Now?'

'Yes, now.' He traced the outline of her lip with his finger, slowly and patiently, seeking the truth in her eyes.

Karla took his finger in her mouth and sucked it gently. Staring into his eyes, she took his hand in hers and sucked again.

'Don't tease me, Karla, unless you're planning on seeing this through.'

Reaching for his face she pulled him towards her and kissed him gently on the lips, biting his bottom one playfully. 'I'm planning on seeing this through,' she mumbled, before kissing him harder.

Matt didn't need any more encouragement. Undoing her blouse slowly, he watched her eyes open wider as he pinched one inviting nipple and then the other. He feasted on them both, taking his time to give them the attention they deserved. As she reached for him, he brushed her hand gently away and grabbed for her pert behind. He squeezed, and her soft moan in response made him do it again. Gently holding her face he drew her in. Parting her soft lips, she groaned and opened willingly. His tongue played with her lips first, drawing her to meet him. The kiss deepened, softness turned to eagerness, eagerness to passion, and then want and need combined.

Matt slowly pulled away, watching Karla's face, her eyes opened questioningly.

'Not here,' he panted. 'I want you in my bed again. This time you're not going home until we're both ready.'

Karla pushed her hands against the door to steady herself and watched Matt redo her blouse buttons.

'We could do it here and at your place.' She put her hand on his chest and rubbed tenderly.

Kissing her forehead he turned and walked toward his desk. 'Nope, we can't. I want time with you, Karla, and I've work to finish here first.'

'You're saying the right things, Matt, but I'm feeling like you're still angry with me.' She sashayed to the desk and leaned toward him.

'Not at all. I have plans for us and it doesn't include doing you against my office door. At least not today.' He winked and smiled at her before sitting down. 'Now how about a raincheck 'til Friday? We'll go on a date, then you'll come to mine and bring a weekend bag?'

'I...' She shook her head and smiled. 'Matt, you continue to surprise me.'

Karla walked around the desk and leaned over him planting a long smouldering kiss on his lips. 'Yes, to the weekend. I'm looking forward to it already.'

He watched her leave. Once the door was closed, he heaved a sigh of relief and started laughing. A satisfied grin crossed his face.

♥♥♥

Fergal hesitated. The key was poised at the keyhole. Unsure if it felt weird to just walk in, or even weirder still to ring the bell. Shaking his head, he turned the key in the lock of his own front door, opened it and called out. 'Anna? You here?'

'I'm in the kitchen.'

He knew this was going to be difficult, but just hearing her voice sent his head into a spin already.

Anna arrived at the kitchen door. He stood stock still. 'Aren't you coming in?'

'Eh, ye, OK. I wasn't sure if I should use my key or not. But then, it would have been too weird to ring the bell in my own home.' Fergal was pointing at the door and returned his gaze just in time to see Anna saunter back into the kitchen. Following her, he crossed the hall and surveyed his home. It felt a little uncomfortable to be back, yet familiar at the same time.

'Would you like a glass of wine?' She didn't turn from stirring the pot.

'Sure. Are you having company?'

'Yes. You.' She turned now and fixed on him with those brown eyes. 'I thought we could have dinner while we chatted. A little more civilised that way, no?'

He certainly couldn't argue with her and was happy to enjoy any experience that felt like normal. Even if it was an illusion, and it was going to disappear again.

'Sounds good to me. Can I do anything to help?'

'Pour the wine? I'm plating up now.'

The familiarity pulled at his heart. Silently they moved around each other, instinct told them how. Anna placed the plates on their table and they sat facing each other.

Neither spoke for a time.

'Cheers.' She raised her glass.

Fergal held her gaze and replied. 'To the future, whatever it may hold.'

Anna didn't answer. She sipped her white wine and continued eating.

'Are we going to talk? That's what I'm here for, isn't it?'

'Well, yes. That is why I asked you over, but I thought a pleasant meal would be good first. No?'

'Sure, but we may as well talk while we eat because, at this stage, there is no point in making small talk when our marriage is hanging in the balance, now is there?'

'Really, Fergal, why so dramatic?'

'You think I'm being dramatic?'

'Yes, actually I do. I understand we are here to talk about our marriage but really, there's no place for histrionics. Let's discuss it like the two adults we are.'

'Yes, agreed. Let's discuss it like adults. Why don't you go first?'

'What do you mean go first? It's a conversation, Fergal. We will both talk, no?'

'Well, I'll start then.' He took a large swig of wine. 'Have you changed your mind?'

'Are we going to start there?

'Where else would you like me to start? What about, are you still fucking Harry?'

'Incredible. I knew it was too much to expect that you would be mature about this.' Grabbing her plate, Anna put it on the countertop.

Fergal turned and watched her. 'You haven't answered either question, Anna.'

'Because they are childish and stupid. You do not get to just come in here and demand answers like that. There is a bigger issue here.'

'A bigger issue? I'm confused, enlighten me.'

She leaned against the counter, wine glass in hand. Sipping slowly, she observed him over the rim. 'You changed the goalposts, Fergal. You, not me. You said you could handle it. Then you decided you couldn't deal with it anymore. You were the one who changed the rules. So, whether I have changed my mind, or who I am fucking is irrelevant.'

'It's certainly not irrelevant to me.' Fergal hung his head. 'I can't do it, Anna.'

She didn't move. He sat still. The air was heavy with resignation between them.

Anna came to him and placed her glass on the table by his side. She placed her hands on his shoulders.

'Don't,' he mumbled half-heartedly and shook them off.

'Let me?' She kneaded his shoulders gently and stroked his neck, he couldn't hide the stress.

'Don't, Anna.'

She sat by his side, lay her head in his lap and crawled into the foetal position. It was an automatic reaction, but he found his hands tenderly stroking her hair, brushing loose tendrils away from her face. Looking down at her beautiful sallow skin, he found himself desperately wanting to kiss her. Knowing he should stop, and still, his hands stroked her. 'Anna.'

'I know.' Her eyes closed, and she tenderly touched his hand. 'Don't stop.'

'Goddamn you. I love you so much, Anna.'

'And I love you.'

Lost in their thoughts, time passed and then Anna spoke. 'Can we start again? I don't want to fight. I do have something to say though, and I wasn't entirely convinced of it until this very moment.'

'Go ahead,' he whispered.

'Ferg, I'll try it your way. But I can't guarantee I can do it.'

His hand stopped mid-stroke. 'You will? You mean it?'

Anna rose and looked at him. Touching his cheek she drew her hand down the side of his face.

'I do, I mean it. I will try.'

'Should I ask what brought the change of heart?'

'I don't want to lose you from my life. I've missed you too much. If this is what it takes, I'm certainly willing to give it a try. But I can't give you any guarantees.'

'I know.' He reached for her hand and kissed the palm.

'We need to talk more about it though, Anna.'

'We will, but not tonight. Tonight is for us. No?'

'Tonight is definitely for us.' He leaned in and held her chin, touching his lips tenderly to hers.

He could hardly believe they were doing this. He had given up all hope of ever being able to kiss his wife again, let alone do anything else. Reaching down, he took her hand and walked towards the stairs. Stopping in their hallway he took her face in both hands and drew her in. Savouring her, he placed a long, slow kiss on her lips, keeping his eyes open, as he watched her face for the sign he needed.

She sighed, smiled, opened her eyes and saw him. 'I'm here. I'm yours,' she murmured.

'I know.'

The following morning Anna was running late for work.

Fergal wasn't planning on letting her go anytime soon. Knowing she would be seeing Harry today didn't help either, but he put that to the back of his mind. 'Stay. They can do without you for a few hours, I'm sure. Reschedule your clients.'

He reached out to grab her arm when she passed the bed on her way to the ensuite.

'I can't. You know that. I promise I'll try and leave early today. We'll take a long weekend soon, go away somewhere nice.'

He felt like a teenager again. Giddy with excitement he jumped up and grabbed her. 'Kiss me.'

She laughed softly and protested gently, pushing his chest with her hands, but her open mouth and willing tongue told a different story.

'I've missed kissing you, Anna.'

'And I've missed kissing you, Ferg, but I really do have to go. Don't worry we will continue this later.'

She gave him a long kiss before pulling back and looking at him. 'I love you.'

'I love you, too.' He kissed her nose. 'Until later.'

'Later, my darling.'

CHAPTER 35

'Knock, knock.' Harry walked in smiling and gently closed Anna's office door behind him.

'Anna, I'm glad you asked me to come in,' he said as he crossed to her desk. Something in her look told him this wasn't the type of call to Anna's office that he was expecting. 'What is it? Has something happened?'

Anna walked around the desk and took Harry's hands in hers. 'Harry.'

Just the sound of his name on her lips drove him crazy.

'I'm sorry, but we have to end this.'

'End it? Why?'

'It's run its course.'

'You're not serious? This isn't close to having run its course. What's happened, Anna? Something must have.'

'Fergal and I are back together, and I've promised him I'll try it his way this time.'

He dropped her hands and walked towards the drinks console. Pouring himself a measure of scotch he knocked it back before turning to face her.

'So that's it? Just like that?'

'Yes, I'm sorry. You knew I was married, Harry. This was never going to go anywhere.'

His breathing slowed, 'I thought we had a real connection, Anna. I'm surprised that's all. You've been quite vocal in your stance on marriage and what an open one meant to you. You've certainly rowed back on your beliefs fairly quickly.'

'I haven't rowed back, as you say, Harry. I'm just trying things a different way. It's the only way I can save my marriage, so I owe it to Fergal and myself to give it a try.'

Harry didn't say anything. He couldn't. He poured another drink, knocked it back, and walked towards her. Grabbing her he kissed her, her surprise at the intensity was quickly replaced with anger at his audacity.

'Harry!' She forcibly pushed at his chest.

'We're not done, Anna. Don't kid yourself.'

He stomped out of the room slamming the door behind him.

'Mate, how about a swifty before heading home?' Harry had his desk phone on loudspeaker talking to Matt. His head was in his hands, and his computer was blinking with ignored messages on the desk in front of him.

'Sure, I can do that. But I'm not having a late one. Need to be good to go tomorrow night when Karla comes over.'

'Sure, sure. Just one or two.'

When Harry arrived at Café En Seine, the Thursday night after-work crowd were in party form, which made his mood even lousier. Seeing Matt at the end of the bar he sauntered over and slapped his back in greeting. 'Jesus mate, it's wedged in here already. What's going on that we're not aware of?'

'Hey,' said Matt. 'It's some company retreat from the US. Chris behind the bar there was saying there's two hundred of them here for pre-dinner drinks.'

'Americans you say? Could be just the distraction I need tonight. You fancy chatting to your fellow citizens and bigging up your Irish mate?'

'I don't think you need bigging up. But I'm not going to be much of a wingman tonight. I'm conserving my energy for the weekend with Karla.'

Matt took a swig of his pint and handed Harry his. 'So, what's up? You sounded pissed off on the phone.'

'All good now. Water under the bridge. Anna and I are done.'

'Oh? You or she finish it?'

'She's making a go of it with her husband.'

'Ah, was bound to happen. You OK?'

'Yeah, I'll be good.'

'You want a chaser with that pint?'

'Yeah, why not? It's nearly the weekend and I've got some Americans to chat up.'

'Sounds like a solid plan, my friend.' Matt caught the bartender's eye, held up two fingers and mouthed tequila. It was just enough information for the bartender to know what they wanted. He loved Irish bars.

CHAPTER 36

Matt knocked on Karla's door, held his shoulders back, and checked his breath again, probably for the third time since coming from the car.

Laughing at himself, he shook his hands and arms to let some of the nervous energy out.

The door opened and Karla stood on the other side looking radiant in deep blue.

Matt swallowed hard and let out a breath before speaking. 'Wow, Karla.' It was all he could manage, and then he leaned in and kissed her.

The lingering kiss meant they could both savour each other before coming up for air.

'Sorry.' Matt pressed his head against her forehead. 'I couldn't stop myself. You're stunning.'

Laughing, Karla leaned into him and this time it was her turn. She took a step closer, grabbed his face in her hands and kissed him. He responded eagerly. 'Don't be sorry when you kiss me the way you do,' said Karla.

'I won't ever say that again so.'

'We have to go, or we'll never make it for dinner at this rate.'

Karla eyed him questioningly. 'Would that be such a bad thing?'

'Oh, Karla, don't tempt me. Are you ready?'

'Let me get my bag and coat, and I'm all yours.'

'Words I like the sound of.'

The drive to dinner felt easy and relaxed, and when they arrived at the restaurant Matt felt like the luckiest man alive walking in with Karla on his arm. Knowing that all eyes were on the woman he was with made him feel invincible. They ordered a drink at the bar while waiting on a table.

'A toast.' Matt held his glass aloft. 'To a great night and an even better weekend ahead. To you, Karla, you are beautiful, inside and out. You are intelligent, and sexy as all hell, and I am so glad we find ourselves here tonight. To you.'

Karla was taken aback. Blushing she held her glass up and looked at Matt, she smiled and touched her glass with his. 'Thank you, Matt.'

'Karla, I meant every word. I'm glad we're getting the chance to do this.'

'Me too. What made you decide to ask me after I'd made you so angry?'

'Just because I was angry, it didn't mean I stopped wanting you. I was disappointed when you left that Saturday, and I wasn't sure I could handle any more rejection from you.'

'I know. And as I said, I was sorry for walking out the way I did.' She saw the look on Matt's face.

'OK, OK, running out the way I did that day, but I had my reasons. And then I just didn't know what to do after that. I was embarrassed by my behaviour, so I decided to compound it by acting the way I did in 37 Dawson at the work night out.'

'Well, as long as you understand that it was you being a jerk, I'm a happy man.'

'Hey, cheeky.'

'No seriously, Karla. You know how I feel about you now. I was so disappointed but I wasn't about to let you walk all over me.'

'I get it. And for the record that was never my intention. I was confused about what I was feeling.'

'Are you still confused?'

'I'm here now, aren't I?'

'Yes, you are, and might I add in case I haven't said it enough tonight, you look sensational.'

Dinner went from great to fantastic and the conversation was easy and fun. Matt loved how flirtatious, yet ladylike Karla was, and now and again took a moment to look at her when she didn't know, just so he could admire her. Returning to his apartment after their meal, Karla accepted the drink Matt offered, grabbing him, and kissing him full on the lips. 'I've wanted to do that ever since that toast you made at the start of the meal.'

'Well, if I knew it would have had that effect on you, I would have made that toast weeks ago.' Matt wrapped his arm around her waist, drawing her in.

'I've had a lovely evening, Matt.' Karla gave him a peck on his right cheek. 'You are a very interesting man.' She kissed his left cheek. 'You are a very handsome man.' She kissed his right cheek again. 'I want you to take me to bed.' She kissed his left cheek and pulled back to look at him.

'I think I can do that.' Matt grabbed her face and kissed her. 'I want you, Karla.'

'I'm yours.'

Matt took her hand and led her to the bedroom. He kissed her lips tenderly. Responding eagerly, she traced the lines of his body with her fingertips. Her tongue entwined with his as tenderness turned to eagerness, and their rhythms increased. Matt groaned loudly at her response. 'Karla, you're amazing.' That was all he managed before the need took over. The knowledge of what they could do to each other drove him wild.

He expertly undid her blouse revealing beautifully encased breasts in the silkiest baby pink lingerie he'd ever touched. 'Karla, baby.'

She smiled at him. 'For you.'

Her pert breasts moulded to his hands perfectly. His lust building, he grabbed her butt and Karla instinctively wrapped her legs around his waist. They fell to the bed together in a hot sweating mess of limbs, laughing, kissing, and enjoying each other. Matt stopped and looked down at her. 'I'm glad you're here.'

'I can tell.' She grinned back at him.

Karla woke to a warm tingling sensation that took her a moment to comprehend. Opening her eyes, the realization dawned on her, and she felt for the top of Matt's head between her legs. She smiled and groaned as pleasure coursed through her.

Looking up he grinned. 'Morning, sexy lady.'

'Morning.' She entwined her fingers in his hair. 'Don't let me stop you.' She gently pushed him back down and laughed. Karla let her head rest against the silk pillowcase. *This isn't a bad way to wake up,* she thought when she felt another wave of pleasure flow through her.

Later that evening as they strolled together, Matt reached out for Karla's hand and placed it to his lips. 'I've had a really great day.'

Karla's steps slowed. 'Matt, I have to say you've surprised me more than once.'

'In a good way?'

'Yes, very good.' Stopping, she turned, reached for his face and kissed him. His hands rested on her hips. 'I'm sorry it took me some time to really see you.'

'That's OK, you can spend some time making it up to me. In fact, maybe we should go back to mine so you can start properly?' He tugged her hair playfully and tapped her bum.

'I can work with that,' she said and smiled.

CHAPTER 37

Harry threw the racquet onto the couch, slammed the bag on the floor and stomped to the fridge.

Grabbing a Heineken, he flipped the lid off and guzzled. He sauntered to his ensuite, turned on the nozzle in the shower, stripped and tossed his damp sports clothes in the basket. *Let's see if this can help clear the head because Squash certainly didn't.*

Knowing his mind would continue to drift back to Anna and what she was doing to get back on track with Fergal, was driving him nuts.

Only one thing for it. Picking up his phone it didn't take long to get a response to his, 'Hey, you free?' text.

'Yes, baby.'

'Get your fine ass over here so ☺'

'When you ask so nicely. C u in 20.'

Two hours later Harry kissed Sophia goodbye one more time and escorted her to the lift. He closed his apartment door and leaned against it. *Sophia has outlived her usefulness. I shouldn't have called her over. The release wasn't worth the incessant chatter.* He was annoyed at himself.

Fucking Sophia hadn't helped to get Anna from his head at all. He'd had good sex before. He'd had sex with someone he loved before, and he'd definitely had his share of bad sex. Sex with Anna had been on the good side of the scale. If he was honest, it was probably on the mind-blowing side, but that was that.

Dropping his head in his hands, Harry fought hard with the feelings that refused to leave him in peace. He knew it was more than hot-as-fuck-sex; he was crazy about her.

Strolling to his couch, he took the remote from its holder and flicked on the Sky Box. Flopping into the seat his thoughts drifted to Abigail. He knew she felt like unfinished business, and now he had another experience to add to that, Anna.

With Abigail it was different. Wondering whether they would have gotten back together was always a question for him. Would he still be in New York if the accident hadn't happened? Despite the questions, he'd known he'd never get the answers he wanted, so he'd mostly stopped wondering what would have been different if she hadn't died that day.

Catching feelings for Anna hadn't been on the agenda, yet here he was, on his own, trying to process what the hell was going on, and what was glaringly obvious to his psychologist brain. Unavailable women were the bane of his life.

Flicking through the channels, he put on Wimbledon and hoped he could switch off long enough to give his head some peace.

CHAPTER 38

Anna woke early Monday morning before the light. Stealing a glance at Fergal's strong jaw and handsome face, she smiled softly. The warmth of his skin against hers felt so good she folded herself into him and stroked his chest tenderly.

Sometimes all you needed was a reminder and for someone to fight for you to appreciate what was right in front of you. A brush of her lips to his showed her what she already knew. She was right where she belonged.

Matt didn't knock. Swinging Karla's office door open, he walked in and within three strides reached her, then he grabbed her into a long, deep, lingering kiss. Her eager response was even more than he could have hoped for. He saw her laugh as he retreated back, her head nodding in sweet agreement. He shook his head chuckling and shrugged his shoulders wondering, could it just be this easy?

Harry sat in his car looking at the building where Anna had created her dream. The Love Lab was taking off, and clients were being helped just as she'd wanted. Harry was incredibly happy for her.

He was glad he had his best mate working with him and delighted that Matt and Karla had eventually worked through their issues and were making a go of it.

He was also happy that despite his love life being in the toilet, he had a job he loved and was grateful for. That said, he knew what he needed to do, he took out his phone and punched in the number he'd gotten. It answered after three rings. 'You've reached the office of Dr John Lauer, psychologist. Please leave a message and we will get back to you as soon as possible.'

Harry took a deep breath. 'My name is Harry Eames and I'd like to make an appointment. My number is 086 5557575. Thank you.'

Satisfied with his decision, he hung up the phone and stepped out of the car. Despite how he was feeling, he planted a smile on his face, knowing that it would make it a little easier to face whatever the day would bring.

ACKNOWLEDGMENTS

I loved writing the story of *The Love Lab*. Seeing it all come to life on these pages is a dream come true.

It's a story about a woman who forges ahead regardless of what others think of her. I do feel an affinity with Anna, because ballsy women can sometimes be mistaken for hard, unloving women.

But it's also about sex & love and the many guises it comes in.

In the spirit of love it's important for me to acknowledge all of it that surrounds me, and in turn helped me get *The Love Lab* out into the world.

My darling son, Dylan. A young man now, who came into a chaotic, unsure world, and in the process changed mine irrevocably. You are the reason I pushed forward when I was tired or feeling lonely on dark mornings & winter nights. To be a writer is my dream. How could I look at you and tell you to follow yours if I didn't at least try to follow mine?

To my mum. Your love of family and resilience is an inspiration. Your help, guidance, unquestioning loyalty and your own faith in taking a chance on love, despite what others may have thought, make me so proud to call you Mum. That faith brought Pat into our lives. Someone we will be eternally grateful for.

My dad, your search for meaning in an unjust world, your belief & support in all your children's creative endeavours and your unwavering quest for connection is inspiring.

My amazing second parents, Syl & Kev. You have loved & supported me unconditionally. I can't imagine going through my life without you both by my side.

I am so grateful for the amazing siblings, cousins, aunts and uncles and extended family I get to call my own. My tribe of amazing friends who support & love me & in turn who I love dearly. This book wouldn't have come to pass without you all.

To Amanda, www.amandajevans.com. Thank you for your guidance in the initial stages and for introducing me to Jeremy & the team at JM Agency.

To Brona, www.bronamills.com. You offered wonderful advice to me without even knowing me. You gave me the confidence to move forward as a writer.

Declan O'Donoghue, @declan_mindset. Joining your programme changed everything.

My *Mastermind* buddies. So much gratitude to you guys for my weekly accountability and so much more.

Michael Heppell & all the Write that Book Alumni. Thank you. I can't wait to see a copy of *The Love Lab* on your shelves Michael!

To my amazing bosses & the team at 47 Medical. You have all championed *The Love Lab* for that I'm so very grateful.

To my beta readers. The early ones, Adele & Ramona & to the lovely group from 'The Drogheda Dolls'. Thank you all for your wonderfully helpful feedback.

And finally, to borrow from Snoop Dog, I want to thank me. When it comes down to it none of this would have happened without me sitting down and putting pen to paper and chasing my dreams. In all my years I've never been my own best friend. So, I'm taking this opportunity to say, thank you, well done & I'm so proud of you Jill.

Love Jill x

ABOUT THE AUTHOR

Meet Jillian Stout, a 52-year-old debut novelist hailing from the coastal town of Stamullen in East Meath. A dedicated and loving Mum to an 18-year-old son, Jillian finds joy in family life, spending time on the beach and taking a dip in the sea with her lab, Cooper. Jillian's life would not be the same without her close-knit family and circle of wonderful friends.

An eternal believer in romance and its boundless possibilities, she has a soft spot for romantic novels that whisk the reader away to fantastical worlds filled with hope and love. Jillian began writing *The Love Lab* to explore both her love of escapism and insatiable desire to learn more about people's inner lives.

Beyond her literary pursuits Jillian finds peace and expression through her art. Her abstract paintings, which use acrylics on canvas, have helped her foster the creative side she has put to exceptional use in both her entrepreneurial and literary endeavours.

She is an active member of The Julianstown and St Brigid's Drama groups. She loves the opportunity to perform on stage and bring stories to life in front of a live audience.

In her quest for balance and wellness Jillian is an avid gym goer, cyclist and walker.

Despite the demands of her current role as a manager in a bustling doctor's surgery, she has tried to foster a supportive and encouraging environment for all and she is happy to report they eagerly await the release of her debut novel.

DEAR READER

To you, the reader, thank you for reading *The Love Lab*. I hope you enjoyed reading it as much as I enjoyed writing it. I'd love to hear from you, so feel free to reach out to me via the links below, and tell me your thoughts and impressions of the book. Follow me on Instagram and TikTok for news, updates and other interesting content. I also have some signed copies of *The Love Lab*, which I'm looking forward to gifting to some lucky readers. Just scan the QR code below, which takes you to where you can win a signed copy.

I'm looking forward to going on an adventure with you again soon, with the follow-up to the Love Lab ...

– Jill

www.jillianstoutauthor.com

@jillianstoutauthor